REVENGE OF THE TEACHER'S PET

YELLOW SHOE FICTION Michael Griffith, *Series Editor*

DARRIN DOYLE

REVENGE

of the Teacher's Pet

A Love Story

LOUISIANA STATE UNIVERSITY PRESS ❖ BATON ROUGE

PUBLISHED BY LOUISIANA STATE UNIVERSITY PRESS
Copyright © 2009 by Darrin Doyle
All rights reserved
Manufactured in the United States of America

LSU Paperback Original
First printing

Designer: *Amanda McDonald Scallan*
Typeface: *Century Schoolbook*
Printer and binder: *Thomson-Shore, Inc.*

Library of Congress Cataloging-in-Publication Data
Doyle, Darrin, 1970–
Revenge of the teacher's pet : a love story / Darrin Doyle.
    p. cm. — (Yellow shoe fiction series)
"LSU paperback original."
ISBN 978-0-8071-3434-4 (pbk. : alk. paper) 1. Teachers—Fiction.
2. Love stories. gsafd I. Title.
PS3604.O95475R48 2009
813'.6—dc22   2008044005

Two lines from the song "Fish Heads" are quoted in chapter 2. Written
by Robert S. Haimer and Bill Mumy. Published by Music Spazchow.
Copyright 1978.

Two lines from the song "If You Wanna Be Happy" are quoted in
chapter 3. Written by Carmela T. Guida, Frank J. Guida, and Joseph
F. Royster. Copyright 1963.

The brief quote in the epilogue was taken from Richard Mooney's
article "A Limb Loss Primer." Copyright Richard L. Mooney, 2000.

The paper in this book meets the guidelines for permanence and dura-
bility of the Committee on Production Guidelines for Book Longevity
of the Council on Library Resources.♾

For Courtney

ACKNOWLEDGMENTS

The author would like to thank the following people: Michael for the wisdom; Brock for the scribbles; Rebecca for the title; Chris, Steve, Jason, and John for the corn; the Sewanee Writers' Conference and the New York State Summer Writers' Institute for the friendships and libations; the Western Michigan University posse for removing the training wheels; the University of Cincinnati posse for pushing the bike into traffic; everyone at Louisiana State University Press for the generosity and dependability; Jo Ann, for her eagle eyes; Simon and Charlie for the "My neck!"; Carol and George for the patience and guidance; Tim and Brian for the pain and gain; Pat and Beth for the porch; and Courtney for everything.

REVENGE OF THE TEACHER'S PET

ONE

1

Sleepy-eyed, ample-bodied Mary Ann opened the front door one morning at her husband's urging, expecting nothing more than the dewy suburban lawn, but found that the yard had been toxically whitened. A vast web of toilet paper covered the walkway, grass, and tethered sapling. If their Ford Escort were a corpse it could not have been identified, it was so buried beneath Angel Soft and Barbasol. Scrawled across the Escort's windshield, in giant soap letters, were the words *I LOVE EGGS*.

A balloon had exploded on the front door of the house. A cold, heavy dollop of mayonnaise dropped onto Mary Ann's bare foot. Swooning under a wave of anxiety and revulsion, she wondered what the new neighbors would think, how costly and embarrassing it would be to clean this apocalypse, and most important, *why* they'd been targeted.

Mr. Portwit, standing behind her, swallowed his toothpaste to speak. "Like the ejaculations of a mythical giant. Don't you think?"

"How did I sleep through this?" she asked.

"That space heater's loud," he said, pointing with his brush toward the bedroom.

"You slept in the basement. Did you hear anything?"

"Come inside," Mr. Portwit said. His lips were ringed with white froth, making him appear rabid. "It's chilly."

He boiled water for tea, inserted bread into the toaster, and poured two tall glasses of orange juice.

"I stood at the living room window and watched them do it," Mr. Portwit said. "It was three boys from Mrs. Jennings's class. Rick Fletcher, Donald Peterson, and Sedgwick Reynolds, to be exact. They were surprisingly professional," he mused, dropping Lemon Zinger tea bags into the mugs. "Like guerrillas carrying out some secret operation in the dead of night. Thrilling, in a way. They spared no expense. Three dozen eggs, eight rolls of toilet paper, two cans of shaving cream, one bar of soap, and four mayonnaise-filled balloons."

"You watched them destroy our yard?" Mary Ann said. "That shaving cream will eat the paint on the car. That mayonnaise is going to curdle on the door . . ." She put her fingers to her eyes, either to stem the flow of tears or to initiate it; she couldn't tell which.

The water boiled. Mr. Portwit poured it, then came into the dining room and set one of the mugs in front of Mary Ann. He held the other and blew on it while seating himself at the table. So casual, so composed. To a stranger, Mr. Portwit might appear intimidating in the way he mastered his emotions, remained cool and rational even under duress. But Mary Ann knew better: beneath the rhetoric and posturing was an uncertain man seeking approval. He was performing for her, performing his new role as husband. And, she had to admit, doing it rather convincingly. He was responding with calm and mastery to a strange (and of course *unprovoked*, she told herself) nighttime incursion. As she watched him dunk his tea bag up and down wearing a thoughtful expression, a rush of pride quieted her doubt. For a moment, she let herself believe that they were exactly what they appeared to be—a suburban couple in middle America greeting a weekday morning at the breakfast table.

"It's upsetting," he agreed. "Believe me, I wanted to kill them. How ballsy, especially when we're *home*. They probably peeked in the bedroom window, thought we were sleeping.

"You see, I was this close"—he positioned his thumb and forefinger an inch apart, then thought better of it and shrunk the distance to a half-inch—"to sneaking out the back door and ambushing whoever was nearest." His eyes were invisible behind lenses that held the reflected stars of the two hundred-watt bulbs suspended above the table. "But then I realized that that's what they wanted. I'm their number-one laughingstock already, and truth be told, you're not far behind. But this isn't about you, it's about me. Anyway, a fifty-year-old man running in his briefs at 3 a.m. can only appear foolish."

She smiled at the image of Dale pouncing from the shadows to menace three kids who each had at least ten pounds and three inches on him. By his own admission, he had always been small. At five, he was mistaken for a preschooler. At eleven, he couldn't ride the roller coasters at Cedar Point. And when his growth spurt finally came, at seventeen, it was disappointing. He leveled off at 5'6", well below the national average of 5'9.2". Dale knew the exact number because he was an avid gatherer of facts. He read the *World Almanac*, owned the *Encyclopaedia Britannica*, watched *Jeopardy!* and taught middle-school science. He believed strongly that any disadvantages from his diminutive stature, slight build (138 pounds), and thick glasses could be offset by exuding confidence and poise. Confidence and poise, he'd told Mary Ann, could be manufactured from within, which was "where the magic happened."

Though she wasn't in the mood to say it now, Mary Ann found his bravado endearing. It was his misguided way of assuring her she would be protected, that she'd backed the right horse when she hitched her wagon to him. Ironically, until they started dating she'd had very little recent trouble in her life. Since then, her weight had dramatically increased, he'd been officially reprimanded at school, and now their new house was the target of disgruntled, egg-lobbing students.

Mary Ann knew she needed to speak now in a manner Mr. Portwit would understand—without condescension, certainly, and with great care to obscure the fact that she was second-guessing what he would surely call his methodology.

"The police station is four blocks away," she said. She took a noiseless sip of tea, then reached for the newspaper and pretended to browse the headlines through splotches of mayonnaise. A dozen seconds passed. She was proud of her self-control; she would match him, detachment for detachment. Then she added, under her breath: "You wouldn't have had to actually go outside and chase anyone."

"Sweetheart," Mr. Portwit said. He reached for her hand as if to hold it but only patted it like a puppy's head. "You know I have our best interests in mind. I'm not afraid of three preteens whose collective age adds up to their individual IQs."

Without warning, her chest tightened. This was a moment for *action*, not math problems. She was unable to censor herself: "It's not an issue of fear. Bottom line is you *did nothing.*"

He seemed to ponder. With the untrimmed fingernails of his right hand he stroked his cheek in an upward motion, going against the stubble. "You're right," he answered. "I do tend toward histrionics. I apologize." He stood from his chair and exited the room.

He tended toward histrionics even in his apologies, apparently.

She called after him in her best imitation of a pleasant voice, "We have to be at work in forty-five minutes!" She guzzled her Homestyle Tropicana and resisted the urge to slam the empty glass onto the table.

Mr. Portwit returned, breathing heavily. "Had to run downstairs." He held his camera—the 1993 Kodak Cameo that he had boasted was the only one he'd ever owned or ever would own. "So as I was saying," he beamed, excited as a kid who'd just lost a tooth, "in response to your assertion that I did nothing . . ."

"You took pictures."

"Yes. Twenty pictures. Official documentation. They were professional, as I said, but not smart. They did not wear ski masks."

"So you're going to show these to Principal Foster."

"That's one option," Mr. Portwit said.

Mary Ann scooted her chair from the table with more force than she intended, and she hoped her heavy body hadn't dug trenches into the imitation-wood laminate. "I don't have time for your games," she said.

She went to the bedroom to dress. It was a hell of a way, she thought, to spend one of their first mornings in the house. They hadn't even unpacked all the boxes, and already they were fighting. Not to mention that he'd slept in the basement last night. She chose to see this as an anomaly and to give it no further thought before school.

Clothed now, Mary Ann frowned at the full-length mirror, turning this way and that, running her hands down her torso as if to press herself into a different shape. The pantsuit was only three months old, and already too small, suffocating. She had to face facts. Nearly fifty pounds over the past five months had been dispersed over her body—most of it in her rear and thighs, although her face bore some of the brunt. Leaning toward the mirror, she plucked at her cheeks, wishing she could rip off the excess flab and reveal the beautiful girl inside. It was enough to make a person cry.

She'd always been large, but now it was embarrassing and, if she was to believe the news, dangerous. The last time she'd dared mount a scale, it had groaned and creaked while the spasming needle took its sweet time deciding upon *237*.

But what did it matter, now that she had a husband? And a husband who encouraged her—beseeched her—to eat? From their first date, the "sunset picnic," as he'd called it, Dale had shown his desires clearly.

The April 1 dusk had been unseasonably springlike, for Michigan. With the blanket spread beneath them, Mary Ann and Mr. Portwit had reclined on elbows. The horizon was bloody and purple and magnificent. The hilltop park's location provided a wide, hazy overview of Kalamazoo. After two glasses of wine, Mary Ann's stomach and face were warm. She'd only eaten a few crackers before her appetite had run away with its tail between its legs. Good riddance.

"I hope it doesn't bother you to have dinner on a pile of corpses," he said. "Back in 1923, they built a factory on this very spot. A small plant, for manufacturing shoes. One night, the janitor dropped a lit cigar into a bucket of primer—WHOOSH!" He wiped the air with his hands in a simulated explosion. "Twenty-seven men died, but by far the most tragic thing is the thousands of *soles* that were lost!" He socked Mary Ann's shoulder.

"There's the Radisson," Mary Ann said, pointing.

"Think of the people in there," Mr. Portwit remarked. "All the lives, all the dramas. Just beyond those windows."

The wine made Mary Ann's voice act before her brain had time to shut it down. "You're more of a romantic than I ever suspected." She attempted a flirtatious smile, but she worried that it came out as a leer.

Mr. Portwit apparently didn't notice. His gaze lingered on her until Mary Ann had to look away. "You haven't eaten," Mr. Portwit said. "Don't tell me you don't like falafel."

"Oh, I love falafel, it's just—"

Mr. Portwit silenced her with a pad of pita bread. "You're hurting my feelings," he said as she nibbled from his hand.

Self-conscious since childhood about eating in front of strangers, Mary Ann took small bites and covered her mouth.

"Come on," Mr. Portwit said. "Like you mean it."

She finished the bread, and Mr. Portwit's hand was there again, bearing a stuffed grape leaf.

"You don't have to be shy around me," he said. "At least pretend you like it."

Wine-buzz filling her head, Mary Ann rent the grape leaf in half. She chewed openmouthed and with passion, like a starving animal.

"Now *that's* a picnic!" announced Mr. Portwit.

The following Monday, she was greeted at her desk in the third-grade classroom by a single red rose and a box of chocolate turtles, attached to which was a handwritten note: *A treat for the treat of your company.*

At the end of the day, a crackly voice over the intercom said, "Mary Ann."

She looked up from her desk at the dusty speaker mounted on the wall. The children were long gone, and Mary Ann was indulging in her fourth turtle.

"Mary Ann Tucker," the voice repeated, "I must demand that you accompany me to Charlie's Crab this evening. Please dress formally. I'll pick you up at seven. That is all."

Mary Ann's footsteps now thundered through the living room. Personal comfort be damned, she'd resolved to make it through the day in the pantsuit. Dale was still sitting at the table, still not dressed for school. She watched as he pointed the camera at his own face, bared his teeth, and snapped a photo.

"Smile," Mr. Portwit said when she entered. He clicked.

"Are you coming? We need to hose off the car."

"Take a big bite of toast for me. We need to finish this roll."

His lopsided grin somehow managed to be both annoying and reassuring. *For better or worse,* she remembered. Here, in gray sweatpants and a ratty T-shirt, sat the living embodiment of that vow. Mary Ann placed her bag on the floor, lifted the slice of toast from her plate, and crunched, imagining that she was eating Mr. Portwit's hand. The shutter clicked. The camera buzzed like a time bomb as it rewound.

As they entered the Elkhart Elementary and Middle School teachers' lounge, Mr. Portwit had reached the crescendo of his tirade detailing the impending capture of the "toiletry gang." "They will learn," he announced, index finger wagging, "that the quiet one is always the most dangerous."

Mr. Portwit did not stop talking until he and Mary Ann were seated in their usual places at the corner of the lounge table. In the silence that followed, Mary Ann realized that everyone—all K-8 teachers, auxiliary teachers like music, art, and gym, even Ramone the custodian and Principal Foster's secretary—was staring at them. Oblivious, Mr. Portwit unzipped his soft leather briefcase and drew forth his dog-eared copy of *A Brief History of Time.*

"Good morning," Mary Ann offered, dropping her eyes to the table.

Betty Passinault, the librarian, grunted a "Hmm" of disapproval. Her subsequent intake of breath signaled that she wanted to add a verbal lashing, but aborted in favor of a damning head shake.

"Principal Foster's got throat cancer," whispered Mrs. Ogilvie, the second-grade teacher seated beside Mary Ann.

Mary Ann gasped. Mr. Portwit continued reading. The Golden Rule of Tragedy Coping (like three years ago when fifth-grader Barrett Burger was diagnosed with leukemia), that any unrelated utterance would constitute a breach of etiquette, was under strict, though wordless, enforcement. One had to be sullen. Joy, or anything that could be construed as joy, or even a lack of sullenness, was a no-no. Rude as Mr. Portwit was for burying his face in Hawking, this clearly stood within bounds of the Golden Rule, so Mary Ann relaxed her upper body and felt her feet strain against the insides of her shoes.

"Now that everyone's finally here," Mrs. Jennings said, "we've got exactly two minutes. Why don't we say our prayer?"

The teachers joined hands. Mr. Portwit refused, leaving Mary Ann and the gym teacher unpartnered.

"Honey," Mary Ann pleaded, with as much desperation as she could muster at 1/100 her normal speaking volume.

Without looking up from his book, Mr. Portwit gently joined Mary Ann's hand with that of Mrs. Jungslatter, across the table in front of him. "I can't pray to a God that doesn't exist, for a man I don't like," he said. "But don't let me stop the party."

Mary Ann's face became like a heating coil.

"Let's pray," said Mrs. Jennings, one of two seventh-grade teachers at Elkhart. She was declaring herself the surrogate leader. Mrs. Jennings closed her eyes and bowed her head. The others followed suit. "Heavenly Father, bless Jim Foster during this trying time, and keep—"

The bell clanged for a torturous five seconds, during which Mr. Portwit stood, bagged his Hawking, kissed Mary Ann's cheek, and headed toward the door.

"Keep the . . ." Mrs. Jennings had lost her words. ". . . the family members and those of us here to . . . remember that within . . . even in our diseases, you are the source of health. Amen."

"Amen," echoed the chorus.

Mary Ann scrambled to find a clear path to the hallway. Her mind was filled with images of sickness—a lawn strewn with toilet paper, a swarm of flies dancing upon a pile of rancid mayonnaise, Principal Foster yellowed against a hospital pillow, his throat gone.

Betty Passinault had positioned herself in the doorway. Her trademark shoulder pads seemed doubly thick, and her helmet haircut gave her the look of a linebacker. She wasn't afraid of confrontations. Like a dog, she could smell Mary Ann's fear; she homed in on it with her reddened eyes. Crumbs of granola flew from her mouth when she spoke.

"Maybe you could tell your husband that his outbursts aren't as cute as he thinks." Her flat chest heaved. "Or maybe you also think it's cute to belittle a sick man?"

Mrs. Jennings materialized to cradle Mrs. Passinault in her arms. "Now, Betty, let's not sink to that level," she said.

Mary Ann offered, "We've had a rough morning."

"Let's just put it behind us, shall we, hon?" Mrs. Jennings said. "We've got children to teach."

As the day progressed inexorably toward fourth hour, Mr. Portwit's excitement disrupted his lectures. He stuttered, hummed, hemmed and hawed, his train of thought derailed again and again by the implications of the plastic canister in his pocket.

He hadn't formulated a plan of action, but he was charged by the possibilities. One thing was certain: he wasn't going to show his hand yet. If the vandals knew what he had in his pocket, they would get desperate. They would bribe him; they would burgle the film; or, worst of all, they would attempt to cry their way out of the mess. It was best to convince the vandals, through obfuscation, of course, that he possessed certain information that they didn't have—after all, the ignorant were the easiest to control. Through coded hints, he would convey that their proverbial balls were in his very real grasp, and there was nothing they could do about it. The canister alone could accomplish this task.

In fact, he had concerns about dropping off the film for processing. What if one of the vandals' brothers or sisters—or parents—worked at the photomat? What if an inept clerk exposed the film and ruined the prints? Yes, Mr. Portwit would wait until absolutely necessary to drop that final hammer—until then, he would have some fun.

The bell chimed the end of third hour. The six minutes between classes felt like an eternity or—since Mr. Portwit had never been able to imagine eternity without feeling nauseated—a googol of years. One hundred zeros. What a wonderful word, "Googol." He wrote it on the chalkboard, then erased it and used the same letters to spell, "Go, O Log!"

The students barged into the room en masse, clucking like poultry. Mr. Portwit mused that mindless human chatter was always likened to birds or monkeys. Never to fish, because fish didn't talk. They didn't need to talk. They knew the dignity of silence.

Mr. Portwit could see, lurking outside his room, Mrs. Jennings. He was the dedicated science instructor for sixth through eighth graders, and so all day he remained in the lab while teachers dropped off and picked up their kids. Mrs. Jennings had her students for Homeroom, History, Social Studies, English, and Math, and brought them to Mr. Portwit three days a week; to Music and Art twice a week; to Physical Education four days a week. Her arms were folded over her chest as she visually confirmed that each student's rear end connected to his or her assigned seat. For Mr. Portwit, she forwent the acknowledgment wave that teachers normally offered when dropping off their kids. It was official, then. He was an outcast. Well, what did it matter? He'd always been an outcast here, only no one had said it to his face. Or, rather, no one had not-waved it to his face.

So why did he push Mary Ann, his only ally, so often? And for such petty reasons? How hard would it have been to keep his mouth shut, join hands with his wife and Mrs. Jungslatter, bow his head, and go through the motions? He didn't have to turn everything into a battle, especially at the risk of losing the one positive development his life had seen in decades.

And yet, he reasoned, pretending to pray would've demeaned the faiths of everyone in that room. If a dyed-in-the-wool atheist was expected to partake in prayer without an ounce of true belief, with no one calling him to task—and in fact implicitly *demanding* such sanctimony—well, he was doing them a favor by walking away.

Mr. Portwit looked up from his attendance book, where between classes he'd doodled a series of anthropomorphic beakers with arms, legs, faces, and jagged cracks down their centers. Beside one he'd drawn a speech bubble: "I break for Elkhart science teachers!" He made a mental note to present this as a bumper-sticker idea at the next staff meeting.

He scanned the room and was overjoyed to see that despite their lack of sleep, the three perpetrators had made it to school.

He stood. "Ladies and gentlemen," he said, "and others." His eyes fell on Rick Fletcher. "Today I have planned something special. Today this teacher"—his gait as he paced the front became an old man's doddering shuffle, evoking giggles—"this ancient teacher is going to relinquish the class to one of *you*." He stopped, straightened, and surveyed the room, hand visoring his eyes like a guide on a safari. "I think I see one! Yes, over there!" He pointed to the back. "I see a teacher in his native state, as yet untrained and unformed. Let's see if we can get him to educate us."

He strolled with thumbs in pockets (his right one just touching the lid of the film canister) to Rick's desk. The class tittered. "Mr. Fletcher, I can't wait to see your lecture. What will be the subject today?"

"I ain't teaching," Rick mumbled.

"Not yet, but you will! You're a leader. You have a strong influence on others. So please," Mr. Portwit said, bowing his head and sweeping his hands toward the front of the room.

"No way."

Donald Peterson and Sedgwick Reynolds, in front of and next to Rick, respectively, stifled their laughter. Donald coughed into his hand the word "Freak."

"Your friends don't think you can do it," Mr. Portwit said. "And you know what? They're right. Never mind." His heels clicked up the aisle. He clenched his teeth together to refrain from smiling. It was working. They were fraying like yarn. "Let's just do things as usual. Would everybody open their textbooks to page 47, please?"

His hands trembled; he concealed it by standing behind the lectern. He instructed Veronica Vogel to read aloud. As she read, Mr. Portwit recalled the incident with Rick Fletcher eighteen days earlier that had gotten him reprimanded and which was the motive, no doubt, for the vandalism. He'd been giving what he considered to be one of his most compelling lectures, beginning with:

"The egg, people, is the most perfect architectural design in the universe. The Egyptians, the Romans, our own U-S-of-A—no one has come close to inventing a superior vessel. Strong enough to resist twenty pounds of direct pressure—that's 160 times its own weight—yet delicate enough to be cracked by the beak of a baby bird. It preserves life, it creates life. To many cultures it *is* life. The perfect symbol, anyway."

Mr. Portwit, as he'd done for twenty years, had opened his hand slowly, with solemnity. The Grade AA Medium lay like an enormous pearl upon the clam of his palm. Despite his rousing speech, the students were indifferent. Legs jutted into aisles; backs slouched; heads tipped in every direction, wearing the faces of lobotomy recipients. Mr. Portwit turned and began writing intently, with swoops and taps, upon the board. A student called out, "Mr. Portwit!"

"Yes sir?" Mr. Portwit said, still writing.

"My mom says that you and Mrs. Tucker don't have sex."

Snickering from every corner. Gasps from the girls.

Mr. Portwit spun to face the class. "Who said that?" The question was a formality; no name other than "Rick Fletcher" had come into his mind. However, without proof he could only attack indirectly.

"Okay, Mr. Anonymous," Mr. Portwit said. "I respect your cowardice. And I will answer you. The truth is 'no,' Mrs. Tucker and I don't have sex. And that is because Mrs. Tucker is my mother-in-law. It doesn't surprise me that a pig like yourself would suggest such a thing."

Murmurs of indignation. Someone said, "Oh my God."

"And if you were attempting, Mr. Anonymous, to question the nuptial relations of my *wife* and me, then her name is Mrs. *Portwit.* And to answer *that* question, no, we do not have sex. We *make love.* It is our ability to make love, face to face, with our minds as well as our bodies, which makes us human. It distinguishes us from the beasts. Of course, an animal like *your* mother could never make such a distinction. I feel sorry for her and all her doomed offspring."

The next day, it had been wrist-slapping time in Principal Foster's office. Mary Ann had tagged along. She claimed that she wanted to "lend moral support" and "defend him against any wild accusations." Mr. Portwit suspected that she wanted to babysit him, to protect him from bumping his soft skull against any administrative table corners. However, this notion wasn't entirely unpleasant, so he allowed her to come.

"Dale, we've had a number of *very* upset students and parents." Principal Foster tried unsuccessfully to clear his throat once, twice. The third time was a charm. He was famous for his throat problems. He'd been a three-pack-a-day smoker before being hypnotized into quitting the year before by an expensive Russian who ran a clinic in Boston. Principal Foster was younger than Mr. Portwit, but his fingers and teeth were yellow, his voice like a burned motor. "The complaints are from Mrs. Jennings's kids. They make some rather alarming allegations." He lifted a stack of papers to a legible distance from the reading glasses perched on his nose. "Let's see. They allege that you verbally abused them." He flipped to the next page, coughed wetly. "One report says that you called people's mothers 'animals'? Specifically, 'pigs'? And that you discussed sexual relations with your mother-in-law?"

"It's all true," Mr. Portwit said. "All of it."

"I know you're angry, Dale."

"Will you please call me Mr. PORTwit? I don't remember giving you permission—"

"Please," Mary Ann said. She took Mr. Portwit's hand.

"I know kids, Dale." Principal Foster set the papers down, removed his glasses, leaned back in his leather chair, crossed his hands, his legs, and probably even his toes. He was trying to make Mr. Portwit feel relaxed. His bodily attitude was screaming, "Dale, look at me! I'm calm and cool. Shouldn't you be calm and cool, too?"

"I've been at Elkhart for fifteen years," Principal Foster continued. "Kids lie. They exaggerate. They gang up on you. I know all of this."

"Then why are you saying it?" Mr. Portwit said. "I've been teaching for twenty years, and I'm keeping my mouth shut."

"Honey, you don't want to lose your job over this."

That was Mary Ann. His Mary Ann. Mr. Portwit looked at her muffin face, her beautiful pale skin that with nightly applications of Oil of Olay felt smooth as a butter stick. She was right. Sometimes inaction was the best action. He gave her fingers a squeeze.

"I apologize, Principal Foster. It's been stressful—we haven't even had our honeymoon yet." He threw his new bride a fawning glance, then reset his eyes on Foster. "*Closing* on a new house last week, moving in this week. It won't happen again."

"I don't think anyone's going to lose his job." Principal Foster coughed a chuckle. "I mean, these *are* seventh graders."

An incident report was filed, but Mr. Portwit escaped disciplinary action. His track record, both at Elkhart and at his previous job at Riverside Junior High, remained clean. Unremarkable but clean. Historically, students and parents had enjoyed Mr. Portwit's argyle socks and bow ties, his bald pate and coffee breath. To them, he was a cartoon character. Certainly, Rick Fletchers through the years had ridiculed him, but only in small doses. Even during Mr. Portwit's "dark time" (a term he shared with no one, in part because he wasn't sure he'd emerged from it yet), when he was his most stumbling, his most absentminded, his most anemic and pathetic, the students' mockery had never amounted to much more than snickers in the halls. Mr. Portwit believed that preteens could sense, perhaps on a chemical level, invisible lines that should not be crossed. This was not a man to taunt. Not to his face.

The bell rang, and the seventh graders exploded out of their seats before Mr. Portwit could officially dismiss them. He shouted the next day's reading assignment as the mass of bodies, heading toward the lunchroom—toward freedom, however illusory—bottlenecked at the door. He tried to engage Rick Fletcher in a staredown as Rick exited. The vandal wasn't biting. Mr. Portwit recalled a line his father used to say: "When the boy is growing, he has a wolf in his belly."

He fingered the undeveloped roll of film in his pocket. How odd that proof of anything could exist in such a tiny vessel.

Mary Ann had grown weary of saying it every forty-five seconds, but she would say it a hundred times more, if necessary: "We're not having sex tonight." The stench of turned mayonnaise lingered under her fingernails. Her arms and back felt stiff from raking toilet paper off the lawn, from scrubbing the windows, the door, the car. Below her skin, her heart ached, and not only because it was working overtime to disperse blood through her ever-ballooning body. "You humiliated me in the teacher's lounge," she said. "You need to apologize."

Mr. Portwit—tightly and whitely briefed—reposed on his belly beside her. "Mrs. Portwit, what have I said about forced apologies?"

"I wouldn't dream of *forcing* you to do anything. Heaven forbid Mr. Perfec-twit would admit he was wrong. I'm going to sleep."

"Mr. Perfec-twit—not bad! OK, OK. I apologize."

"Do you even know why you're apologizing?"

"I won't pretend that I care about those piranhas, but I do care about you. I'm sorry."

Mr. Portwit had propped himself onto his elbows. He leaned toward her. Mary Ann half-expected him to bark for an airborne smelt.

"Your eyes are crossed," she said. "And you look like a seal."

Mr. Portwit smiled. He had a kissable smile, when he bothered to show it, so she kissed it. "I have tunnel vision," he said. "I can only focus on one thing at a time. Right now it's you."

"We need to take our honeymoon," Mary Ann said. She opened her arms, allowing Mr. Portwit to come into her fold. "We need to get away."

"Four more days," Mr. Portwit said, touching her neck with his lips. "Now I think we should *seal* the deal." He clapped with his forearms, barked, "ARR ARR."

His face found her breasts, and his hands freed them by unzipping her nightgown and peeling it from her shoulders. His left thigh nuzzled between her legs.

"There's still wedding cake in the freezer," Mary Ann whispered.

The bedsprings groaned along with Mary Ann as Mr. Portwit slid downward. "I eat first," he said. "You eat second."

As his mouth went to work, he thought about what it would look like for a boy standing outside on tiptoes, squinting through the narrow gaps in the blinds. The boy's breath would mist the glass; the patter of rain on leaves, just a whisper, would feel like a godsend, covering mistaken shifts in weight that caused the gravel to squeak beneath his sneakers.

The boy's hand drifts downward; heavy breaths stutter as they escape.

Mrs. Brandmal being mounted, beyond the thin glass, by the faceless husband. Only a flash of skin visible at any given moment, yet the heat (What is happening in there?) wells in him, the knowledge that something—damn the curtains, her mouth most likely an 'O,' unable to control herself, taking him in hand, commanding him to do it to her—is happening.

Led by his erection, Mr. Portwit walked barefoot to the kitchen, opened the freezer, removed a Tupperware platter, unwrapped, positioned three slices of wedding cake upright on a plate, placed the plate in the microwave, selected DEFROST, 30 SECONDS, and START, stroked his penis until the *ding!* opened the microwave, took out the plate, closed the microwave, rewrapped the platter, returned it to the freezer, closed the freezer, carried the plate into the bedroom, smiled at his wife, set the plate on the queen-sized mattress, asked his wife "Frosting first?" studied her expression for signs of abandon, found only an eagerness to please him, decided to proceed anyway, ran a fingertip along the top of one slice of cake, and imagined Mrs. Brandmal's lips as Mary Ann allowed him to insert his frosting-covered finger into her mouth.

❦

He showered for a long time, his hairless head bowed like the teachers in their prayers for Mr. Foster. The hot water always induced thought, provided occasion for meditation: it oiled the rusted gateways in Mr. Portwit's cerebrum. Mary Ann would become weary of him, of the food, the sex, and the food sex. A marriage needed to be more than a fulfillment of animal desires. His father had lectured on this principle on more than one occasion, in his eloquent manner. "Marry a broad who can hem your pants," he told Dale on one of their deer-free deer-hunting trips, as they sipped black coffee at the foot of an elm, their bottoms cold and wet, "and you've got yourself a wife. A woman who's all whistles and bells will leave you hungry. No matter how filling those bells appear." Dale, eight years old, had nodded. Dale, half a century old, scrubbed his pubic region, attacking with a soapy cloth the crumbs and frosting smeared there.

Time had moved too quickly. High school had become college had become the working world had become climbing three flights of stairs to an attic apartment, bearing a sack of white bread as soft and pale as the hand that carried it, with a *Juggs* magazine brown-bagged and pinched under his arm.

When he was first hired at Elkhart, Dale had already crested what he'd perceived as the hill of his existence. He was forty-seven years old. He had never married. His apartment in the finished attic of a house in Kalamazoo's student ghetto felt each day more like a cave. Battered books spilled from the crowded shelves; his desk blocked the pathway from the living room to the kitchen, where his cupboards held pancake batter, Oreos, and a bottle of Tabasco. He could've afforded to buy a house in the suburbs, but a single man in a neighborhood surrounded by pregnant women, ice-cream-truck-chasing children, and lawn-mowing husbands? The concept was depressing, perhaps even illegal in some states.

He had believed then that everything after this point was gravity, a downward free fall to his end. He couldn't have said how he knew this; he merely sensed it. Pinpointing his life's peak was impossible, and he consoled himself with the thought that there would be no memory of a perfect apogee that he would never again reach.

He was forty-nine when he finally noticed Mary Ann Tucker, third-grade teacher. They'd been coworkers for two years, but he'd been in a funk all that time, burrowing into books at every free moment and avoiding eye contact with everyone but his mailman, Rufus, his only friend.

Gray-bearded Rufus, stomping up the walkway through the snow, breath pouring like pipe smoke from his mouth, had resembled a wiry Santa Claus. His was an old-fashioned mail-delivery style. At each house, he called out the resident's name. In Dale's case it was either "Mail's here, Mr. Portwit!" or "No mail, Mr. Portwit!" If greeted by an erect red flag, Rufus would holler, "Thanks for the outgoing!" while emptying the box.

A man like that, Mr. Portwit thought, could have no enemies, no disease, no reason to linger in bed until noon on weekends. A man like that, while undoubtedly saddled with the burdens of every aging person—unfulfilled dreams, regrets, poisonous memories—could step lightly, love deeply, and live bounteously. Day after day, perched at the window, gazing down at the street, Mr. Portwit awaited the faraway voice that heralded Rufus's arrival. Their brief exchanges became the happiest part of Mr. Portwit's life. He would arrive home from school, change into comfortable sweatpants, boil water for tea, open the window a couple of inches—just enough to let in sounds of traffic and a touch of the chilly air—and wait. When Rufus's voice rang out, Mr. Portwit would throw on hat, gloves, and boots, and go downstairs to clear icicles from the eaves with a broom, or sprinkle salt on the walkway, or shovel the sidewalk, even though none of these tasks was his responsibility. When Rufus arrived, the two men talked. Mr. Portwit shared opinions on evolution, cloud formations, and cloning, while Rufus, walking briskly to keep warm, nodded with enthusiasm, smiled, and was never too busy to offer his own views on the weatherman's prediction of more snow. Just before Christmas, Mr. Portwit surprised Rufus with a box of Nilla Wafers; he bestowed the cookies upon Rufus and snapped a photo.

It was when Rufus was reassigned that Dale attempted to hang himself. Three days after the new carrier dropped the bombshell of Rufus's relocation, Dale closed the bathroom door on a looped belt, put his head inside the loop, and lifted his legs.

What had he done to drive Rufus away? Dale spent a miserable weekend retracing each exchange of their brief relationship. He critiqued each flippant hand gesture, every careless pun that might've offended his friend. He slept in fitful spurts. He drank a large quantity of cheap vodka. At one point, he spent three hours acting out a handful of their recent encounters, using the coatrack as a stand-in for Rufus. When finished, he felt ashamed and furious. He could think of nothing he'd done to deserve this. He mused that every *action* is, by definition, part *act*. This meant that though he might not even have realized it, Rufus had been a fraud. His actions, which Dale had perceived as honest gestures of love (not love for *him*, necessarily—he wasn't so naive and schoolgirlish as to believe this—but a love for life, for his job, for the minor relations to other humans that formed the fabric of existence)—these had all been a sham. That this falseness, moreover, was built into the language was downright devastating; no one could perform an action without implying that he didn't really mean it.

When Mr. Portwit closed his eyes, inserted his head through the looped belt, and lifted his socked feet from the floor, he expected to be choked painfully as his heartbeat died by degrees in his ears. Instead, the belt slipped from his neck and rode up under his chin. His head was pinned to the door; his jaw was clamped shut. Gravity held him in place with a magnet-like insistence. The position was uncomfortable, but not fatal. It took ten minutes of flailing before he managed to plant his feet, right himself, crack open the door, release the belt, and collapse like a pile of intestines onto the unwashed porcelain.

Afterward, the belt was no longer a mere trouser supporter. It attained a symbolic power, like a fossil or a photograph. Rufus had never been a real friend. He could have refused his route transfer.

Beloved as he was, he could simply have asked his customers to start a petition drive, had he desired to stay. At the very least (down around the level of basic human decency), he could have bothered to *mention* his upcoming relocation, could have slipped a note into Mr. Portwit's mailbox to say, "Thanks for the memories, my peculiar and fascinating friend." But no.

After the suicide attempt, Dale had abandoned the death idea and decided that living was for enjoying, and that he would enjoy life in the basest way possible, which meant cultivating and satisfying his sex drive for the first time. He had, to this point, had sex with two women—both in college, polite girls who were afraid to leave the lights on. So, after indulging himself with pornographic videos, Dale graduated to peep booths at the Portage Adult Book Store and the Velvet Touch. Then to prostitutes, who provided brief moments of intense satisfaction followed by weeklong feelings of soiledness. In total, his sexual bonanza lasted just over eight months, shorter than the length of most human pregnancies.

Then, bored, he'd decided to strike up a conversation with the shy third-grade teacher, who liked to nibble Hostess Fruit Pies. Once he'd set his sights on her, Mary Ann had fallen easily. She was, like him, an over-the-hill loner, an outcast from the reindeer games of the Elkhart staff. Dale had known that his motives weren't based solely upon attraction—not at first, anyway. He was lost. He was seeking direction. Distraction. A safety net. In his mind, he'd fallen as far as humanly possible, and in desperation he reached for the helping hand touted by clergy, classic rock, and commercials alike: romantic love. Of course, the added bonus was that he actually *liked* Mary Ann. She was pleasant and upbeat. She smelled nice. She held him tightly when they kissed.

Then along came the urge to watch her eat, and soon after, he began to feel excited by her exquisitely enormous rear end (as well as her other abundances). While there was nothing morally *wrong* with these new desires, they felt to Mr. Portwit like a swerving back toward the unsavory behavior of his past. So one evening, he proposed. She said yes.

Their whirlwind romance landed them a marriage license and a house in the suburbs. All this in half a year. End of story. Beginning of story.

Now he had a woman to hold, a wife with a brain and a bosom

who happily accommodated his request to watch her devour food and to have sex while different edibles got squished and mangled upon her naked body. He'd objectified, and thus rendered impotent, Rufus's memory by enlarging, then framing, his photograph and enshrining it on his dresser. Mr. Portwit hadn't felt a suicidal urge in fifteen months. His belt, though now on display at the Green Top Bar, still functioned. By all counts, life should feel perfect. Yet here he was, dripping in the shower, unable to shake the idea that something wasn't right. There was a black hole in his universe, and he was beginning to feel the suck of its gravity.

Mrs. Brandmal rewarded the good children by eating a one-on-one lunch with them in the library. That damn sentence. He wished he could charge a toll for the number of times it had driven through his brain.

He'd been eleven years old. Mrs. Brandmal, his teacher, had inspired more erections than any other woman at PS42. Her best skirts stopped at her knee, and a simple positioning of her high-heeled foot onto the low inner shelf of the lectern exposed a patch of thigh that sent every fifth-grade boy into outer space. She had legs, golden, nyloned legs—and she *liked* to show them!

That's what they thought; that's what they hoped for and prayed for and talked about at recess. They didn't care about missiles pointed at Florida, about Communists disguised as classmates. They prayed that Mrs. Brandmal would sit upon the stool and cross those legs and, glory of glories, unleash more flesh than any boy could stand.

This was not to mention her breasts or the tight sweaters that bore them, or the dessert of her confident strut across the room, cherried by a sidecar left hand, her index finger and thumb poised as if pinching shut the mouth of a tiny invisible sack so that no one could discover its contents.

Mr. Portwit felt profound disappointment as he scrubbed his face and thought about Mrs. Brandmal. It was terrific to be here in a new house—1,500 square feet, good lighting, strong water pressure—but his real hope had been that Mrs. Brandmal would be left behind in that attic apartment along with his other shameful behavior. He dried his face. He inspected his nose hairs in the mirror. He couldn't recall exactly the first time he'd thought about killing her, but he was certain it had begun during the prostitution era, or perhaps right after Rufus left. At the time, it had been a fleeting impulse; nothing more than a bizarre, unformed notion that he pushed from his mind.

He slid deodorant under his arms, then brushed his teeth. Mary Ann's brand—Crest Ultra—tasted more pleasant than the baking soda he normally used. And yet—was it as effective? Doubtful. Something so sweet and minty couldn't truly get at the plaque buildup. Progress, repair, cleansing—such things required pain. Or, if not pain, at least a disagreeable flavor. No one had ever cured their cancer with lollipops.

So Brandmal had pursued him here, into his new marriage, into the womb of suburbia. He had tried to run, but she'd tracked him like a bloodhound. If he traced backward through the years, her presence (albeit only a mental presence) was the one constant in his life. It surprised him to think now that his long-standing dissatisfaction and his deep and inexplicable periods of depression could be blamed on a single person: he had only to declare it so, and it would be so. It was in his power, wasn't it? That's what self-help, pop psychology, and shoe commercials were all about—telling us something about ourselves over and over until it becomes the truth: *I'm a strong person. A happy person. I can do this. Just do it.*

Was she still alive? What about her husband? Did she still live in Saginaw? If she was alive, it would not be difficult to find her. If he could find her, couldn't he murder her? Her death wouldn't erase the past, but it would be like destroying an abandoned hornet's nest; no hornet could ever live there again, so this would *relieve* the past of its significance. It would be easy. Mrs. Brandmal would be—what—seventy-five, give or take? He could nullify her for nullifying his life.

Once Dale's body was dry, he draped the towel over the shower curtain rod. He entered the bedroom and navigated to the bed, not bothering to turn on the light. Mary Ann's backside was a wall beside him. Her breathing was slow, deep. He nestled close and pressed against her. The world sloped in her direction.

A wind sucked through the caverns of Mary Ann's lungs as she inhaled. Exhaling, she became a boiling teakettle, or a tooting train. A person could be many things, even when she was unconscious.

2

Mary Ann's mother owned a cottage tucked deep in the woods, invisible from Highway 57, near the northeast shore of Lake Michigan. Mary Ann and Mr. Portwit arrived there to spend their honeymoon strolling along the state park beach and fishing for bluegill in Bass Lake.

The days were short and chilly. November loomed three weeks away, promising to shrivel every remaining leaf and turn trees into skeletons. The town of Pentwater was similarly terminal. The ice-cream stand had boarded up for the season; restaurant hours were cut in half; only a handful of RVs could be seen, and they roamed the empty streets like lost dinosaurs. Besides the local high school kids paired on car hoods in the parking lot to watch the sunset, the beach was abandoned. Mr. Portwit noted that the area merchants, finally allowed by the off-season to don apathetic faces for customers, were "eagerly relaxing their orbicularis oris muscles."

In recent years Mary Ann's mother had repainted the cottage the same shade of mouthwash blue as Betty Passinault's SUV. She'd altered the interior, too: new tile had been laid on the expanded kitchen floor, which now reached halfway into what used to constitute the dining area. Gone was "Big Brown Bear," the enormous sofa where Mary Ann had regularly fallen asleep in front of the ten-inch black-and-white TV after playing horseshoes with her father. In the sofa's place was an expensively frail-looking, faux fox fur loveseat that Mary Ann could barely fit inside. The ten-inch TV had grown to thirty-six inches and had sprouted color.

"It feels like a different place," Mary Ann said, removing clothing from their suitcase and stacking it neatly in the cherry-wood bureau, one of the few items she still recognized.

"It *is* a different place," Mr. Portwit answered from the kitchen. "It's not a museum. Your mother isn't dead."

"But my dad built this cottage. She could've consulted me about *some* of these things."

"Did you ever ask her?"

"No, Answer Man, I didn't," Mary Ann said, looking out the bedroom door at her husband—her husband! such a foreign phrase; she might never get used to it—as he rinsed the dinner plates and loaded them into the dishwasher. "Wait, wait. Don't tell me; I need to start speaking my mind and stop being dead."

"Bingo," Mr. Portwit said.

At five-thirty in the morning, Mary Ann awoke. Beside her, with his eyes closed and the blanket pulled up to his chin, Dale looked like a little boy. He was at peace, his expression softened, his crinkles ironed. Of course, she was reminded of her father in his coffin, but not too much, only in passing. If one focused on things like this, life was reduced to a parade of reminders; every Pontiac Catalina, blue architectural drawing, or half-eaten English muffin became dark symbolism. Admittedly, for the first few years after the accident, she had broken into hysterics upon seeing Don Johnson's three-day shadow (her father had, in her eyes, invented that look) or a box of Swisher Cherry Cigarillos (he enjoyed one whenever he was in a celebrating mood). Now, however, such reactions were under her control.

"Time to wake up," she whispered. No response. She put a hand on Mr. Portwit's shoulder. His eyes snapped open. He turned and stared at her in horror.

"It's the first time," he said, his ragged voice tremolo, his eyes unseeing. "I swear it's the first time."

"Honey, it's me. Everything's OK."

"I'm scared," he whispered. "I don't like this anymore." His eyes were open, but they showed no recognition of anything in front of him.

Then all at once he noticed the sheet throttled in his hands. He noticed Mary Ann. His breath quickened. He scrutinized Mary Ann. Gradually, his mouth formed a smile. He seemed embarrassed.

"You were dreaming," Mary Ann said.

"You bet."

"Do you want to tell me about it?"

He licked sleep from his mouth. "There's nothing more boring than another person's dreams."

"I don't mind," Mary Ann said, careful not to sound too curious.

"Those fish aren't going to catch themselves," Mr. Portwit said.

They rowed toward the center of Bass Lake in the dull gray twelve-footer whose familiar identification sticker, CY13Y26, still clung tightly to her bow.

"See . . . Why 13? . . . Why 26?" Mary Ann said, as Mr. Portwit's oars dipped in and out of the black water. "I used to say that every time we went out."

"Did you ever get an answer?"

"They were rhetorical questions, sweetie."

"Is that so?"

"I'm huge," Mary Ann said. Her whisper felt loud on the motionless lake. "Look at how tilted the boat is."

"The world loves you. It wants to pull you closer."

Mary Ann opened the plastic container of worms. Her fingers burrowed into the soil, a rich, fecund, sticky dirt, its odor pungent enough to make her mouth water. She took hold of a fat worm. It writhed stupidly but with passion even after it was impaled three times. Mr. Portwit also baited his hook. He enjoyed the dirt under his nails, the worm goo on his fingers. They cast their lines onto what looked like spilled tar stretching to the shoreline. They were alone. They concentrated on locating their bobbers in the half-light.

"Happy honeymoon," Mary Ann whispered.

"This is enchanting," agreed Mr. Portwit, his voice still thick with sleep. "No people. Not even enough light to see the sky in the water. There might be a heaven after all."

"It's weird. I haven't fished in twenty-five years. How did I get so old so fast?"

"You know of course that you didn't age any faster than anyone else in history."

"So my perceptions don't count for anything? Even if it feels fast, it's not? Even if I'm full, I'm not?"

"Old, young. Full, hungry. The important thing is that you're fishing now, aren't you?"

Mr. Portwit was quiet for a moment. From a bed of weeds along the nearest shoreline, a bird took flight with a furious flapping sound. It soared over their boat and across the lake.

"Adjectives," Mr. Portwit scoffed, continuing his thought, reeling in his line. "What can you do with them? Line them up against a wall and shoot them. That's why I pursued science. Remove the subjective."

"But I never would have loved you based on your looks. Sorry, honey. You *needed* my subjectivity. And if you'd come up to me and just said, 'Ooga booga,' I would've run away."

"That's the first time language has done me any good."

"We have a strange marriage, don't we?"

"There's that adjective junk again."

"I'm not having sex with the bluegills," Mary Ann said.

"What if I catch a few sunfish?"

Three hours later, seventeen bluegill and two sunfish filled their bucket. Mary Ann, as a finale, reeled in a speckled bass, but it was two inches short of regulation. Mr. Portwit kissed it and tossed it back into the water. The sun peeked over the trees and turned the lake into the sky. They stuck the fishhooks into the cork handles of the poles, and Mr. Portwit stepped cautiously to the boat's middle seat. Mary Ann pulled up the yellow nylon rope, hand over hand, until the rusted Folger's coffee can filled with cement rose to the surface. She stripped the wig of weeds from its crown. The surrounding cabins had come to life, and the chatter of children echoed over the water. Mr. Portwit took up the oars and rowed.

The air in the cottage smelled of ceramic tiles and toilet water. Mary Ann's lower back throbbed, her fingernails were black, and though Bass Lake was only a five-minute walk, she felt like she'd completed a triathlon. Lugging a pail full of water and fish, even with a partner, was brutal work. She felt used, but in a good way. Mr. Portwit entered the utility room as she began unfastening her life jacket.

"So . . . tight . . ." she said, huffing, frustrated because she couldn't breathe. "I am so. Damn. Fat."

Mr. Portwit dropped the tackle box into the corner. "You complain, I tell you it doesn't matter, you complain, I say everything I can to make you feel better, then you complain some more. For shit's sake, I like you fat! I LIKE YOU FAT. Where are the knives?"

Mary Ann stopped fidgeting with her life jacket. "Sorry," she mumbled.

He didn't hear, or just didn't respond. He was busy foraging through drawers in the kitchen, making a profound racket. Mary Ann left her life jacket on and went into the bathroom. She sat on the toilet. She wanted to cry, which she knew was ridiculous. It took virtually nothing to break her—just raise your voice and criticize something, anything, and BOOM, she turned on the waterworks.

Besides, he was right. Every instinct she'd ever had about her body had been incorrect. Every diet had failed, every mirror was warped, every food other than raw vegetables was apparently bad for her. When it came to her body, her recent incredible weight gain was the only thing that *had* worked, the only thing that had ever made another person *pleased*, for Christ's sake. Why was she fighting her only success story?

"Another interesting fact about the shark? It never gets full," Dale had told her at Charlie's Crab, the upscale restaurant where many high-schoolers dined before prom. "It's always hungry. It eats. And eats. And eats. Whenever it can."

"I didn't know that," she'd said. Even though it was their second date, she still felt surprised that he was sitting across from her, surprised to be eating, let alone sharing, a fancy dinner (drawn butter, cloth napkins). He'd asked her out so suddenly, after years of genial silence.

Mr. Portwit had ordered a lobster for himself, grilled shark steak for Mary Ann. For appetizers: a bowl of garlic butter encircled by frog's legs, jumbo shrimp quotation-marked over a bed of greens, sautéed mushrooms, and a basket of steamed clams. At Mr. Portwit's prompting, Mary Ann ate voraciously, pausing between bites to offer a bashful smile and wipe her mouth with a linen napkin that matched the color of their drinks.

She stuffed her face partly because she didn't know what to say. She was still processing the fact that he had ordered the main course for her. What did it mean? Was his concept of masculinity rooted in the 1950s? One part of her wanted to take offense, to make it clear that she could make her own decisions, thank you very much. At the same time, she couldn't help but see his backward views as a sort of innocence, as if he'd learned dating protocol from Gary Cooper movies as a child and was now at last getting to play the role of cavalier romantic.

"You look beautiful when you chew," Mr. Portwit said, himself not chewing but sipping at his Burgundy. "The muscles in your jaw are magnificent. Like a heartbeat that can't be contained." His eyes, brown and deep, captured the candlelight, flickering like a banjo at a bonfire. In many ways, he reminded Mary Ann of a bald Jeremy Irons—an actor Mary Ann passionately loved—without the accent. Mr. Portwit's manner was polite, his speech rhythmic and imbued with hidden meaning. His brow was bold, well-defined. His teeth were perfectly white. His cratered pate, ringed by a halo of grayish-brown hair, was like a miniature of the moon. Mary Ann wanted to reach out and touch it, so she did.

"I've been wanting to do this since our picnic," she giggled, pistoning her fingertips on his cranium.

The meal was exquisite. Lean Cuisine fettuccine and a bag of Cheetos were a typical dinner at Mary Ann's house. From the end of her fork now, a wedge of shark steak dripped lemon juice. It virtually melted upon hitting her tongue.

He cracked open the lobster's claw. "If you think about it . . ." He speared the meat with his tiny fork. "You *have* to have another bite of this," he offered. She mouth-grabbed, she chewed.

"If you think about it," he continued, "there's no better way to enjoy life. The shark is a metaphor for heaven. Always tasting, savoring, never needing to stop. Getting pleasure out of every bite."

"Couldn't you look at it another way?" Mary Ann had answered. "Doesn't it mean a shark is never satisfied? It always needs more, more, more." Her fingertip traced the lip of her wineglass. "Sounds like me, actually." Rich desserts, fatty potato chips, donuts—since she was a girl, Mary Ann had battled her appetite as if it was a demon living in her belly. Until now.

"Yes, that's it!" Mr. Portwit said. "You're blessed. It's a blessing." He put down the lobster claw and palmed Mary Ann's knee under the table. "I know that you're *large*," he said, reading her expression, noticing the shocked darting of her eyes. "Yes, I'm saying it right now. Out loud. To your face. You are a large woman. Since when is the adjective *large* a bad adjective? Seems harmless to me. Even good. I'd love a *large* sum of money right about now." He laughed heartily. "Did I say you were *ugly*? Or *gross*? Of course not. You are large, and to me, large is beautiful."

That night they made love, and Mr. Portwit whisked her into his world, leaving hers behind. It wasn't until their third encounter, however, that he brought out the whipped cream and cherries. Soon the erotic edibles became more imaginative. Schuler's cheese spread. Lightly toasted bagels. Asparagus spears. She reasoned that her mother, if she knew (mortifying thought), *should* be proud (in theory)—not of their unconventional sex life, but because Mary Ann was finally doing something for herself. Mary Ann had found her sacrifice. She was letting someone be nice to her. She enjoyed Mr. Portwit's company. He made her smile, he gave her gifts, his kisses brought her to her knees, the sex was a rush. Gorging felt terrible, but if that was the price of true love, she would grin and bear it.

More than once, she asked—delicately, offhandedly—where his fetish had come from. There was no special reason, he said. None that he was aware of, anyway. He only knew that watching Mary Ann eat made him exceedingly happy. It roused his blood, he said, making it feel charged with electricity as it coursed through his body. He swore that he'd never had such desires before, not with any woman.

Through the end of the school year, she and Mr. Portwit spent every weekend together. He showed no restraint in broadcasting their relationship to the other teachers. He sat beside Mary Ann during lunch. He watched her, whispered random thoughts into her ear as she chewed. His manner created a bubble around them, shutting out the other teachers, who made no effort to hide their amazement. For the first time since Mary Ann had known her, Mrs. Passinault was speechless. The other teachers reacted similarly; a queer silence fell over the lounge, punctuated only by the crackle of wrappers and the clearing of throats.

In the middle of the summer, he proposed, and on September 1, they were married. Mary Ann didn't write a list for five months. They postponed their honeymoon because of work and because Mr. Portwit had found them a house in the Kalamazoo suburb of Portage. He had lauded the safety, the quiet, the large yards, and the name, "Portage."

"It means 'the transport of cargo and goods,' often with ships as the load-bearing vessel," he had said.

He admitted that as a bachelor the notion of moving to such a neighborhood had been abhorrent, but that marriage had opened his eyes to its benefits. He could see himself guiding a lawn mower, waving to neighbor Nick who stood on a nearby back patio, flipping burgers. Mary Ann wondered why he'd reversed his position on the subject. Was it another of his inscrutable changes of heart, or was he making a sacrifice for her? She chose to believe the latter.

Mary Ann had been thrilled at the prospect of the suburbs. Her previous neighborhood had been worn and dingy, with dark houses so packed together they appeared to be straining to touch each other out of loneliness. It was a neighborhood populated by retirees, unweddeds, and the widowed, not distant enough from the halfway house to discourage the homeless mental cases from using her bushes as a toilet and her yard as a part-time disco.

Hard to believe that she'd bought that house at thirty, and that she'd lived there, alone, for ten years. Hard to believe that at twenty she'd promised herself she would be married by thirty. Or that at ten, she'd sworn on a pile of her mother's panties to be married by twenty.

Hard to believe how easily people altered their dreams so they wouldn't feel that they'd failed.

That's why Mary Ann had kept her lists—seven boxes, each stuffed head to foot with binders, each binder labeled with dates. Mary Ann, still seated on the toilet of the family cottage, felt a shudder of accomplishment thinking about the day she'd finally brought them into their new home. It had taken only twenty-five minutes to haul the boxes into the back room of the basement. It took six hours to unpack them.

Mary Ann recalled her mother's eternal insistence that Mary Ann never did anything for herself. If ever a picture-phone would've come in handy, it would've been at that moment, viewing the grand display: two decades of self-serving labor, fifty-four binders lined up like soldiers on the basement shelf of her new home.

"This is what I've done for myself," she would've said, spreading her arms to display them in all their glory.

Each list was more than just its content; each evoked far more than a place and year; each represented the mental landscape and emotional backdrop that made her, distinctly, "Mary Ann Tucker."

Six Boys I'll Never Be Able to Neck With (1978)—her very first list. It was the night of her sixteenth birthday. She had sat up in bed, squinting, writing by the sliver of light that filled the gap under the door. Her notebook was as virginal as she, but its cherry was popped that night. (Mary Ann's wouldn't be for another twelve years.) She and Bernette Fargas had gone to the Plainfield Roller Rink, where Bernette necked with both Ronny Weidenfeller *and* J. P. Cornelius. Mary Ann got to hear about it from everyone at the roller rink, Bernette included.

Four Songs I Need to Be Happy (1979)—Funny. "Maybe I'm Amazed" at Number 4. "Fat-Bottomed Girls" at Number 3. "Time in a Bottle" at Number 2. "And now" (in Casey Kasem's rich baritone) "the Number 1 song that Mary Ann Tucker, of Grand Rapids, Michigan, needs to be happy: 'Lovin,' Touchin,' Squeezin'' by Journey." She had compiled this list while seated on the grass in front of the house, waiting for the city bus to take her to a recital. Mary Ann was second-chair trumpet in the high school band. Her pencil lead had just broken off when her dad stepped out the front door. He waved to Mary Ann. He yelled, "Good luck today! Remember to have fun." He didn't normally work on Saturdays. He had an important meeting with city planners and commission board members. He was the head architect for the new downtown amphitheater. Around the Tucker house, this was a major deal.

Nine Ways Mother Should Change (1980)—1980 was the year that the lists became more frequent. That summer, just after graduation, Mary Ann had felt birthed, naked and trembling, into a world where people wouldn't feel obliged to be polite because they had to sit beside her in class. Mary Ann had never been good at making friends. During senior year, Bernette had been absorbed into a popular circle that apparently stopped taking applications after her acceptance. Mary Ann ("Tucker the Trucker," to a few of the less tactful, based on her brick-house frame and short-cropped hair) was left without a close relationship with anyone her age. Her once-a-month list-writing hobby turned into a weekly habit.

Exacerbating her loneliness was her father's new job, which demanded long hours both at home and at the office. Mom turned tense and humorless; she demanded quiet so Dad could get work done in his study. Mom had been poor (relatively) her entire life, in part because she had never wanted to pursue her own career. Jack was the earner; she was the housewife. She'd been known to announce, with gusto, "I'm just not good at anything!" followed by, "I'm more of a support scaffold." (She was proud of the architectural pun.)

But Mom enjoyed having money, loved the new paychecks, and looked forward to all future income this project was slated to provide. She wanted Jack to have no distractions from an attention-starved daughter, or an attention-starved anybody, for that matter. If Jack needed to hunch over his blueprints and calculator seventy hours each week, then that's what he had to do. If Jack had to miss his daughter's band recital to update drawings, so be it. If Jack had to eat his breakfast on the run, Mom would stuff a half-toasted English muffin into his hand and shove him out the door.

And if licking the jelly overflow from one of these muffins, or swatting at the crumbs in his lap, rather than concentrating on the road, had indeed sent Jack over the yellow line and into the path of the Keebler truck, then wasn't his death actually, technically, Mom's fault?

Ten Things I Miss About My Dad (Parts 1 thru 10) (1980)—The night of his funeral, with her mother's muffled offstage sobs as the sound track, Mary Ann wrote ten lists. Ten lists of ten. She wanted to capture him in her mind. Photographs were nice, but whatever the camera saw, that's what you got. A person had no control. Besides, photos were shared memories, shared with Mother. Mary Ann wanted her own portrait, a private one. For eight hours that night, she wrote, cried, listened to music in her headphones, curled up on the bed, and tried not to blink.

For the remainder of the summer, her mouth ached from frowning. Her stomach hurt from overeating. Her face wrinkled from the anger toward her mother, anger toward herself; she realized she was a loser. She had lost her Dad, lost the security of high school, lost her best friend Bernette, lost her sex drive (the thought of kissing a boy nauseated her) all in the span of a couple months.

She packed her belongings into the Ford Tempo she'd bought with $478 earned bagging groceries at Vogel's, and sped out of the driveway with no intention of coming back. She was off to Kalamazoo, to Western Michigan University, off to see the world. Her most prized possessions, sharing the front seat on the forty-five-minute drive, were her photos of Dad and the ever-growing binder labeled *Mary Ann's Lists.*

Mary Ann heard a commotion in the kitchen. She continued digging the dirt from under her fingernails. Judging by the urgency of the clangor, Mr. Portwit was trying to find something, and getting irritated at his failure. He would soon be pounding on the door, asking for help. She didn't have the energy to face him just yet.

Mr. Portwit finally found the knives. For twenty minutes, he'd rifled through the kitchen drawers, but of course the utility room was the obvious choice. There, along with the rest of the gear, the knives had been hibernating. From a dust-covered wooden case that resembled an oversized cigar box, he retrieved the filleter and the scaler. He paused to tell the bathroom door that he was going outside to clean the fish.

"OK," the door said, with hastily assembled, utterly unconvincing good cheer.

The job was more brutal than he remembered. In the bucket, the nineteen fish were piled on top of one another like football players on a loose pigskin. Whenever Dale tried to reach into the water, they splashed furiously. He tried three times before getting a firm grip on one of the bluegills. He marveled at the power of its muscle as it flexed for freedom. And its smell was so ripe, like fresh fruit. The smell was *fish*. No other word to describe it. It was unmistakable. He wondered if his own smell was as distinct. *Does it smell Portwitty in here? No, not adjective, but noun: the smell was Portwit.*

He laid the bluegill on the cutting board and sawed below the dorsal fin. With the "pop" of its spine, the head came off. The fish never changed expression. Its gills worked to consume oxygen, and its mouth tried to sing a song. Mr. Portwit improvised a three-bar tune: "*I am a fish / With on-ly one wish / I don't want to die / Without see-ing you cry.*"

How quickly these old rituals were remastered. He hadn't fished in forty years, give or take, yet this process had remained tucked inside the gray folds of his brain, buried beneath "set the alarm clock," "lather and shave," "pants before shoes," "take attendance," and other similar rigmarole. He had fished as a child on Pretty Lake (such a simple and, as adjectives went, nearly inarguable name) during his father's annual vacation from the caulking glue factory.

Oscar Portwit had been a tie among T-shirts, head of Payroll and Inventory, and he liked it that way. Though he'd never done hard labor (at age eleven, he told Dale, he'd run the only lemonade stand in town that was squeeze-your-own), through a combination of calisthenics and genetic inheritance he kept his body tight as the drums of caulk that lined the factory floor. He was a short man who breathed, stared, and barked like a bulldog, and his flash temper kept the boys from seeing him as a pencil pusher. "The men respect me," Oscar liked to say, "because they can count on my unpredictability." The only thing soft about Dale's father was his mind, these last few years. Then again, Dale didn't really know much about that; he kept his contact with his parents to a minimum. A five-minute phone call every three months seemed to do the trick of maintaining the semblance of a blood relation.

He sliced, gutted, scaled. The pile of fish heads grew in the center of the sheet of newspaper, their eyeballs peering as if making sure he would do unto all others as he had done to them. Even ten minutes after beheading, the mouths continued to open and close. It's what Oscar and Adeline, Dale's mother, were doing this very moment, at any given moment; they were staring, opening and closing their mouths for food, water, or conversation. They were dead, and either didn't know it or didn't let it interfere with their mouthly activities. They were both eighty years old, and Dale had no tolerance for people who lived beyond the average life span. He termed them *life hogs*. They were the reason that more and more deaths were referred to as "tragic." When an old person died, it was "natural." When a young person died, it was "tragic." People like Dale's parents—and Mrs. Brandmal, if alive—were turning a sixty-year-old's heart failure into a movie of the week. Pretty soon there would be black armbands for dead centenarians.

The scales came loose in sticky gray clumps, which Mr. Portwit swished away by dunking the knife into the pan of clean water. The blade was new again. It was that easy.

Strange the way children are such robots, so programmable, linking emotion with everyday actions so that even twenty, thirty, forty years later, people feel sad or happy or angry when they repeat the acts. Sad. Happy. Good. Bad. He truly hated adjectives. Adjectives weren't provable. Period. For the man in the batter's box, hitting a home run was as "good" as an ice cream sundae. For the guy who threw the pitch, different story.

He finished cleaning the fish and rose to his feet, surprised that the dull pop at the base of his spine was not audible. He stretched to the left and the right. His fingers, painted with soil, blood, scales, and fish eggs, smelled delicious and dead. Overhead, the sun raged impotently, giving little more heat than the 75-watt bulb Mr. Portwit occasionally fell asleep beneath at his desk. Still, he was drenched in sweat. He wiped his pate with the sleeve of his flannel and looked at the pile of fish heads. All of them had given up on trying to breathe. Mr. Portwit had a sudden, wonderful idea.

"You are not eating the fish heads, Dale," Mary Ann said. "End of discussion."

"Not tonight, of course. I won't ruin our bounteous honeymoon dinner."

"Not tonight, not tomorrow, not the day after."

"OK, you've spoken your mind. I respect your mind. In the end, I'm controlled by mine."

One thing Mary Ann knew about Mr. Portwit was that arguing with him was futile. But whom was she kidding? She had never argued with *anybody*. She would duck into the ladies' room, fake a bout of diarrhea, escape to college—anything to avoid a confrontation. And well, who cares anyway, she thought, as she puttered toward the faux fox fur loveseat, intent on collapsing, reading a book, possibly napping. If devouring fish heads in order to, what did he say, "absorb the energy of an entirely new consciousness," was going to make him happy, then let him gag on scales all he wanted.

She could hear him in the kitchen, singing, "*In the mor-ning, laughing happy fish heads / In the eva-ning, floating in the soup.*"

The head-filled colander sat in the sink. With the full force of the cold tap, Dale blasted the guts, scales, and dirt from the goggle-eyed noggins; he dropped each shiny clean head into a Crock-Pot, which he filled with water and stored in the refrigerator.

After the sun went down, Mary Ann batter-fried the fish they'd caught. A $12.99 bottle of Merlot and two foot-long candles stood in the center of the table.

"Smells like fish," Mr. Portwit said, bibbed napkin tucked into the neck of his shirt, a fork and knife in his clenched fists.

Mary Ann recognized this as a compliment. She thanked him, set the heated dish onto the table with mitted hands. She considered herself a lousy cook, and seeing the tiny fried bluegill arranged as haphazardly as an unassembled jigsaw puzzle made her question her decision to serve the feast from a casserole dish. Mr. Portwit didn't appear to notice.

"To the fish-head people," he exclaimed, raising his glass, "who don't know they're dead yet!"

"And to the rest of us, who don't know what the hell you're talking about," Mary Ann said.

They both drank deeply, reddening their lips.

Mary Ann's cheek was in a puddle. Her mouth had spilled over. Her ears were tickled by the sizzle of frying fish. The fish were whistling in the pan. Whistling a tune! How funny.

Then the mattress quaked, and she opened her eyes. Mr. Portwit, standing in his briefs at the foot of the bed, eyes trained on the door, wearing neither glasses nor shirt, pear-sized fists clenched in front of his face, body bouncing in place on the springs of his legs, looked like an old-fashioned pugilist. The sizzling, the whistling, and now the odor of—yes, it was bacon, not fish—came from beyond the closed door. The whistler whistled "Tie a Yellow Ribbon 'Round the Old Oak Tree."

"Stay put," Mr. Portwit breathed, at a volume so low that a spider in his mouth would have trouble hearing.

Disgusted, Mary Ann flung back the blankets and rolled onto her side so she could raise her body in one fluent motion. She'd gotten adept at this and was certain she could spring out of bed as quickly as any normal-sized person. Her feet found her slippers. "I can't believe it," she said. "It's my mother."

As the bedroom door opened, Mrs. Tucker spun as if on an axis to face it. Her smile was wider and toothier than a shark's. "Good morning, newlyweds!" she trumpeted. "Breakfast is almost ready."

Mary Ann and Mr. Portwit, puffy-eyed, stunned, stepped into the kitchen. The table was set with cow-covered placemats, peach-colored plates with matching cloth napkins, and full glasses of orange juice. A bowl of scrambled eggs and a stack of pancakes competed fiercely for the title of Most Steaming. Mrs. Tucker lifted the frying pan from the stove, killed the eye, and with spatula pressing the bacon in place, tilted the pan to pour the thin stream of grease into an aluminum can.

"Everything's all set," she remarked over her shoulder, dividing her eyes in that superhuman way she had, able to view both Mary Ann and the pouring grease at the same time. "Sit down. Sit down. I insist," she insisted.

Mr. Portwit grunted. He scuffled barefoot into the bathroom. The door closed.

"Mom, what are you doing?" Mary Ann said.

"I know, I know," Mrs. Tucker responded, bringing the plate of bacon to the table. "I'm sorry to drop in on you like this. It wasn't my intention, believe you me. Janie Eichler—you remember her, she lives three doors that way, she was the one who took you to the doctor when you stepped on that nail. You were small. Your father never forgave himself for taking so long at the post office that day. He was so upset." With a brisk shake of her head, she scattered the memories. "Anyway, Janie Eichler hasn't been too healthy lately." She lowered her voice. "She's got something in the brain, I believe. Not a tumor, exactly, but something like that."

"Mom, get to the point."

"*Sorry*," her mother said, eyebrows levitating with her pitch, indicating her alarm at Mary Ann's impatience. "I told her son that I would come up before the snow falls and put in the storm windows, turn on the heater so the pipes don't freeze. That kind of thing. I forgot it was your week. I won't stay. I just saw Dale's car out front and figured I'd make breakfast for you."

Mr. Portwit's heavy urination, which had raged behind Mrs. Tucker's speech, finally died, as abruptly as it had begun. Mary Ann imagined that he'd planned it that way. It wouldn't be beyond possibility for Mr. Portwit to have mastered such a skill.

Mr. Portwit came out of the bathroom. Wearing only his briefs, he walked at the pace of a wedding procession along the border of kitchen tile and dining-area carpet. He disappeared into the bedroom as Mary Ann and her mother exchanged looks. "It's nothing I haven't seen before," her mother said, reassuringly.

Mary Ann sat at the table and invited her mother to do the same. Mr. Portwit emerged from the bedroom. Mercifully, he was clothed.

"Who said that after forty there were no more surprises?" he asked, approaching his mother-in-law. He bent to kiss her cheek. "How nice to see you again."

She smiled up at him. "You can call me 'Mom' now, Dale."

Mr. Portwit took a seat between the Tucker women. He scanned the breakfast with eyes and nose simultaneously, sniffing. He mumbled, "Incredible . . ." As he forked a pair of sausage links he added, "It's not comfortable for me, Mrs. Tucker. Calling you 'Mom.' No offense. And you can call me Mr. Portwit."

When Mrs. Tucker chose to take a long drink of juice rather than respond, and Mary Ann shot him a glare designed to blow up his head, Mr. Portwit added, "What's in a name anyway? A rose by any other name wouldn't smell as sweet as this bacon." He nabbed three wrinkled pieces, dropped them on his plate, and began heaping eggs beside them. "Oh no!" he exclaimed. "My wine hangover has made me forget my manners." He passed the bowl to his mother-in-law. "I'm a believer in proper titles, Mrs. Tucker. Not 'proper' as in formal, but—what should I say?—*accurate* titles. Mary Ann calls you 'Mother,' and that is accurate. 'Mother-in-law' is such a mouthful, and so legalistic."

"You certainly have given this a lot of thought," Mrs. Tucker said. Her mother's mind, Mary Ann could see by her flitting eyes, was processing at hyperspeed how exactly she'd allowed this marriage to happen.

"Dale's a bit overanalytical about some things," Mary Ann said, touching her husband's hand. "Aren't you, honey?"

Mr. Portwit ignored the question. "Now you see? Mary Ann calls me by my Christian name. I can tolerate this on occasion. She goes back and forth between first and last, and I can accept it. I'm not a *tyrant*. I just like accuracy. Call me a stickler." He searched the table for the bottle of Tabasco, grabbed it, unscrewed it, and while distributing it over his eggs added, "I believe that first-name usage is a privilege, not a right. It should not be doled out indiscriminately."

"You'll never guess who I ran into in the produce section at Meijer's," Mrs. Tucker said.

"Who?" said Mary Ann.

"Bernette Fargas. Can you believe it? Only now she's Bernette *Straw.* I asked what her husband did. He's a—what did she call him? Every job nowadays has some three-word name . . ."

"Short-order cook?" offered Mr. Portwit. "These eggs, by the way, are as fluffy as brains."

"I know I'll think of it as soon as I'm on the road," her mother continued. "Isn't that the way it always happens? Well, Bernette's back in Grand Rapids for a few months, but her husband just got a new job in Kalamazoo, and they're in the process of moving right now."

"Right now?" Mr. Portwit inserted, looking at his watchless wrist.

"I gave her your number. I figured you wouldn't mind. You should get together. Those two," Mrs. Tucker said, at last directing her words toward Mr. Portwit, but keeping her trademark arched-brow gaze aimed at his plate, "used to be like sisters."

Bernette Fargas. The name was pregnant with meaning, like the melody of a childhood song, attached to a thousand circumstances both remembered and unremembered. Bernette's face appeared as an eight-year-old girl. Then as a seventeen-year-old. She would be forty now.

"I don't have anything to say to Bernette," Mary Ann said. Half-eaten bacon, eggs, and pancake lay mangled on her plate. With Mother around, her appetite felt embarrassing. A weakness.

"Certainly the last twenty years haven't been *that* uneventful," chided Mrs. Tucker. "You've got a career, a house, a *husband*."

"That's the short and long of it," summarized Mr. Portwit. His eyes fell to his wife's plate, and he pointed with his knife. "Aren't you going to finish those eggs, darling?"

Mary Ann, standing at the driver's door of the new Camry, tried to use mind control to get her mother to climb inside, start the engine, and push the gas pedal to the floor. By some miracle, the slow cooker of fish heads in the refrigerator had thus far remained a secret, but with each second she stayed, its discovery—even though mother and daughter now stood outside the cottage—remained a possibility.

"What in the world happened to *that* machine?" her mother said, referring with a nod to Mr. Portwit's '93 Escort, which looked as if it would crumble in a rusty cloud if molested by a falling leaf. The shaving cream and eggs had stripped patches of paint, and the rear windows were milky as cataracts. "It looks like a burn victim."

"We got vandalized."

Mother didn't seem to care. The injured car merely gave her an excuse to say, "Sweetheart, you need to call Bernette." She peeked around her daughter to be certain Mr. Portwit wasn't watching from a window. She slid a folded sheet of paper from her purse and placed it in Mary Ann's hand. "Here's her number. I worry about you. You don't have friends anymore."

Don't have friends anymore? Like she didn't have legs anymore. Like it was an inarguable fact, obvious to any person with eyes. "My husband isn't my friend? And why are you being so sneaky? He won't care if I call Bernette."

"I wouldn't be so sure," her mother said, lowering her voice in Agatha Christie–mystery fashion.

"I've never had friends," Mary Ann said softly. She wanted to add, "And you never cared before," but she kept her mouth closed.

"Mary Ann, come here." Mrs. Tucker moved in for the hug. They stood, motionless and connected. Her mother, with mouth pressed against Mary Ann's bosom, managed to say, "When I die, I want you to move back home."

"What?"

"Don't worry, I'm not dying. Hearing about Janie Eichler, I suppose. Makes me think about things." She sighed.

In the quiet that followed—her mother maintaining the embrace, not letting go—Mary Ann was left to interpret. What would make her mother sigh? What "things" could she be thinking about? Perhaps those pesky pounds Mary Ann had accumulated? Her sigh, then, was a wordless expression of frustration, worry, and disappointment.

"I know you don't think I'm happy," Mary Ann said. "But I am. Mr. Portwit treats me well." Her mother shuddered at hearing Dale's preferred appellation. Mary Ann continued, "Our house is nice. You need to visit once we get settled."

"I could help with the decorating," her mother said, stepping back to look into her daughter's eyes. "I like doing that sort of thing."

"I told you before, we want to do it ourselves," Mary Ann said. "But as soon as it's ready, you're coming to dinner. Maybe we should just say Thanksgiving right now, so we don't need to worry about it."

"You're going to put on Thanksgiving?"

"I'm never too old to try."

3

A few coworkers from Elkhart had attended Mary Ann and Dale's wedding. Their presence had been a surprise; Mary Ann sent staff invitations—even, grudgingly, to Mrs. Passinault and Mrs. Jennings—but she hadn't expected any of them to come. Mrs. Passinault and Mrs. Jennings had stayed home, of course. But Mrs. Ogilvie and Principal Foster, as well as Ramone the custodian, watched from the rear pew.

The ceremony took place at Grand Rapids' Holy Name Church. The wedding party consisted of a Matron of Honor (Mary Ann's mother) and a Best Man (a 10 x 12 framed photograph of Rufus the mail carrier). During the hasty planning, Mr. Portwit had defended his choice with "Find me where it's written that a Best Man can't be a Polaroid?" and Mary Ann had refrained from pressing a sensitive subject; obviously, Mr. Portwit had no close friends, no brothers. She would let it slide. People would get a kick out of it.

After the ceremony, the twenty-four guests fanned themselves with their programs in the church entryway, waiting for a chance to congratulate the newlyweds. Mr. Portwit's family members were accustomed to his quirks, so most of them, after hugging the bride and shaking hands with the groom, cracked jokes as they passed the photo of Rufus, which was displayed on an easel borrowed from the Elkhart art class.

"Nice job up there, Rufus," said Mr. Portwit's cousin Josh, who for ten years had worked for a heating and cooling company. With his sledgehammer-sized fist he gave Rufus a playful punch on the chin. The easel wobbled.

"I can't wait to dance with him," said old, shaky-faced Nancy Kleinenberg, one of Mr. Portwit's aunts.

Mr. Portwit understood that their jokes weren't mean-spirited. Nobody knew the real story behind the photograph. When asked about the Best Man (which was often, in the receiving line), Dale simply said, "He was the greatest mailman in the world."

To Mary Ann, he had described Rufus as a friend he'd lost touch with when the mail carrier switched routes. He didn't mention the suicide attempt. Mary Ann had resisted the idea at first, but he assured her that people would laugh it off as another example of "Dale the Nut." "Let's give them something to talk about," he said. He was the mild-mannered, seldom-smiling oddball whom no one expected to make small talk but whom everyone expected to crack the ribald joke on Thanksgiving while digging stuffing from between the turkey's legs.

Not that there were many Portwit holiday gatherings. He was an only child. His father and mother each had one sibling; those siblings had produced one cousin apiece. All four of Mr. Portwit's grandparents had died within the span of one year, when he was seven. After this, the families kept to themselves except when one of them died or got married.

Oscar and Adeline Portwit came through the receiving line. It was Mary Ann's first opportunity to meet them. Dale had brushed off all her early attempts to arrange a get-together, and the night before the wedding, the Portwits had pulled a no-show at the rehearsal and the ensuing dinner. When Mary Ann offered her cell phone so he could make sure they weren't stuck in traffic, lost, or in an accident, Dale had politely declined. "They're adults," he shrugged. "They can take care of themselves." She understood then that he had never invited them.

Adeline stepped up to Mary Ann, wearing a modest ankle-length dress; its color was either dark green or light brown, depending on the light. Adeline flashed a closed-mouth smile, gave Mary Ann what felt like a supremely affectionate embrace. She stepped back and looked into Mary Ann's eyes: "No question about it. Dale's got himself a beauty."

Mary Ann was warmed by the comment, though in subsequent days she would question again and again the tone of the delivery, wondering how on earth Adeline could've meant what she'd said, wondering why Adeline chose that and not something more normal, more conversational.

Oscar's pin-striped suit and black bow tie softened, somewhat, the hardness of his countenance. He was short—the same height as Dale—with square, narrow shoulders and a wrinkled neck pinched by his tight collar, making his head appear too large for his body. He resembled an ancient sea turtle that had popped his head out into the sunlight for the first time in years. His eyes were intense, but they didn't project anger or meanness—just a determination to knock people onto their behinds with the utter seriousness of his gaze. He shook Mary Ann's hand, appraised her dress, nodded, and formed a half-smile with his lips. "You look nice," he said.

Dale didn't hug his parents. They both told him "Congratulations" and "You look really happy," and then they went out the door. Dale didn't ask them to be in any wedding photos.

At the reception, Mr. Portwit danced with Adeline. Mary Ann danced with Oscar. Jimmy Soul's "If You Wanna Be Happy" was the song selection. At the opening chorus, "If you wanna be happy for the rest of your life, never make a pretty woman your wife / So from my personal point of view, pick an ugly girl to marry you," Mary Ann heard gasps and chuckles from the darkness, where silhouetted guests populated the tables. She concentrated on her feet, on the way they worked so well together despite being separate from each other. Her feet shimmied; her hips swiveled. She couldn't stop the gasps, but she would turn the crowd to her side, make them gasp for different reasons.

The song's quick tempo possessed her legs. She jigged, jagged, swung her arms, allowed Oscar Portwit to spin her (shaky and spindly as he was), even spun herself when necessary. The crowd got into it: They had certainly never seen a 230-pound woman move like this. Mary Ann launched her shoes to the sidelines, for fear of breaking a heel, and the onlookers' rhythmic claps turned to a roaring cheer.

When the song ended, Mary Ann received a standing ovation. The DJ raised his arms as if parting the Red Sea, milking all he could from this glorious, spontaneous moment. Mr. Portwit rushed up and bear-hugged his new bride. He planted a kiss on her lips.

"I told you," he whispered into her ear. "You have to embrace who you are."

Mary Ann wanted nothing more than to say, "So I'm ugly and I need to come to terms with it?" Instead, she squeezed Mr. Portwit so hard that the breath expulsed from his lungs.

After the buffet dinner, Mary Ann's mother gripped the microphone in two hands and proposed a toast.

"Everyone who knows Mary Ann knows that she is completely selfless. Some of us might even say that Mary Ann tries *too* hard to please other people." She smiled broadly and winked at her daughter. A ripple of laughter crossed the room. "*She* knows what I'm talking about. But if you have to have a fault, then that's about the sweetest one a person can have." There was a dribble of applause. "Mary Ann's going to kill me, but I have a surprise from the Tucker vaults." She beckoned toward the doorway. Every neck in the room craned.

A small girl appeared. She wore a bright red, floor-length evening gown. She entered bashfully, looking straight ahead and chewing on her thumb.

"When Mary Ann was eight years old, she made this dress for me," Martha Tucker said, misty-eyed. She looked at Mary Ann, who covered her mouth with one hand and clutched Mr. Portwit's arm with the other. Tears rolled down Mary Ann's cheek, and she wondered if her mother would mention her father in the toast.

"She gave this dress to me, and she was so proud," Martha continued. "It's quite beautiful, especially coming from an eight-year-old. I said, 'Sweetie, Mommy's way too big to wear that dress,' and Mary Ann just looked up at me—this was the cutest thing—and she said, 'But the dress will grow into you, won't it?'"

The people clapped and said, "Aww."

"Just the cutest—" and her voice cut out as the DJ, thinking she was finished, attempted to take the microphone from her. Before relinquishing it, Martha added, "And I want to thank our photographer, whose lovely daughter is wearing the dress." She gave the microphone to the DJ. Then she took it back again. "Oh, and what I was going to say is that now, finally"—she paused to catch her breath—"finally, Mary Ann has done something for *herself*, like I always told her she should." The DJ took the mike and tucked it into his armpit. Martha Tucker walked to the head table and leaned across it to hug her daughter. Mary Ann stood and leaned to receive the hug, and her breast knocked over a glass of water.

The happy groom circumnavigated the floor, stopping at each table. He was complimented frequently on the "Best Man's" toast. Cousin Josh went so far as to disclose, "I think I pissed myself a little bit during your speech." He slapped Mr. Portwit's shoulder. "Hi-LAIR-ee-us! I can't wait to tell the guys at work."

Dale didn't mind doling out giggles, but his toast had been

sincere. He had stood before the congregation and held the framed photograph face out, at chest level.

"I am NOT Rufus Moore," he had said into the microphone. He waited for the laughter to die down. A voice, which he recognized as Cousin Josh's, bellowed "Who the hell *is*?!" and there was another eruption of laughs.

"Rufus, unfortunately, couldn't be here tonight," Mr. Portwit said, which killed the crowd noise. Until this moment, they'd never considered that Rufus might be dead. It was one thing to make a photograph your best man; that was eccentricity, was Dale. But to choose a photo of a dead man? That was going too far. Society had rules. He let them think this for a five-count, then continued. "Rufus couldn't be here because, tragically . . . he's got to get up early tomorrow to deliver the U.S. mail." A round of relieved guffaws. "But now, before your very eyes, I will channel my friend and ex-mail carrier, so that he can add his voice to this wondrous ceremony."

Mr. Portwit paused, handed the picture to the DJ, closed his eyes, lifted his face ceilingward. His hands floated up, up, up, at the careful speed of an ascending scuba diver, until they quivered above his head. He held this position dramatically; then, abruptly, his body slouched. His hands reached into his pant pockets and tugged out the white lining. He snorted the air as if his nose needed clearing, and cast his slitted eyes about as if just waking from sleep. When he spoke, it was in a distended Yooper drawl. "Mr. Portwit's a fella with two tickets to paradise. He's the smartest man *I've* ever met, and I even met Gerald Ford once. Mr. Portwit's a little guy, sure. Comes up to about here on most people." He chopped his solar plexus with a flattened hand. "But he thinks *big.*" He looked over at Mary Ann, "*Real big.*"

The room went dead except for a lone giggle from the back, where Josh was seated.

Rufus wound up his body to deliver the final blow. "This woman's got the *biggest* heart, the *biggest* mind, and the *biggest* amount of love . . . that I have ever seen!"

The tension bubble burst all at once, accompanied by a many-tiered sigh, followed by enthusiastic applause and chatter. Rufus had redeemed himself.

"Dale Portwit was my closest friend," Rufus said, in a newly somber tone. "And I know I abandoned him when he needed me most. That's why it's such an honor, such a privilege"—he hesitated, grimacing as if the search for the right words was causing a terrible headache—"such a *relief* to be invited back into Dale Portwit's life in order to raise a glass on this most sacrosanct evening. To Mr. Portwit and Mary Ann!"

As a finale, Mr. Portwit hugged himself.

Later, Mary Ann and her mother sat alone at the head table. The DJ was spinning soft, cozy dance songs that Mary Ann had selected, although aside from their ceremonial first dance, she and her husband hadn't stepped onto the floor together.

"He wasn't always like this," Mary Ann said, between sips of champagne from the bottle. "When I first met him, he was as meek as a lamb." She fought back an image of Mr. Portwit sliding his erection over a rack of barbecued baby-back ribs. "I don't think he said a word to me during his first three years at Elkhart." The wedding dress creaked as she readjusted her body on the office chair they'd wheeled into the room especially for her. "He was depressed for a long time, just before he asked me out on our first date. I get the impression it was pretty bad."

"Growing pains," her mother said. "We don't call them that when we get old, but that's what they are."

"That's exactly what he said about me," Mary Ann said. "You two aren't as different as you seem."

"I went through my own midlife crisis," her mother continued. "You know what I did? You know what *my* dirty midlife secret is? I started wearing a bikini."

"Mom, you did not!"

Laughing, she held up her fingers in a peace sign. "Two times. Just twice I actually tormented those poor people on South Haven Beach." She caught her breath, wiped a tear from her eye. "But that was it. That was my crisis. I got off easy."

"You think that's why I've gained all this weight, don't you?" Mary Ann said, eyeball dangerously close to the mouth of the black champagne bottle. She could never tell how much was left in these damn things.

"Mary Ann, I haven't said Word One about your weight! You should talk to your husband about that. Lord knows he refers to it enough."

"We make each other happy, and that's what matters." She was

46

crying again, for the tenth time today. She couldn't be bothered to wipe her face anymore.

Her mother hugged her shoulders. "You were a beautiful bride."

The Monday after the wedding, the teacher's lounge had been the same as always. Mrs. Passinault and Mrs. Jennings retained their domination, butting into conversations whenever possible. No one treated Mary Ann differently. "To human beings," Mr. Portwit theorized, "novel things that happen one time are considered strange. Twice, intriguing. Thrice, thrilling. After that it gets progressively more annoying each time it happens. They're annoyed by the idea of us, as a couple."

Mary Ann had thought (naively, she realized now) that the other teachers would at last welcome her into their fold. After all, she'd proved she wasn't the old maid they'd believed her to be. She had bagged a man. They'd put in a bid and with any luck would soon be paying mortgage on a suburban home, a house with grass on all four sides. Mary Ann's concerns were their concerns, her life their lives. That's how it was supposed to work. Instead, she was ignored just as always. Mr. Portwit was like a nevus or a goiter, a growth on Mary Ann's body that they were obliged to acknowledge—which they did once a day with a polite nod. .

Growing up, Mary Ann had gone both noticed and unnoticed, liked and disliked. Her schoolmates knew her name, but rather than saying, "Mary Ann, do you want to stay over tonight?" they said, "Mary Ann Tucker is a Fucker." Then one day her mother sat on the edge of her bed and told her that when someone teased you it meant they liked you. So the dirt-covered boys who lobbed pebbles at her were actually head-over-heels? What about the kids who acted like friends at school, then ditched her at the mall?

For as long as she could remember, Mary Ann had had a love-hate relationship with herself—specifically, with her physical image. The mirror always told two stories. One moment she was a voluptuous, sultry woman. Fifteen minutes later, an inhuman blob stared back at her in the glass. Nothing was clear; every conclusion was attached to a "but" or an "or." So when Mr. Portwit had come along, insisting on her ability to sexily chew her pita bread, commanding her to masticate while he watched, imploring her to rethink her definitions of appropriate weight and proportion, what was a girl to do?

Perhaps because she'd lost her father early, she felt an attraction toward men who came across as authorities. Network anchormen like Peter Jennings and Tom Brokaw, with their bemused, almost sardonic grins and unequivocal delivery. Her college professors. Men who could answer any question with confidence, men unswayed by the pressures of the world. To achieve this end, Mr. Portwit simplified life—life was either/or with him. He always had new "theories" about himself, and, more often, about others. His theories chose sides, made divisions. He simplified and categorized until every problem sat in a tidy compartment. "How should I respond to harassment from a student? Well, let me pull out the answer book and tell you. Let's see, page 1: 'It's better to be disliked than to be unnoticed.'" To Mary Ann, it didn't matter that he had no theories about his own fetishes; in fact, this only added to his mystery.

The five months before the wedding had been dizzying. They were both too old to slow down. Three months after their first date, he proposed by writing *Will You Be My Bride?* in vanilla hazelnut letters across a chocolate cake. After she said yes, they destroyed the cake in a furious bout of lovemaking.

Then had come the planning. As usual, Mother had wanted things done her way. After all, it was *her* daughter marrying *her* son-in-law. If Mary Ann had a nickel—a penny—for every time her mother said, "I don't want *my* daughter to (*fill in the blank*)."

Inspired by these thoughts on that first Monday after her wedding, Mary Ann took out her notebook. She chewed her ham sandwich and scrawled out her first list since her courtship by Mr. Portwit began.

Ten Things Mother Didn't Want Her
Daughter to Do for Her Wedding

10. Wear flat shoes
9. Get married outdoors
8. Hire a rock band for the reception
7. Write her own vows
6. Have a nondenominational wedding service

5. Serve vegetarian lasagna

4. Put disposable cameras on the tables

3. Do the chicken dance

2. Tie cans to the limousine

1. Let Dale use a photograph as a best man

She finished the list and reread it, sipping from her juice box. Mr. Portwit, beside her, was scrutinizing a book about the origin of the pyramids. The teacher's-lounge chatter was at its usual barroom level. As soon as Mary Ann finished reading the list, Mr. Portwit glanced up.

"Writing something, I see," he said. When it became apparent that she wasn't handing it over, he sang, "*Sharing . . . rhymes with caring,*" in a soft voice that no one else could hear, in a melody only he knew, "*I'm despairing . . . it's a red herring . . .*"

"You wouldn't be interested," Mary Ann said.

"*I'm preparing . . . to get daring . . . and start tearing . . .*" His hand opened and closed like a mouth. "Sharkie's getting hungry."

Mary Ann handed it to him. She had never shown Mr. Portwit any of her lists. Even when she'd hauled boxes into the basement and spent six hours filing binders and rereading her life story, he'd never asked what she was doing. She didn't mind if he saw her newest one, though. In fact, she wanted him to be a part of this tradition. She was ready to put into practice all the abstract promises she'd heard about marriage: growing together, uniting as one, abandoning all secrets in the name of trust. She had nothing to hide.

Her eyes remained on the table as Dale read. Would he laugh? Would he think she was cruel? Demeaning? Incisive? Whip-smart? Poignant? A flock of modifiers took flight in her head, but none of them prepared her for the one Mr. Portwit chose.

"Cute," he said, returning the notebook to the spot on the table where Mary Ann had fixed her gaze. He resumed his reading.

Mary Ann stared at the notebook. It looked different than it had before.

4

Driving home from the cottage, Mr. Portwit was sullen. He chewed the inside of his cheek, steered with his good hand. His other wrist was mummied in athletic wrap. He hadn't gotten to eat any fish heads. After Mrs. Tucker's departure, he and Mary Ann had caught *My Big Fat Greek Wedding* at the one-screen theater, followed by a stroll along the harbor, through neighborhoods, past tennis courts carpeted with dead leaves. A sudden thunderstorm had sent them running to a nearby elementary school, where they sheltered in the entryway until the rain stopped.

When they got back to the cottage, the power was out. Dale insisted that this would not stop him from enjoying his symbolic dinner. Mary Ann searched for candles while Dale opened the refrigerator, gripped the heavy Crock-Pot, pulled it from the rack, and promptly dropped it. A flood of bluegill heads and ceramic shards gushed across the kitchen floor. Mary Ann, in the utility room, heard the racket, ran to look, saw Mr. Portwit take a step forward. His legs flew out from beneath him and he splashed to the floor.

Mr. Portwit's wrist was sprained. He gouged his fingers as he collected the daggers of stoneware, then used curse words Mary Ann had never heard as he gathered the fish heads. Some heads were squashed underfoot; others were coated in dust balls and carpet hair. The air in the cottage was rancid. In the dim candlelight, it took three hours to clean and deodorize. First the toiletry apocalypse, and now this, Mary Ann thought. Two messes in as many weeks. With only minor prodding, Mr. Portwit conceded that his plan had come to ruin.

For much of the two-hour drive, Mary Ann thought about Bernette Fargas. The possibility of seeing Bernette again opened a floodgate in her head, a rush of images, sensory impressions, feelings long buried. The name whisked her to that happy time—it seemed happy now, at least—when there were things she could depend on: a soft pillow, heavy blankets, and the low, soothing tones of her parents conversing in their bed across the hall; her father emerging from the steamy bathroom, his face lathered, towel around his waist, asking Mother to brew the coffee; the yellow nose of the school bus peeking from behind the corner pine tree, blinker flashing, destined to stop at her feet. Time had taken these certainties away, but nothing had replaced them.

Maybe that's why she taught elementary school. She craved routine, structure, and dependability. The classroom was governed by the rule of rules: trust in authority. The bell rang; the teacher took charge and guided the children through the day. This took all pressure off the students, who understood that while adults were granted all authority, they also bore all responsibility. The teacher, too, benefited from the neatness, the ritual, the regimentation. And the answer book was always available.

❦

Certainly he wasn't as mobile as he used to be. As of late, his erections were less steel girder and more rubber tubing. Hair had to be excised several times a month from his ears and nostrils. But the way he'd lost the grip on that Crock-Pot . . . that wasn't *him*. He never *dropped* things. He was no yogi, but he'd taught himself to juggle four equally weighted spherical objects, like oranges or stress-relief balls. He could write, shave, and eat ice cream with his left hand just as well as with his right; he could raise each eyebrow individually. Even when drunk, he was *coordinated*.

With one bare foot resting on the glass coffee table, and toenails dropping at each *snap* of the clippers, Mr. Portwit mollified himself about the fish-head thing. It wasn't important. Like everything he did lately, the fish-head feast was an attempt at distraction. One would think that having a first wife and a first house would be enough distraction. The big unknown was this: what was he trying to be distracted from? If he didn't know the answer to *this* question . . .

He looked at Mary Ann. She was locked snugly into the faded green recliner she'd insisted on keeping because of some sentimental attachment to her old life. One of her eyes was on the *Cheers* rerun and the other on the sheet of paper in her lap. She was absentmindedly clacking a ballpoint pen against her teeth. It was Saturday, October 18. He'd been married for one and a half months.

He had inflated the woman he loved from 180-something to over 240 pounds with a food fetish that he cared less and less about each day. How far would she let it go? If she wanted to stop, if she wanted to go on the Atkins diet, or get her stomach stapled, would he mind? Would he allow it? How much was it worth to him?

Mary Ann's complexion was the color of pancake batter. Mudflap bangs draped her forehead. Her hair was flat, bodiless, shoulder-tickling, either "dirty blonde" or "clean brunette" (it had been described in both ways, supposedly, depending on the light). It was a head of Ford Escort hair: unremarkable and in need of maintenance every six months.

Even with her weight gain, everything he had initially liked about her facial structure remained intact. The slight upward thrust of her features gave the impression that she was always sniffing at the air. Her eyes, narrowed to squints, were held in her head by puffed little baskets of skin. This meant that her eyes, and thus her psyche, was fragile, and needed protection. The natural repose of her lips left her teeth exposed. When Mary Ann did bother to seal her lips, they formed an automatic frown. What did it mean to be born with a frown? He hadn't figured out this one yet, but he liked it.

Mary Ann noticed him staring. "I've been wondering," she said. "Are you going to show those pictures to Principal Foster?"

He didn't answer. He had hoped she wouldn't mention the photographs. It rekindled the sudden, funneled anger he had felt, the need to teach those kids a lesson. At the same time, it stirred up a powerful shame he'd been trying to ignore. When, two days before the honeymoon, he had finally stood at the Meijer One-Hour counter and opened the packet of developed film, he found that his beloved evidence was nothing more than twenty shots of a blurry yellow light in a sea of black. He'd photographed the streetlamp. Neither Rick Fletcher, nor any of his friends, nor any human being could be identified—that is, until he reached the end of the roll and saw himself grinning stupidly and Mary Ann chomping into a slice of toast. He handed the pictures back to the clerk and told her to destroy them.

Mary Ann was reading his mind. "Why don't you just put it behind you? Kids play pranks. Even I played 'ding-dong-ditchit' two or three times."

Mr. Portwit arranged his toenail boomerangs into a circle on the table, then brushed them into his waiting palm. "Do you ever wonder where all your body parts end up? Hair, nails, teeth, earwax?" He stood and walked through the dining room, saying, "Excrement, saliva, tears, vomit? Hmmm . . . there have to be others. Semen, obviously."

He opened the cupboard below the kitchen sink, reached into it, sprinkled the toenails into the basket. He closed the cupboard, slapped his hands together. *Menstrual blood*, he thought. How could he have missed that one? When he returned to the living room to tell her, Mary Ann was gone.

"Good morning, students and teachers. This is Mrs. Jennings," came the voice through the intercom. "I want to remind every class to submit their get-well cards by the end of the day. And remember that the most heartwarming card wins a box of Krispy Kreme doughnuts. I spoke with Principal Foster, and he is *very* excited about coming back to work and seeing all of you again. He says that the hospital food is even worse than the cafeteria food."

Mary Ann's third graders giggled. They had asked about Principal Foster. They understood that he was "sick." They felt sad for him and his family, but their emotions, Mary Ann noticed, rarely lasted longer than a few seconds at a time. And how was cancer to compete with the prospect of doughnuts? Seated behind her desk, hands folded in front of her, she was overcome with jealousy. These children didn't know how lucky they were. As they aged, their problems would get messier, more confusing, more expensive, and more difficult to shrug off. For now, however, they wriggled in their chairs, puffed their cheeks, wagged their heads, blew spit bubbles, and forgot all about disease and death.

"I invite everyone to keep Principal Foster in their prayers," Mrs. Jennings continued, "because we care about him. That is all. Have a good day."

The transmission ended with the deep ceremonial *pop* of the microphone disengaging, a sound that always reminded Mr. Portwit of a backbone cracking. Seated at his desk, he was treated to an unfamiliar sight: a full classroom. First hour was normally his free period, which allowed him a chance to soak Exacto blades and

Windex Petri dishes, but with Mrs. Jennings acting as interim principal, he'd been assigned to "help take up the slack," which meant teaching first-hour English to her seventh graders.

They were his least favorite group, not only because of the presence of three vandals, but for simple physiological reasons. Coarse, dirty hairs poked from the boys' faces. From their mouths squeaked broken voices. From their armpits issued spicy odors. They were souls in limbo, not quite boys, not quite men. It was not uncommon to spot a male student leaning forward, writing furiously in a notebook while surreptitiously rubbing his lap with his free forearm.

The girls had problems, too. Shirts revealed sad, unchallenged training bras intended to house the nubs no bigger than avocado pits that had formed on their chests. Entire Shakespearean tragedies were played out between recess and final bell, scripted on folded scraps of notebook paper. Tears rained at the slightest prompt, as evidenced this very morning before the second bell rang, when Rick Fletcher dropped Rachel Vannen's beret into the trash can.

Mr. Portwit was in no mood. On days like this, he wondered why he'd gone into middle-school teaching, even though he knew the answer: laziness. In demeanor, manner, and appearance, he was a prototypical college professor. While an undergraduate at Central Michigan, he was dubbed "Prof" by students and faculty alike. But he'd fallen victim, in the end, to an indifference designed to protect him from failure and obscurity. To teach in college would require publication, research, new theories—all subjected to merciless microscopic scrutiny by overeager pedants.

Here, his theories never needed to leave the womb of his head. For middle-school teachers, mediocrity was the norm. Intellectual rigor was considered suspicious. Questions were asked, of course, but only to the students, and only if the answer could be confirmed in a Rand-McNally book. You weren't expected to *think* about the subject matter. If two plus two equaled four, then goddamn it, that's what it equaled. How could anyone have a question about that? Show up on time, follow the rules, write legibly on a chalkboard, and know more about cell division than your twelve-year-olds. You traded your salary for long vacations, and you slept comfortably knowing that your face, voice, and mannerisms would, whether the students liked it or not, live on in their minds as a swath in the fabric of their existence.

In Mr. Portwit's right front trouser pocket, the empty film canister waited for the chance it would never have. What had once represented possibility and power was now just a hollow plastic container. He felt impotent; he felt cheated. Although it made no logical sense, he placed the entire blame upon Rick Fletcher. The fever of revenge infected him. In his shirt pocket was the folded confession he'd written the night before, after three glasses of wine.

After roll call, Mr. Portwit told the students to open to page 84 in *English and Its Usage.* Today's focus was active vs. passive verbs. As he read the opening paragraph aloud, glancing up to see Rick Fletcher battling to keep his eyes open, Mr. Portwit was visited by an idea almost as inspired as the sacrificial consumption of two dozen bluegill heads. It would both hasten the process and make it much more artistic than cornering the kid on the way out the door and bullying him into signing the confession. Mr. Portwit interrupted his reading.

"As most of you know, the best way to learn is by practical application. Textbooks are good for presenting information, but to internalize that information, we must use it. It doesn't exist to us until we make it a part of our lives. Until we live it."

He told the students to close their books and open their minds. "Mr. Fletcher," he said, beckoning with his hand, "please come to the front of the room."

"Why me?" Rick protested.

"You are the perfect person to illustrate the principles of active and passive verbs. Please select a quality stick of chalk."

As Rick Fletcher scuffled petulantly up the aisle, Mr. Portwit intoned, "Many of the best writers in the world agree that the active form is often, although not always, superior to the passive. Most times, as in 'I ate the cake,' which is active, versus 'The cake was eaten by me,' which is passive, it is fairly obvious that the passive tense is, shall we say, *ungraceful.* Do you have your chalk, Mr. Fletcher?"

Rick showed Mr. Portwit his chalk.

"Wonderful. Now please write the following sentence on the board. *Rick Fletcher vandalized Mr. Portwit's house.*"

The ensuing symphony of gasps told Mr. Portwit what he already knew: that the whole class, probably the whole school, had heard about the incident.

"I ain't writing that."

"Not yet, you're not. But you shall be. Go on. This is just a hypothetical sentence, Mr. Fletcher. Just because we write something doesn't mean it's true."

Rick turned to the board and with embellished, defiant strokes scrawled the sentence.

"Beautiful," Mr. Portwit said. "And I like the exclamation mark at the end. Now can we all read the sentence together?"

"RICK FLETCHER VANDALIZED MR. PORTWIT'S HOUSE!" came the gang vocals, followed by nervous laughter.

"What is the verb in this sentence?" Mr. Portwit asked. He was pleased to see that Rick Fletcher's face had gone pale. "Cindy?"

"Vandalized?" said Cindy.

"Very good. Now when we make this sentence passive, we need to put the object *before* the subject. What is the subject in this sentence?"

Three hands went up. "Yes, Billy?"

"Is it Rick?"

"This is a brainy group. Yes, Rick Fletcher is the subject. Look at him up there. Absolutely he is the subject. No, no, Rick," Mr. Portwit said. "Stay put. We're not through with you yet. So if Rick Fletcher is the subject, then what is the object? What's left?"

"The house?" ventured Janie Perkins.

"That is correct! Mr. Portwit's house is the object. So how do we make this a passive construction? Cindy again."

Cindy sucked in some air, bit her bottom lip, and formed the sentence slowly. "Mr. Portwit's . . . Mr. Portwit's house was vandalized by Rick Fletcher."

Mr. Portwit clapped sharply, causing Rick to jump. Rick's eyes shifted in his head, looking for a way out. He glanced to his accomplices, behind whom Mr. Portwit had strategically positioned himself. "Would you please write that passive sentence on the board, Mr. Fletcher? 'Mr. Portwit's house was vandalized by Rick Fletcher.'"

As the chalk squeaked, Mr. Portwit described the reasons for using passive construction. "Sometimes we use the passive voice when the *object* is more important than the subject. An example sentence: A car accident killed my father. That is active, right? Right. Preferable in most cases, but in this instance, it makes the *car accident* more important than *my father.* I love my father. I don't love the car accident. I want people to focus on my father, so I say, 'My father *was killed* in a car accident.'"

"This is bullshit," Rick said. He said it under his breath, while facing the board, and it was amazing the way these kids knew the exact volume to make an outburst so that you questioned whether or not you actually heard it. The other students knew what they heard, though, and they *ooooh*-ed.

"Mr. Fletcher? I believe you just said that this was BS? Only you said the word, rather than the initials." Mr. Portwit was being careful. They wouldn't be able to pinch him for using profanities. "I've got another sentence for you to write, Mr. Fletcher. Listen carefully. 'Mr. Portwit took pictures of Rick Fletcher vandalizing the house.' Did you hear? Why aren't you writing, Mr. Fletcher?"

Rick wasn't writing because his hands shook as if he were being electrocuted. Tears formed in his eyes, and his jaw clenched. His unfocused gaze swept the room as he searched desperately for any idea that might save his ass. But ideas weren't really his forte. "I ain't writing that. It's BULLSHIT!" he yelled. His face was no longer pale, but red.

"Ooooooooooooooh. . . ." chorused the class. They tittered, giggled, looked at each other with eyes as large as tennis balls.

"OK, let's go," said Mr. Portwit, marching to the front of the room, carefully assembling his sternest face because inside he was all smiles, though he didn't feel anywhere near happy. "We're going to the office. Put down the chalk." He'd never had a confrontation like this—not with a student, not with anybody. He felt injected with some powerful stimulant. His vision was clear and crisp, and everything moved at half-speed. Rather than tightening, as he might have envisioned, his insides felt warm and spongy, as if he were soaking in a pleasant bath.

Rick Fletcher seemed to sense that fighting was useless. He sulked toward the hallway with Mr. Portwit on his heels.

"When I get back," Mr. Portwit announced, one hand spread to display his fingers to the students, "I'd like to see FIVE sentences using active construction. Five from each of you. In your notebooks."

Away from his friends, Rick Fletcher appeared smaller, proportional for the first time to his age. He was shorter than Mr. Portwit, which was a feat. He was also thinner and more athletic, younger and less burdened, better-looking and more popular. In this moment none of these traits, however, was admirable in Mr. Portwit's eyes. In fact, Mr. Portwit saw with utter clarity that these were handicaps for the child that would one day lead to his ruin. Oh yes, right, today was that day. Never before had Mr. Portwit's social awkwardness and physical inferiorities (height, baldness, ruddy complexion) felt like such a godsend as in this silent march toward a much-needed lesson in humility. The back of Rick's neck was beaded with sweat, and Mr. Portwit inhaled his preteen scent, which was not so different from that of the bluegill.

"I didn't do anything," Rick Fletcher said, face pointed at his shoes. "It was Sedgwick and Donny's idea. I only threw one egg."

That was one thing he loved about adolescents. As predictable as a hangover after beer. It took great concentration to fight down the urge to punch the kid's mouth until he gurgled blood. Mr. Portwit put his hand on Rick's shoulder and guided him to the nearest wall.

"Listen carefully," he said. "Consider the propulsion of a fish through the water. You are the fish. I am the water. A fish uses its tail fin to push water backward. But a push on the water will only serve to accelerate the water. In turn, the water reacts by pushing the fish forward, propelling the fish. The size of the force on the water equals the size of the force on the fish." He slid from his trouser pocket the empty film canister. He smiled at Rick Fletcher to show that he meant no harm, but that harm was inevitable nonetheless. This was the nature of nature. It was Newton's Third Law. "It's out of my hands. Once the fish pushes, he's getting pushed back."

Rick was clearly numb at this point. Mr. Portwit glanced at the boy's trousers to make sure he hadn't flooded them. Rick's breath came out shallow and quick, and his rib cage trembled beneath his Ozzy Osbourne *Faeries Wear Boots* shirt.

"You can still control how much I push back," Mr. Portwit said. "Let's keep walking, and I'll show you what I mean."

They entered the office. The temp, Mrs. Vugermann, frowned as they stepped inside. Her eyes hovered above her reading glasses. "Has this one been making trouble again?"

"He'll be telling us momentarily," Mr. Portwit said.

"Mrs. Jennings isn't in right now."

"Yes, I know," Mr. Portwit said. He guided Rick to the door that bore the name PRINCIPAL FOSTER. "Go on in," he instructed.

"Mr. Portwit, you can't go in there."

He dismissed Mrs. Vugermann with a wave. "It's fine, it's fine." Once inside, he closed the door and turned on the light.

Mr. Portwit made certain that Rick Fletcher was seated comfortably, with the PA microphone positioned a reasonable distance from his mouth, before dipping into his shirt pocket and pulling out the confession. He unfolded it and laid it on the desk. Rick finally broke down. He bawled, the tears dropping out of his eyes faster than he could wipe them with his palms. His words were barely comprehensible.

"I'm sorry," he pleaded. "I told—hic—you—hic—I'm sorry."

"Buck up, Mr. Fletcher. We're almost on the air." Mr. Portwit could see, through a gap in the blinds, Mrs. Vugermann's eyeball assessing the situation. Hoping to confuse her, Mr. Portwit gave her a casual thumbs-up along with a somber, professional nod. He looked down at Rick Fetcher. "All you need to do is read the confession. There don't need to be any messy emotions involved. After this, the process will be complete. No more pushing from me. We'll both be purged."

Mr. Portwit switched on the microphone and spoke into it.

"Good morning, students and faculty. I apologize for the interruption. This is your science teacher, Mr. Portwit. I'm here with Rick Fletcher, who has a special announcement to make. Please give him your undivided attention."

In the third-grade classroom, on one knee beside the desk of pigtailed Lucy Barrett, Mary Ann regarded the wall-mounted speaker in a way that to an onlooker would suggest she was watching a meteor shoot toward Earth. From the intercom came the hollow jostling thump of the microphone being repositioned. Then a voice. A scared, undone voice.

"I, Richard Bartholomew Fletcher," the voice mumbled, "do hereby . . ." A pause. "I can't read this word!"

Softer, very soft, in the background, Mr. Portwit's voice—"Impli-cate."

Mary Ann rose to her feet and hurried out of the classroom, telling the students to sit quietly as Rick continued in his robotic voice, "Im-pli-cate myself in the recent vandalism of Mr. and Mrs. Portwit's house. I and my friends Donald and Sedgwick threw toilet paper and eggs . . ."

In the hallway, Mary Ann could hear Rick Fletcher's voice ringing from every classroom.

". . . and we used shaving cream to write . . . in . . . insane? . . . *inane* slogans on their car and garage. We behaved like animals by throwing mayonnaise balloons on their door." His words dissolved into sobs.

Mary Ann could hear, through the PA, Mrs. Vugermann's faint knocking at Principal Foster's office, could hear the temp's muffled, hesitant, "Do you have permission for this?"

Mary Ann moved as quickly as her body would allow, the office door growing before her eyes. She had to get to the intercom. She had to tell them, tell everyone, that she had nothing to do with this, that she was a nice person, a nice person who cared about children and cancer and lawn care, and that just because he was her husband didn't mean she approved of everything he did. While she speed-walked, while in near-sprinting panic, the thought that flashed in Mary Ann's head, for reasons unknowable, was that she and Dale hadn't had sex once during their honeymoon.

"We deserve to be taken to the police," Rick continued. "But Mr. Portwit is a kind man, so he only asked that we apol . . . apologize for our crime. We are sorry, and we hope that all of you can forgive us. Amen." There was a pause. "Why does it say 'Amen'?"

Just as Mary Ann arrived in the main office, where a flushed Mrs. Vugermann spoke animatedly into the telephone receiver, Mr. Portwit's voice returned to the loudspeakers.

"Thank you everyone, for your attention. That is all. You may resume the education process."

TWO

5

Mary Ann drummed the steering wheel to the beat of "(Keep Feeling) Fascination." She exited I-94 at Oakland Drive.

Mary Ann's hands hadn't stopped bongoing since she climbed into her car ten minutes before. Her jaw continued attacking a wad of gum that had long ago lost its flavor. Once the song finished, she pulled the pebble of Trident from her mouth, tucked it into the plastic bag hung from the window handle, then reached into the unused ashtray for a cinnamon Altoid. She sucked the mint. Her eyes fell to the passenger seat, where a handwritten note detailed the directions.

The bottom up. That's how we dress. The shoes come first, the hair comes last. Why had this phrase been running through her mind for the past five minutes? It lit a match beneath her nerves. She had expected anxiety, not terror. Her palms, feet, and armpits were sweaty despite the thirty-seven-degree air that thundered through her half-opened window. She approached the Straws' large back-split home on Timberlane Drive. It was backed by a wall of leafless gray trees. The driveway was shaped like a "U" and touched the road with its ends, like a magnet trying to pull Mary Ann's car to the house.

The bottom up. That's how we dress. The shoes come first, the hair comes last.

"It's how trees grow," Mary Ann's mother says, kneeling, neatly folding the scalloped tops of Mary Ann's socks. "The bottom up. And when your father designs houses, he doesn't start with the roof, does he? Can you think of any more examples?"

"Snakes grow side to side."

"Stop kicking your feet, sweetie. What about flowers? How do they grow?"

"Top to bottom," Mary Ann says.

"You mean bottom to top."

"Bottom to top. What about a pumpkin?"

"Well, I suppose in that case the root comes first," mother says, "And then the whole thing sort of swells up. There are exceptions to every rule. But you don't want to look like a pumpkin, do you? Stand up and let me see."

"I don't have any clothes on."

"Mommy needs to see how you walk in them."

Mary Ann, six years old, white-pantied, stands from the bed.

"Walk to the door, sweetie."

Mary Ann steps uneasily, making airplane wings of her arms, for balance.

"You'll get used to the heels. They look good. Very pretty. Come on back now. Mommy's got a dress she wants you to try on."

"Mom, if Daddy started from his shoes, how could he put his pants on?"

"No no, don't sit down," Mother says, emerging from the closet with a blue dress. "Let me see something." She holds the dress against Mary Ann's midsection. "Oh yes. Isn't that nice? Let me see that on you."

Mary Ann unzips the back of the dress. She begins to step through.

"No no, take off your shoes! You don't want to get it dirty."

"You said we go bottom to top."

"I didn't mean literally, Mary Ann. We *match* from the bottom but—oh, don't worry about it. Just—here—" She kneels and unstraps Mary Ann's shoes.

Mary Ann climbs into the dress.

"Suck in your stomach, sweetie," her mother says, zipping. "Come on, Mary Ann," her mother says, zipping until it will zip no more. Mary Ann protests that she is too big.

"Nonsense. You ate dinner twenty minutes ago. You're a little bloated." Mother steps back to regard the dress. She licks her finger and rubs a crumb from Mary Ann's cheek. As if this tiny crumb has been hiding Mary Ann's true size, her mother suddenly turns sullen. "I just bought this dress. You couldn't have grown out of it already. You haven't even worn it."

"What's going on in here?" Mary Ann's father says from the doorway. "Well, look at that. Who is this stunning lady?"

"Jack, it doesn't fit," her mother says with exasperation. "One hundred twenty dollars, and it doesn't fit, one month after I buy it."

"One hundred what?!" her father chokes out. He isn't really angry—he flashes a smile at Mary Ann, his secretive smile, pulling Mary Ann in on the joke. "Martha, I told you. This is just to meet Bob's family. It's not a formal thing."

"It's your new employer, Jack. We need to make an impression."

"I'd rather give him the impression that we need the money."

"OK, forget it. I give up," Mother says, brushing past Father on her way out the door, sprinkling the air with mumbles. "Heaven forbid the child should do what we ask . . ."

"Dad, how do snakes move around?"

Mr. Tucker sits on the bed next to Mary Ann. His face is dark and unshaven. His smell is musky, full.

"Well," he says, "snakes have hundreds of muscles, all up and down their bellies. Tiny little muscles that move at the same time."

"But I have muscles, and I can't slide on the ground."

"You can't?" Her father lies on the carpet. He squirms on his belly, struggling, huffing and puffing. Mary Ann giggles. "Really," her father gasps. "I was doing it yesterday. Wait, wait. I'm getting it."

"It hurts under my arms."

Her father turns over, panting, onto his elbows. "Let's take it off."

He helps her out of the dress. "Put on your pajamas," he says. "We'll figure out something else for you to wear."

The Fargases' home: two-story bay windows aglow atop a hill, at the end of a winding driveway. Like the castle in "Princess and the Pea." In the backseat, Mary Ann smooths her blue dress. It's tight, but it's necessary. That's what her mother had said. The hairpins pull at Mary Ann's scalp. She wants to look beautiful; not so much for Mom, but for Dad. It's an important night. So important that no one talks, and everybody smells like flowers, even though they don't grow like flowers.

A Mexican woman, a real-life maid, serves dinner. The two Fargas daughters, Bernette and Isabelle, play Paper Scissors Rock as the maid centers the platter of ham on the table. The dining-room ceiling is as high as the one in Holy Name Church.

The adults talk about the children. Mary Ann is the same age as Bernette. They could play together. Mary Ann and Bernette size each other up across the table. The adults tell them to smile at each other, so they do, cautiously. "What do you think? Do you want to play together?" The girls shrug, continue eating. Brick-sized slices of Kentucky Bourbon Pie arrive on flowered china. A third bottle of wine is uncorked. Mr. Fargas shovels his pie and begins talking, full-mouthed, about schematics and blueprints, camber and modinature, catenary arches and sculpted swags. His voice is a trumpet, pitched high, insistent and persistent.

Mary Ann marvels at how many words are being pushed into her head. Mr. Fargas is a word machine. Someone needs to pull his plug. It frightens her. Can her head get full like her stomach? Will her head get fat? She looks at her pie wedge. It's enormous; how can that fit into her stomach? Everyone around her uses a six-beat eating rhythm: cut, stab, lift, open, chew, swallow . . . cut, stab, lift, open, chew, swallow.

Five Things I Used to Wonder About
But Don't Anymore (1982)

5. How snakes move along the ground
4. Why bubbles have to burst
3. Why my stomach gets full but not my head
2. Whether or not people who live in big
   houses are always happy
1. What it's like to kiss a boy

She wrote this list when she was twenty. Three of the items came from that night at the Fargas house, when she was only six years old. Her father had been hired at Fargas & Fargas Developers. Eighteen months earlier, the company where he spent seven years climbing through the ranks from intern to licensed architect had declared bankruptcy and let him go. He crossed picket lines at the Grand Rapids Water Works to serve as night watchman; he delivered Wonder Bread to local supermarkets; he hosed with hot water the hard remnants of bread pudding from the buckets at the Smorgasbord Restaurant. And he read the want ads. He sent out applications. He interviewed. At last, Fargas & Fargas was his big moment, his opportunity to be a head architect, the job he planned to do and to love for the rest of his life. He had once told Mary Ann, after reading "Hansel and Gretel" to her, that "Good things happen to good people." She had believed him.

With a tissue, Mary Ann wiped the sheen of perspiration from her forehead. She cut the engine and checked her face in the rearview. If she'd had a pin, she would have stuck it into her cheeks on the off chance that they might—just might—pop. She licked the back of her hand and smelled it. With an expulsion of air similar to a child blowing out birthday candles, she exited the car; its frame levitated five inches when she stepped out. She hoped Bernette wasn't watching from a window.

Mary Ann pressed the bell, heard the rich, sonorous DING-DONG, and recalled the times she and Bernette would ring doorbells and run across the street until collapsing behind a bush, weak with fear and laughter, to watch the person open the door. The victims always looked so fragile, turning this way and that, clutching their bathrobes, squinting into the darkness, calling out, "Who's there?"

Mary Ann heard Bernette's voice. Through a window she saw the flash of an arm, a sleeve, a hand. The door opened. A glossy-coated Irish setter appeared, bouncing up and down as if on a trampoline. It yelped, either happy or angry to see Mary Ann; it was impossible to tell which. The woman—was it she? the face was turned down, just a jawline, an earring, a white sweater—tugged the dog by its collar and shooed it into the background while saying, "Get in there, Forest." The woman opened the door and leaned outside. It was Bernette.

"May I help you?" she asked.

Of all the first lines Mary Ann had envisioned for the reunion, this had not been among them. She muttered a few "uhs" before formulating anything meaningful. "Hi. I'm. Mary Ann?"

Bernette's eyes crossed the boundary between confusion and surprise. She stepped into the cold air, onto the concrete porch. "Oh my God!" she yelled. "I did not even recognize you! Well, it's only been about twenty years, right? Mary Ann Tucker, come here."

They hugged. Bernette was tiny in Mary Ann's arms, but no tinier than Dale, or her mother, or anyone she knew. The larger Mary Ann got, the smaller—and thus more delicate and precious—everyone else became.

Mary Ann said, "I'm Mary Ann Portwit now. And you're Bernette Straw?"

"Your mother told me you got married." Bernette leaned back and gazed with sudden, frightening sincerity into Mary Ann's eyes. "Congratulations."

Mary Ann received a tour of the house. The family room's vaulted ceiling stood as high as three stacked Dales. The dining room, thirty feet wide, watched a patch of woods through a wall of bay windows. Between the trees glimmered a stream. The dining-room floors were a deep-grained wood, the color of caramel. Each of Bernette's two daughters, who were presently at the mall with their father, had her own bedroom. In the basement, there were two guest rooms and a game room (pool table, dart board, Ping-Pong table). In the master, Bernette and Barry slept on a waterbed under a handwoven afghan from Malacca.

Mary Ann and Bernette sat at the kitchen table, sipping apple cinnamon tea. Bernette had traded her blond ponytails for a taller head of blond hair, fluffed and tousled by gel. Diamonds twinkled in the lobes of her baby-foot ears, which had scarcely grown since she was eleven. Her eyes were the same shade of blue as the berries she'd baked into the muffins.

Eight months ago, Mary Ann would've politely no-thank-you'd any offer of food. For a fat person to snack in front of others was to display denial of an obvious problem. Now, however, she chewed without shame. Maybe it was because of Bernette's disarming warmth and cheerfulness. (After her initial faux pas, Bernette had been nothing but friendly, and who could call it a faux pas, anyway? Twenty-two years, and the pounds that attended them, had seriously disguised Mary Ann.) Or perhaps the lack of shame came from Mr. Portwit, Mary Ann thought pleasantly, detaching a wedge of muffin with her fingers. His dismissal of Mary Ann's insecurities was contagious. He loved her figure. His love gave her a certain power, allowed her the confidence to reunite with an old friend who had always been prettier and more successful. Mary Ann decided she would need to share this revelation with Mr. Portwit. He'd been depressed as of late, putzing around the house in his tube socks, staying up late and sleeping until noon.

"I can't get over how stunning you look," Mary Ann told Bernette. As it came out of her mouth, she realized she was broaching another taboo subject: physical appearance. Now Bernette was expected to throw a compliment Mary Ann's way.

Bernette smiled, said "Thank you," and raised the teacup to her lips.

"Don't worry," Mary Ann said. "You don't have to say the same about me. I know I'm fat." She chuckled at the ineffectiveness of this tiny word to describe herself. "I'm *really* fat. I can't imagine what I look like to you after all these years."

"Well, I admit I was surprised, initially," Bernette said, mouth lilting up on one side in an expression Mary Ann recognized as bemusement. "But I must say you're still the same girl I grew up with. I mean it. Look at you, Mary Ann. There's just more of you to love."

With that, she and Bernette were friends again. They had parted as eighteen-year-old girls, stepped through separate time portals, and been rejoined as middle-aged women. Women with memories and knowledge and distensions and scars and a few carefully hidden white hairs, but to each other, they'd retained the freshness and purity of children. They were living scrapbooks.

On the four-winged bird of popularity, determination, good looks, and intellect, Bernette had soared through Union High. She'd dated three captains of the basketball team, served as Class Treasurer, president of the French Club, and varsity cheerleader. Teamed with two other go-getters named Nicole Hooperman and Jackie Kinsella, she had formed CUT, the Consensually Unselfish Teens, a group that, through charitable work at soup kitchens and homeless shelters, had, in the words of Grand Rapids Vice-Mayor Jeremy Doberman, "helped to surgically remove, with their fine example, the tumor of apathy from the hearts of teenagers everywhere." This bizarre quote had even been engraved on a gold plaque and presented to the trio at a black tie ceremony at the newly opened Amway Grand Plaza Hotel.

After high school, Bernette moved to New York. Mary Ann's mother kept in touch with Bob Fargas, so throughout college Mary Ann had been subjected to frequent updates on Bernette's "amazing" activities: While on a full ride at Sarah Lawrence, she double-majored in French and International Diplomacy. She spent one semester of junior year in Versailles. She spent half her senior year on a tiny French-speaking island in the Caribbean, building bamboo houses and counseling the locals on personal hygiene.

It was on this Caribbean trip that she'd met Barry Straw. From the framed photograph on Bernette's dresser, Mary Ann could see that Barry was unfairly handsome. His eyes matched Bernette's in size and blue intensity. Kneeling on the shore, with the honey sunrise swaddling his hairless, teak-colored body, Barry displayed a freshly painted picket fence of teeth. The photograph could have been the cover of a romance novel.

They'd waited until graduation to get married. Barry had barely finished returning his tuxedo when they took to the skies again: Africa, Egypt, Tibet, Russia, Southeast Asia. For two years, they lived off savings and odd jobs, shared dreamless nights in rumbling, thirty-six-hour train rides from India's toes to its crown. They'd hiked the rims of Indonesian volcanoes, chewed fried locusts on a crowded Bangkok street corner, slept in a Korean alley and awoken to the buzz saw of a leper dislodging one of his tonsils.

After returning to the States, they settled in Chicago. Bernette found work as a sales representative for a cosmetics company (European Division); Barry became the strategic planning analyst for a pharmaceutical giant. How Bernette ended up in sales she didn't know, but she apparently excelled at it, as in everything she attempted, as evidenced by the framed certificates lying in the corner that named her *#1 Regional Salesperson* in four consecutive years. ("Oh, those things," Bernette explained. "Had to clear the office wall. Out with the old, in with the new!")

Five years later, she bore their first daughter. Two years after that, the second one. Barry was offered a transfer to Kalamazoo, with a substantial raise. Since Bernette had quit her job to stay home with the girls, they moved back to Michigan, the circle complete, without plan or prejudice ending up only forty-five miles from where Bernette had "wet my pants because I was so scared to sing at the Holy Name Christmas recital."

Three times a week, Mary Ann went to Bernette's. It became part of her November routine. First she stopped home and changed from her teaching clothes into a pair of jeans that, when unfolded, was as wide as the card table they ate dinner on. Mr. Portwit, clad in one of his four pairs of gray sweatpants, greeted Mary Ann with midafternoon snacks—nacho chips lavaed with melted cheese, sugar cookies cut from a log of dough, buttered wedges of olive bread, pastrami sandwiches slathered with mayonnaise.

He watched her eat. He asked about her day, her students, the weather, but never about Mrs. Jennings, Principal Foster, Rick Fletcher, or any of the others who'd played a role in his suspension.

She searched his tone and detected no cynicism beneath his cheer. He behaved like a man on a well-earned two-month vacation, showering every fourth or fifth day, climbing into bed at 4 a.m., munching celery sticks dipped in peanut butter on the couch with a book spread before his face.

Dale apparently could not feel ashamed, sorry, or mistaken. He could only be proud—proud to have spoken his mind, to have lived for the moment, to have swum *downstream* for a change, because contrary to popular thought, speaking one's mind was far more healthful in the long run than swallowing one's rage and pain, which is what most people did. "People try so hard," he said, "and they fight the current of instinct." The repression of honest feelings, no matter how socially incendiary the articulation of these feelings might be, led to disease, death, and depression. "And not necessarily in that order," he added.

It was difficult to be around him for long stretches, so she avoided him. He kissed her goodnight when she climbed into bed, and she kissed him before she waddled off in the morning. The enormous irony of Dale *not* admitting that he'd been wrong to publicly humiliate Rick Fletcher was that Dale *had* been wrong. Not wrong in any vague moralistic sense, but wrong in Dale's own professed, dogmatic, scientific sense. His hypothesis and ensuing experiment had been founded on an untruth, plain and simple.

He'd based not only his actions but his ability to defend those actions on the existence of photographic evidence. After the Fletcher debacle, he had confessed to Mary Ann of standing at the Meijer counter, opening the packet, and flipping through what he called the "hideous, worthless pictures." Despair had seized him, he said, each time he revisited the moment. He saw no choice but to "force the villain's hand."

Initially, Mary Ann was enraged. Why would Dale sabotage their lives by getting himself suspended? They'd recently closed on a house. They had mortgage payments and credit-card debts for the moving company. For a week, Mary Ann refused to talk to him other than as necessity dictated.

Then, gradually, the Rick Fletcher Affair began to lose its hold on the minds of the Elkhart students and faculty. A competent substitute was brought in to teach Mr. Portwit's classes. Rick Fletcher's parents calmed down and withdrew their litigious motions. Mrs.

Jennings proved a capable stand-in for Principal Foster, who would return to his duties after a ("Let's pray on this") successful surgery and recovery period. The PTA's decision was that Mr. Portwit be given a second chance; he would resume his post after Christmas break. He would be rested and calm, and everyone, including Mary Ann, knew that he would "return to the classroom with the vigor and professionalism he has exhibited throughout his career." Once the administration had issued this official recommendation, and the day-to-day frenzy died down, Mr. Portwit no longer made Mary Ann's blood pressure like mercury at a Zippo's flame.

She only felt sorry for him now, because although he tried to present a carefree figure, his ashen sweatpants, unbuttoned flannel, sandpaper stubble, and crooked glasses gave him a brittle, lost look. The divoted dome of his head, like a lump of clay passed between third graders' hands, seemed vulnerable. Inside that skull was a brain that would not concede fault, would not be wrong. She viewed this not as an admirable trait, but as a disease, one as pitiful and deforming as her own obesity.

But he was sweet to her. He provided snacks (fattening and inelegant as they were), vacuumed the carpets, spun and twist-tied the garbage bags, washed the dishes. He puttered through the house with an impish yet forlorn grin attached to his face. He mumbled to himself as he watered the plants, wagging his finger at the air, making speeches to the fern. By the middle of November, Mary Ann doubted that he would ever want to return to the classroom. Or that she would want him to.

♡

Biggs, aka Mr. Bullshit, wrestled the bottle of champagne between his legs. The cork popped free. He filled a bubbly flute and set it on the bar in front of Mr. Portwit. Biggs wiped the condensation from the bottle, then placed the bottle beside the flute.

"What's the toast tonight?" Biggs asked, counting the bills Mr. Portwit had given him.

"To Rick Fletcher. May he father a dozen children exactly like himself, so he is constantly shown a mirror of his own ineptitude." Dale downed the champagne.

"He's the kid that got you suspended, huh?"

"No, Biggs, I suspended myself. But yes, he was the catalyst.

That's the danger of repeating one's actions. You start to repeat your words, too. I apologize for telling this story before."

"Keep buying bottles of champagne, you can repeat yourself all you want," Biggs answered, turning the television dial until it showed a late-night news program.

"What kind of name is that?" Mr. Portwit mused, fascinated by the rush of bubbles in his glass, how they resembled fireworks shot skyward. "'Rick Fletcher.' Think of it out of context. It sounds like an insult. 'That guy's a rick fletcher if I ever saw one.' 'You ever seen such a rick fletcher before?'"

"Makes me think of a felcher," Biggs laughed. "You know what a felcher is? It's when a guy . . ."

"Why is it that every passion eventually gets boring? Even something as basic as sex. How long have you been a bartender, Biggs?"

"You ask me that every time you come in here. Ten years."

"And you love it?"

"I get to meet nut jobs like you, don't I?"

"Hear, hear!" Mr. Portwit raised his flute, clinked it against an invisible glass held by his invisible neighbor, then turned it upside-down over his mouth.

"Any time you want your belt back," Biggs said with a smile. He nodded toward the nail in the wall to the left of the register, from which the belt hung.

"Give it to the next poor schmuck who comes in without a date," Mr. Portwit answered. This was becoming their regular joke, even though Biggs didn't know the context, and Mr. Portwit didn't understand his own punch line.

Mr. Portwit recalled with embarrassment the first time he'd come to the Green Top. It was less than three weeks after the wedding, on the day after moving into the new Portage house. He'd been depressed. Depressed about the rain. (It was September, sure, but there would still be grass to mow, and now he was responsible.) Depressed about the movers. (He'd felt so useless, thin as a dandelion and gesturing meekly toward the rooms while burly men humped boxes like mules.) Depressed about his earlier depression. (Wasn't a new house and a new wife enough to get this monkey off his back?)

His blues had led him back to downtown Kalamazoo, not far from his old attic apartment, into a bar he'd never patronized.

He'd been seated on this very stool, thinking that the belt noose had been a mistake, thanking his lucky stars (specifically, the ones that made up Orion's Belt—he laughed aloud) that he'd failed to kill himself. To be discovered dead in the same room that you shat in, shaved in, flossed in, soaped your scrotum in? Hanging from a door, strung up by the implement that holds up your pants? There was no poetry to that, not even the cruel poetry of nature, like lemmings walking off a cliff, black widows devouring their mates. To die pantsless in a bathroom would've been pathetic, would've said to everyone who heard about it, "Dale Portwit was a pathetic man. He lived pathetically, he died pathetically."

Just as he had done tonight, Mr. Portwit had asked, "How long have you been a bartender, sir?"

"Probably since you had hair."

"That's a long time."

"I'm just ribbing you. You look good without hair. You wear it well. Not like me."

The bartender pointed to the top of his own head, where a lonely tuft poked upward, an island in a bay of scalp.

Dale had reassured him. "Most people see a bald head, a scar, a lisp, an amputation . . . and they see faults. I see these as advantages. What's your surname, sir?"

"Why?"

"It's where your history hides. It tells a stranger what you love, what you hate, your disposition, your psychological makeup, your secrets. It's all in the surname, sir."

"Bullshit."

"Mr. Bullshit," Dale had mused. "That's easy to remember."

That first conversation had been interrupted by a gust of wind. Two young men coming through the door. Jackets over their heads. Feet scratching the floor mat like dogs burying turds.

"How's it going?" Mr. Bullshit had said.

"Raining like a son of a bitch."

"You got the game on?"

"Sure." Bullshit whacked the television with his palm. "Just about to start."

The men: jacket removal, synchronized nods at Dale. Beer ordered: two bottles of Bud Light.

"How the hell did the Lions get to play on Monday night?"

"Season opener, too."

"It's all about who they play."

Dale had listened, unable to talk. Verbal constipation. Two strangers arrived, and all ideas fled his mind. He was like a newborn baby. But hell, even a baby could coo; he was soundless, comparable to the stack of washed ashtrays at the end of the bar. He was the small drunk with a failure of a belt holding up his pants. He had wanted to tell the bartender about his own last name. He had wanted to explain its meaning, but now the words were gone and Mr. Bullshit was having a grand old time chatting with his new friends.

Dale hammered the bottle onto the bar. Stood from his stool. The men's heads looked at him. Diseased cantaloupes with hair. Nothing natural about hair. Hair was dead. Covering your head in death. Waste tissue.

"I'm not taking off my pants," Dale had announced. "I'm only removing my belt. My pants will stay up. I'm not taking off my pants."

"Hey!" said Mr. Bullshit. "Take that outside!"

Dale placed his belt on the floor. "I don't want it. You can have it. Throw it away. You should probably throw it away. It's no good."

Mr. Portwit had left the bar. Great brooms of rain swept the pavement, powered by a steady wind. He started to cross the street, stopped on the center yellow line, turned his eyes toward the sky. The rain drenched his face. He squinted. One massive, colorless cloud covered the stars. Mr. Portwit turned this way and that, to get his bearings, to figure out which direction was north, to calculate where Orion might be hiding. A car horn blared a warning. He staggered out of the street and into a puddle. The car sizzled past. The pale figure hunched behind the steering wheel appeared to be melting.

Mr. Portwit shuffled down the sidewalk, hands stuffed in the pockets of his too small denim jacket, the world wavy and murky beyond his rain-spattered lenses. His beltless pants threatened to fall around his knees. He found his car. Flapping like a pinned bat under the windshield wiper was an orange parking ticket. Mr. Portwit freed it and let it fly away.

The morning after, he hadn't been able to will his eyelids open; they were welded together. A bird had built a nest inside his skull. The nest was being eaten by flames. He was sick; beer was poison to Mr. Portwit. Mary Ann, no more than a touch and a voice beside him, said that she would call Elkhart. They would find a sub. He should rest and drink lots of fluids. She had kissed his cheek. As soon as the click of the front door sounded, he had leaned over and vomited on the floor.

But that wasn't a pleasant memory. Tonight, the Green Top operated at its usual reposeful pace. On the main floor, three of the circular tables, populated by shadowy figures, vibrated in the candlelight. The bar stools were empty but for Dale. It was Tuesday, moments past midnight. He always waited until Mary Ann was tucked beneath the comforter, slumbering and twitching in her dream life. Then he slipped into a pair of slacks, took the keys from the kitchen hook, and marched out the door.

He'd taken a liking to the Green Top—the quarter video poker on the bar, the 1980s Bud Light mirrors and framed vintage Pabst Blue Ribbon "Beer Wolf" ads. The hinges of the Green Top's door were called into duty only a few times a night, and the jukebox bounced between plaintive Willie Nelson and solemn Johnny Cash. The bar matched the speed of Mr. Portwit's life during suspension. Last week, he'd felt comfortable enough to smuggle a Sharpie into the men's room and write on the inside of the stall above the toilet paper dispenser, *Some come to sit and wonder / I come to shit like thunder.* He did not consider it vandalism, but rather an attempt at dialogue. The bathroom walls were too pristine for a dive like this, and Mr. Portwit believed that bathroom graffiti was one of the few remaining exchanges of ideas that weren't influenced by capitalistic or political motives.

He fingered the stem of his champagne glass and wondered why Mrs. Jennings (and/or Principal Foster) hadn't fired him outright. Several theories were plausible. The most likely hinged on the faculty and parents' unspoken consensus that Rick Fletcher had indeed vandalized the house. Rick's parents were upset, but their furrowed brows and tough talk of lawsuits clearly masked guilt for the monster they'd bred.

Still, Rick Fletcher's naughtiness could scarcely outweigh the faculty's general disdain for Mr. Portwit in recent months. He had refused to pray for Principal Foster in the teacher's lounge. He had skipped countless mandatory training sessions designed to deal "officially" with all the newly named conditions, including the acronyms and initialisms (ADD, ADHD), the disorders that were entire meals of words (Gerstmann's Syndrome, Central Auditory

Processing Disorder, Nonverbal Learning Disorder Syndrome, Bulimia Nervosa), and disorders of the Dr. Seuss variety (Dyscalculia! Dysgraphia! Dyslexia and Dyspraxia!).

And then, the reason most hurtful: Mr. Portwit had wooed and wed the most unpopular woman at Elkhart. This flew in the face of everything the women teachers held dear. If someone like Mary Ann Tucker could be pursued by a man, a man who by all rights should be hitting on *them* but hadn't said more than a "Lovely day, isn't it?" in three years . . . well, then *they* weren't so special, were they?

Last but not least, he had humiliated *a child* (such a cardinal sin these days as to goosebump flesh in the way that cross-dressing had when he was growing up). And the nail in the cake, the final icing on the coffin, was that poor Rick Fletcher had been recently diagnosed as ADHD.

Since when had children become porcelain dolls? When he was a child, Mr. Portwit and his contemporaries were second-class citizens who behaved with appropriate humility or got paddled. Nowadays, it made no difference that the "child" (a term he questioned) displayed both the simplistic gaze and the intellectual fiber of the sacred cow he'd become.

But all of his controversial acts, Mr. Portwit believed, were reasons for celebration. He'd sworn after the Rufus debacle that from then on, damn the consequences, he would *do* rather than merely *be;* his days of quiet stagnancy were over. He swished a fresh helping of champagne around in his mouth, felt the sting of the bubbles. He'd escaped unemployment, too, and had done so without engaging in the intolerable act of an apology—not to Rick, Rick's parents, Principal Foster, or Mrs. Jennings. These seemed like major victories, and they were why he bought a bottle of champagne when he went to the Green Top. Besides, champagne didn't make him vomit.

Rick Fletcher, however, because the evidence never surfaced, had also escaped punishment. Public humiliation, according to Mary Ann, had even elevated him to minor folk hero. The younger children, she said, could be heard on the playground chanting little ditties about his glorious rise and fall. Surely it was something along the lines of: *Fletcher told the teacher that his wife was fat / His mayonnaise balloons went splat splat splat!*

Mr. Portwit didn't want to think about any of it. He would enjoy this abeyance, manufacture some kind of routine out of the chaos of free time, ignore the niggling fact that he seemed doomed to fail at everything he tried.

The bar television showed a shirtless, obese man jogging toward the camera in slow motion. A title appeared, superimposed over the colossal undulation of flab that was the man's torso: *Fat of the Land?* The male voiceover said, "Americans are even fatter than they think, with nearly one-third of all adults—almost 59 million people—rated obese in a disturbing new government survey based on actual body measurements."

"You might want to listen to this," Biggs said. "You're looking a little soft there, Mr. Portwit." Biggs was a good guy. Mr. Portwit liked him, looked forward to viewing his circular head, his unpretentiously messy hair, his taut, hirsute forearms ending in ten stubby fingers, the absentminded way he flogged himself with a damp dish towel while his eyes absorbed the cathode rays.

"One in five Americans, or 19.8 percent, considered themselves obese in a survey based on people's own assessments of their girth. The new survey puts the real number at 31 percent—a doubling over the past two decades. The new number is considered more reliable, since people consistently underestimate their weight."

"The problem keeps getting worse," said Health and Human Services Secretary Tommy Thompson. "This has profound health implications."

The concluding thought before the McDonald's commercial was that obesity increased the risk for a number of serious ailments, including diabetes, heart disease, stroke, high blood pressure, and some types of cancer.

Mr. Portwit unfastened three buttons of his flannel shirt and allowed a hairy island of gut to peek out. "You might be right, Biggs."

"They're gonna need to redefine what's obese and what's not," Biggs offered.

"I don't know if you mean it," Mr. Portwit said, nudging his glasses to the top of his nose. "But you're exactly right. See, that's the problem with adjectives in general—"

The tinkling of the bells. The chilly breeze on the back of Mr. Portwit's neck. Biggs's eyes moving from Mr. Portwit to the door. A nod of acknowledgment, a clasping together of Biggs's thick, hairy hands. "How's it going, fellas?"

Always fellas. Always a different pair of fellas. Always pairing at the bar, double-fucking Mr. Portwit's conversation. Was there a Fella Farm nearby, breeding these goateed blowhards in hay-strewn wooden pens, growing them big and strong, slapping base-ball caps on their heads, branding their biceps with barbed-wire tattoos and herding them to the Green Top for an inaugural taste of the trough?

"Ain't you gonna finish your bubbly, Mr. Portwit?" Biggs asked, hopeful perhaps, as Dale stood from the stool, discreetly rebut-toned his shirt, and wrapped a scarf around his throat.

"Sorry, Biggs, I've got places to go."

The gum-chewing fellas, not yet masters of mouth closing, watched without interest as Mr. Portwit donned his wool coat and fedora. Mr. Portwit felt proud to call Biggs by name. These fella-cattle would certainly note this exchange, causing, somewhere in their subpar gray matter, nerve endings to communicate, electricity to zap the next lobe in line. Conclusions would be drawn—not this instant, but soon—that this mysterious "Mr. Portwit" was an impor-tant man, secure enough or reckless enough to abandon a bottle with two inches of champagne still in it, a man who knew bartend-ers by their first names and rushed into the cold 1 a.m. November air to tend to pressing business that they would never know.

"See you tomorrow," Biggs called out.

With the windows of the three-season porch opened halfway, the breeze almost succeeded in cooling Mary Ann's overheated head. Bernette, jovial and unfazed, fanned Mary Ann with the November *Better Homes and Gardens,* a double issue featuring an exten-sive middle section devoted to "Turning Your Bathroom into a Blastroom!"

"Your color's getting better," Bernette said, placing the magazine on the table and a reassuring hand on Mary Ann's knee. "You scared me. Your eyes rolled up, and you were shaking. Do you want me to take you to the doctor?"

"I'm fine," Mary Ann said. She took a sip of water. It hadn't only been embarrassment—that was the trigger, of course, but it was much more than that.

They'd stepped out onto the porch to observe the quiet shed-ding of leaves, to nibble lemon squares and peruse a bevy of home improvement magazines. Bernette offered Mary Ann a teak Adirondack. Had Mary Ann seated herself in it, or more accurately, atop it, the chair would now be firewood. The unguarded mutual realization, the sudden "oh!" as Bernette blushed and sprinted into the house for a different chair, made Mary Ann so ashamed that her head began to lose blood. Her eyes flitted around the room, over the matching end tables, the Japanese lanterns strung above the windows, the Ecuadorian wall hanging, the silver-framed 8 x 10 of Bernette and Barry wearing puffy yellow coats atop Mount Kilimanjaro. It felt like she'd swallowed a lead meatball. Mary Ann's own life was like that kitten on Sesame Street who couldn't climb the step—a cute life. Tiny. Pity-worthy. Precious because it was so insubstantial. Bernette, meanwhile, had it all. If Bernette wanted to talk to her father, she picked up the phone and pressed seven buttons: he answered with a cheery "Hello"; he would know, without asking, that his daughter had been thinking of him.

As Bernette stepped into the porch, dragging the recliner, Mary Ann saw herself reflected in a window. She witnessed as if for the first time the unnatural immensity of her body, a mountain even the Straws couldn't climb, a walking whale they would not photograph. She fainted just as the recliner was scooted up to the back of her legs.

"I'm so sorry about your chair," Mary Ann said. Any shifting of her rear caused the broken springs to *boiiing* like a cartoon. "I'll buy you a new one, I promise."

"Don't be crazy," Bernette said. "It's some old thing Barry had in college. I've been trying to get rid of it for years."

Mary Ann excused herself to go to the bathroom. After she urinated, she inspected the tub and shower (separate entities, each pristine), the linen closet (precisely folded towels in every color of the rainbow), and the drawers below the sink (mercifully cluttered). In one of the drawers, behind the Calamine lotion, cotton swabs, witch hazel, and First Aid kit, Mary Ann found a bottle of prescription pills: STRAW, BERNETTE F. LIBRIUM 550MG CAPSULE, TAKE (1) CAPSULE TWICE DAILY.

"You know, Mary Ann," Bernette said when Mary Ann returned to the porch. Her concerned expression made Mary Ann feel like a burn victim. "Everybody's got something about themselves that they don't like. Sometimes it's real, sometimes it's in their head." She thought for a heartbeat. "I don't know if that makes it any less real."

"Mine's real."

"So's mine." Bernette extended her left arm. She drew the shirt-sleeve toward her elbow. Scaly red patches, shaped like teardrops, ran the length of her forearm. "I don't wear bathing suits in public any more. It's all over my arms, my legs. On my ass, for Christ's sake."

"You used to have it on your elbows and knees, I remember."

"*Only* my elbows and knees. *Little* patches. I thought I had it bad *then*. God, in elementary school all anybody does all day is dissect the kids they sit by. I remember I sat in front of Kenny Kennedy, so I had to turn around to give him the handouts. One time he asked about my elbow. I told him I fell and scraped it." She laughed, hiding her arm again with the sleeve. "It looked nothing like a scrape. When you're a kid you try anything."

"Isn't there some new medication for psoriasis?" Mary Ann asked. "Supposed to be really good? I thought I'd read about it recently. Some pill?"

"There isn't any pill," Bernette said. "Just ointments."

Mary Ann decided to push it. "What am I thinking of? I swore that something called Liborium or Librium had something to do with psoriasis . . . or eczema?"

"Librium's one of those Prozacky drugs. Makes you *happy*." Bernette formed an exaggerated smile and touched her dimples with her fingertips. "It's one of Pfizer's biggest sellers. You've probably seen the commercials. It'll put Hype through college. I hear it doesn't even work that well."

6

For a scientist, correlation was not, and could not be, equal to causation: conflating them was a liberty taken by juries, journalists, and average Joes like Mr. Biggs the bartender, Oscar Portwit, the Elkhart teachers, and the farm-bred fellas. For those types, if

    A) an acorn fell from the tree, then
    B) the cat darted into the road, then
    C) a passing car crushed the cat
    . . . then they could sleep well knowing that the acorn spooked the cat and caused it to run into the path of the car and become fly food. Causation. The acorn killed the cat.

Scientists did not have this luxury.

Since his suspension, Mr. Portwit's days had shrunk. He awoke a few minutes before noon and lay, corpselike, staring at wrinkles on the sheet near his eye that reminded him of a cresting ocean wave, or a chain of hills, or human lips. He stared for ten minutes, then flipped to his right side, located a ball of dust nesting against a floorboard, and stared for another ten. Eventually he dragged himself out of bed, his face heavy, his steps scuffling. It took enormous effort to squeeze the tube of toothpaste and jam the brush into his mouth.

His teeth were his close friends. He licked them, ground them, used them to chew at his cheeks. His teeth were his connection to the world during the day as he strolled through the living room, looked at soap operas on television, stared out the window at the suburban landscape he possessed no language to describe. By the time Mary Ann came home from school, he always managed to tap a core of energy and affix a pleasant face onto his head. He whipped up snacks for her to devour; he asked polite questions about Elkhart. He still watched her eat, but the effort required for sex seemed to be out of both their ranges.

One day, Mr. Portwit awoke with this cause-and-effect idea on his mind. He needed to find the mechanism that had led him, once again, to emotional atrophy. The place to start, logically, was with the nonsensical, fairy-tale-ish sentence that had lingered for so many weeks now: *Mrs. Brandmal rewarded the good fifth graders by eating a one-on-one lunch with them in the library.*

Rather than stare at wrinkles in the bedsheet, Mr. Portwit decided to start every day by aiming his body and mind at the white ceiling above his bed. Like a jumbo sheet of paper, this ceiling would now be used to calculate the formula of his life. Freshly wakened, he would search his hot-off-the-presses dreams.

Could the nameless anxiety be Miranda Brandmal? The thought of killing her made Dale feel sick now, so how could it have reentered his head so naturally just weeks before? And a more difficult question: if the idea was so repugnant, why was it still in his mind? The answer came without effort. He envisioned the murder of Mrs. Brandmal as a star in the sky: quiet, unobtrusive, not always noticeable . . . but always there. Even if the notion had died the moment he stepped out of that shower, like a star its light was reaching him and would continue to reach him for a long, long time.

His dreams were elusive. When, on occasion, he was able to summon specific content from the blurred fringes of his mind, they had nothing to do with Mrs. Brandmal, nor the fifth grade, nor those special lunches. Still, he reached to the nightstand, set his glasses on his face, and took up pen and paper to record the fragments of his nocturnal wanderings.

For ten days he logged everything, which amounted to very little: *Something about a loaf of French bread that I needed to sharpen. . . . I was going to write with it?* And *Roman candles exploding to the left and right, fizzlewhistlepop, in the darkness of a field? Or a backyard? Not any backyard I've seen before.*

On the afternoon of the tenth day, while seated at the dining-room table, indulging in a microwaved bowl of Campbell's clam chowder, he realized with panicked certainty that dreams could never be considered evidence. Even if he experienced a "significant" dream, it would still be just that—a dream. What self-respecting scientist would trust the mad stew of the unconscious to prove a truth? Mr. Portwit's desperation to find an answer had turned him into a moron and a hippie, a sucker for murky guesswork. He ripped every page of "research" from his three-subject notebook and condemned it to a Tuesday-morning death in the green hurby curby.

Next he delved into his memories, but these were forty years old. His Mrs. Brandmal experiences were the same age as his wife, a coincidence he seized upon. He speculated that he, as a person, had really been "born" *after* the Brandmal experiences, and that his choice of Mary Ann as a bride had been a sign, an arrow with the aggressive dictum emblazoned above it: "Mrs. Brandmal is the reason you are who you are, the reason you cannot ever be truly happy."

On the other hand, it was ridiculous—looking to birth-date coincidences for evidence? He chuckled while shaving his neck, chuckled because this kind of thought process was what turned rational folks into astrologers, palm readers, and believers in the predictive powers of carefully arranged goat entrails. As he wiped foam from his jaw, he said aloud, "You aren't going to kill Mrs. Brandmal." Thinking back on the shower that had rekindled his homicide plan, he chuckled at how in that moment it had seemed so easy, so right.

He'd gotten married, in part, because he thought it might suffocate the creature inside himself. But it hadn't worked. When he recalled his depression of ten months ago, of one year ago, of ten years ago, those days didn't seem any worse than the present. Certainly he had good feelings about Mary Ann, but those feelings existed in a separate compartment, prohibited from interacting with the nameless anxiety that walked beside him every day.

In order to find reason *not* to murder Mrs. Brandmal, he searched his memories. Her physical image came easily: buxom, ample-hipped, milk chocolate hair cropped short in the style of *The Trouble with Harry*–era Shirley MacLaine, cat's-eye glasses, nyloned legs like golden statuettes, a full, red mouth bordered by smile creases. However, when he tried to summon what Mrs. Brandmal was doing, saying, touching—the memory emerged as a shapeless, corroded hunk of metal, a process like raising from the bottom of the Atlantic a salt-eaten remnant, unidentifiable as stern or hull, an object entirely different from when it went down.

This is what he remembered with clarity:

Every boy in the class professed to love her or to have kissed her. The lovers were in the majority. Only Frank Peltz and Dan Morgan claimed to have kissed her, but their stories were widely discounted as braggadocio. The fact was that Mrs. Brandmal, despite her sensuous air and provocative lectern posture, was a stern presence. During lessons she smiled at you, but when you chanced to be alone with her, if she pulled you out of class and leaned to your eye level to hand you a note from your mother, she spoke brusquely and without humor, and you forgot instantly that you'd ever imagined her in a sexual context.

Then there were the special lunches. Every week, the class had a contest. Spelling bees, arithmelympics, history mysteries, musical chairs—these were Mrs. Brandmal's games. Dale thrived at the competitions, winning either often or always (he couldn't recall which).

The other students, especially the boys, were jealous. While Dale disappeared into the library with the voluptuous teacher, they remained on the playground, dangling from the monkey bars like wet laundry, likely reaffirming to each other that Dale was a sissy and would never make a move. Their next step, after days and weeks of this, was to exclude Dale from in-class conversations. Finally, they ridiculed him to his face.

Sometimes, Mr. Portwit could recall fragments from the lunches. Over a bottle of champagne or a fifth of vodka, Mr. Portwit found that these would rise occasionally to the surface as bloated, unrecognizable corpses. At 3 a.m. on the evening of the thirtieth day of his suspension (November 19), he attempted to write down his memories, however incomplete.

He sat at the computer—Mary Ann's because he'd never felt the need to buy one—and typed in the form of a narrative, with himself as the main character. He soared through one long paragraph, then got bogged down by which person to use and deleted the mess. Next, he tried poetry, but aborted when the verse became too free—the line he read just before clicking "No" to the screen prompt "Save changes to Untitled?" was:

Those sweatered bosom balloons below the ready-mouth catch crumbs like flypaper

He tried Mary Ann's listing method, but ended up with only

Ten Memories of Special Lunches

10. Sitting at a table in the library, with . . . some food,

probably I ate cheese sandwiches, because that's what Mother used to make for me.

9. She is eating an apple? Something is crunching in her teeth.

8. The clock is up on the wall, ticking above the unstaffed checkout counter.

7. She is beautiful; she will soon be touching your leg under the table.

6. I am scared, she is looking at me, her eyes are unnatural.

5. Blue dress, another day blue blouse.

It was pathetic, unhelpful, pointless. Dale deleted the list, deleted it all and would have deleted it twice if he could've borne writing it again. Even in his own head, he couldn't discern real from fabrication. Especially in his head. Trying to summon the past through a series of words on a page . . . it was a faulty system! Unknowns, variables, discrepancies between what he *wanted* to write and what his vocabulary and experience would *allow*, which was to say nothing of the years, months, weeks, hours, days, nights, showers, bus rides, graduation ceremonies, hangovers, toothbrushings, hanging attempts, marriages, pecan-pie fuckings, house-in-the-suburb-buyings, etcetera, that had stepped between him and the truth. Memory—what a cruel joke. To tease humans with the ability to preserve their lives on a private reel—then to discover that the damn thing didn't work!

Mary Ann's perceptions of schooldays as daylight shortened: waking and driving in darkness as deep as midnight; sunrise imminent; hints of pink and yellow along the horizon; classroom heaters reborn in whiffs of burnt dust; children's coats fat like squirrel's cheeks; coats piled together on too-small hooks; a snow flurry here and there, flakes like black bugs swarming the dirty sky outside the window; Principal Foster no longer a man but an ongoing intercom saga.

His saga had characters:

Kay Foster—faithful wife of twenty years, active in paper drives and bingo nights. According to Mrs. Jennings: "bravely fighting by her husband's side."

Joe Kazuhiro—superintendent of Kalamazoo Public Schools,

second-generation Japanese American, smiley and generous and a frequent intercom interpolator ("I saw Principal Foster yesterday, and he was full of get-up-and-go, and he told me to tell all of you that he keeps a copy of last year's yearbook by his hospital bed and looks at your faces three times a day just to remind him of everything he has to live for").

DOCTOR BROMAWAY—mysterious, white-coated savior about whom the women speculated; the composite, from conversations Mary Ann overheard, made him 6 feet, 2 inches tall, with broad, soft hands, thick lips, a European accent, long eyelashes, serious brown eyes, unshaven cheeks, curly hair the color of Guinness.

LOUISE "WEEZY" FOSTER—nineteen-year-old daughter (her nickname too much, too screwed-up funny, an ironic screwed-up funniness that you didn't want to laugh at now that our hero Principal Foster had developed, as a period to his death sentence, emphysema on top of the throat cancer). In one respect, though, Mary Ann envied Principal Foster's daughter: her premortem "good-byes" and "I love you's" were something Mary Ann never had.

The saga had drama, comedy, suspense, pathos. It was narrated with engorged emotion by "Principal" Jennings, which the kids now called her. The children—bless their hearts—were oblivious to the morbidity of such a title. Or were they? Their seamless transfer of this title to Mrs. Jennings, along with the sudden death of Tyrannosaurus the first-grade gerbil, signaled to many of the superstitious/religious faculty (everyone but Mary Ann and Ramone the maintenance man) the innate premonitory powers of children and animals. Foster was doomed. So spake the innocents.

The teacher's lounge was hushed and reverential, transformed into a hospital waiting room, or a funeral home, or some combination of the two. Even the popcorn thupping in the microwave seemed to have turned itself down a notch. Talk of possible snowfall, of mental and spiritual encouragement, of school activities (the paper drive, the Halloween Costume-vaganza)—these were allowed because they were necessary and pragmatic. Mentioning buck-toothed Benjamin Wright's forays into ruler gnawing was met with a polite smile and a pair of raised eyebrows that translated to, "I'd love to talk about your student, but since this would take my mind off our diseased Principal, I'm going to continue nibbling my pocket pita in silence."

It was compulsory, apparently, for everyone to wage solemn inner protest against Cancer and Emphysema, foot soldiers serving a bigger, darker, evil—Death Himself, that bony wraith in his fluttering cloak. Death had no right to come here, to this school! This Elkhart family of teachers and friends was going to dial up The Big Man, send a few thousand "knee-mails," summon Him on flaming chariot to rearrange Old Cloaky's face one bone at a time.

These were Mary Ann's bitter, cynical thoughts, and she didn't enjoy them. But it was happening: She was mutating. While she munched take-out Reuben sandwiches and pretended to read, her mind sounded, to herself, exactly like Mr. Portwit. She realized how much she missed him. If only he were here to provide the sarcasm, she could go back to being that nice, quiet lady that nobody liked.

These days she sat at the end of the glossy imitation-oak table in the teacher's lounge. Her nine-hundred-dollar chair had been paid for by a government fund for people with special needs and ordered directly from Steelcase. Standard padded folding chairs could no longer hold Mary Ann, not because they failed structurally, but because, at 263 pounds, she couldn't fit onto them. She had shed them like dead skin.

She wasn't embarrassed about her new double-wide leather office chair. It made her feel regal. Its legs were like tree trunks (as were hers). It wouldn't fail. It held all of her, with room to spare. She could breathe again. She was, however, embarrassed about her body. Her position at the head of the table made her feel conspicuous. The chair also altered the traffic pattern in the lounge; the teachers had to squeeze past it to get to the microwave. They didn't voice disapproval, but by their glances she suspected they were praying for her.

♡

Dale dismounted the bed and, socked but otherwise nude, walked to its foot to begin his jumping jacks, a routine Mary Ann hadn't witnessed in a month. A month was an insignificant amount of time in most relationships, but for theirs it was—what—12 percent of their time together? Mary Ann was struck by the realization that this marriage business was just beginning for them and would result in countless minute alterations of each other's behavior, routine, mental and emotional state, and diet. Nothing was stagnant anymore.

Every action would change the other person in unpredictable ways. They were like sculptors in the dark, whacking away with hammer and chisel upon a flesh-and-blood human.

This metaphor was thrilling, terrifying—like a triple-layer fudge cake—and seemed tied to an image of Mary Ann's father folded between the driver's seat and the dashboard, half-eaten English muffin in his hand, the miraculous radio playing "Coward of the County" while strawberry-scented breath escaped his blood-filled mouth. What had happened to his final puff of air? Was it still floating around in the atmosphere? She would have to ask Mr. Portwit sometime, ask what happened to our breath after we set it free.

Thump, thump, thump, like a heartbeat. After eighty-seven jumping jacks, Dale stopped, breathing valiantly. Eighty-seven— an odd integer, and Dale had never, to Mary Ann's knowledge (she hadn't counted every time, but she did have a habit of counting rhythmic noises that surrounded her), stopped on an odd number during after-sex jumping jacks. Usually it was ninety. So it was an oddly-odd odd number that Dale had stopped on. She was really starting to think like him.

"Was that eighty-seven?"

"What do you care?"

"Aren't you impressed that I noticed?"

"I knew you could count," he puffed with finality, with no regard for the month that had just passed with little interaction, no sex, and then this surprise three-orgasm pasta explosion. He stepped to his dresser and selected a pair of clean underwear from the top drawer.

Mary Ann reached to the nightstand for the roll of paper towels. She wiped her belly, breasts, vagina, and thighs. To get at the food remnants, she lifted and rearranged handfuls of flesh. Her flesh was thicker, denser than ever. Her body had become a foreign material. But there was a certain erotic quality to its unruliness, the fact that no number of hands could hold it all at once, and that there would always be unchecked—even unseen—spillage. She would never run out of her.

She had at last resumed her list writing, happily returning to her Friday-night routine. Though she knew that on weeknights he had been sneaking out to drink, on weekend evenings he was as much a homebody as she, and they orbited each other "like the earth and moon," as Mr. Portwit said, tied together but never touching, following their natural paths, she writing lists in front of the television, he drifting from chair to chair, textbook to textbook, wineglass to Internet, stairs to floors, until sometime after 2 a.m. when they crawled into bed and fell asleep on opposite sides of the mattress.

"I made a date for us to go to the Straws," she called, with conviction and volume.

The door to the bathroom was closed, and Dale's toothbrushing was a muffled, high-intensity buzz, like a fly's wings.

"Tomorrow afternoon," Mary Ann continued. "We thought maybe a late lunch. Two o'clock or so." The rushing water ceased, followed by a spitting noise, then the rushing water again. Then nothing. Nothing. Then Mr. Portwit snorted forcefully to dislodge phlegm from the back of his throat. He spat it into the sink. He ran water again.

Dale went along. Like a chauffeur or a cabdriver or a second cousin at a funeral, he went along. It was all Mary Ann could hope for, and she was, in actuality, happy for it. Dale was driving, both hands gripping the wheel. The unheatable Escort floated along I-94. Each breath lived briefly as a cloud in front of Dale's face before vanishing and being replaced by the next. Once again, Mary Ann recalled her father, crushed against the steering wheel. If he had died in winter, he would have been able to see where his final breath had gone.

Dale stared ahead, slow-blinking, ignoring the sunlight that buttered his eyes and face. So sullen! So brooding! He was really one of the bad boys, Mary Ann thought with more than a little pride. He was the wolf in sheep's clothing, the rebel inside the nerd, but he could be tamed.

She had warned, and he had promised: he would *not* make a scene, would not criticize the Straws' lifestyle, would *not* question their ideologies, denounce their brand of air freshener, or ridicule their bookshelf size. He had promised with a smile on his face. He would be polite, nonjudgmental, engaging (as was his natural demeanor, she had assured him).

Mary Ann checked over her shoulder every ten seconds to make certain the recliner wasn't bounding into the distance. By her reckoning, she owed Bernette a chair, and she was happy to repay the debt today. They hadn't bungee-corded the trunk, so the lid thumped the recliner with every minor divot in the expressway. The noise lent a sense of urgency to the journey.

They arrived at the stroke of two. "I told you," Mr. Portwit said, turning the key and killing the engine. She had wanted to leave ten minutes earlier, had even stood in her coat, clacking the bedroom door frame with her wedding ring. Mr. Portwit had insisted that the drive would take eleven minutes; Mary Ann insisted on more than fifteen minutes. "Trust me when it comes to clocks," Mr. Portwit said now, unbuckling his seat belt.

Lesson taught and learned, they leaned to each other and kissed the lips they found waiting.

Mr. Portwit insisted on bringing the recliner inside. Mary Ann held the trunk open while he embraced the chair and gave a mighty tug. It didn't budge. Mr. Portwit's hands slipped, and he stumbled backward. Mary Ann quietly suggested that they leave it until Barry could come out and help. Waving off her advice, Mr. Portwit again bear-hugged the recliner. Between grunts he insisted it was only a matter of leverage. Head veins bulged, and perspiration beaded on his crown. Mary Ann watched anxiously for two minutes as he finally managed to wrestle the green beast onto the pavement, at which time, panting with exhaustion, he wiped his brow with his sleeve and said, "Okey-dokey. We'll leave it here until after lunch."

The Straw family was arranged in the entryway like a Christmas card. Bernette swung open the door, her smile stretched to the point of potential pain. She ushered the Portwits inside with a kiss that, though aimed at Mary Ann's right cheek, did not, Mr. Portwit noticed, actually make contact.

"Mr. Portwit," Bernette gushed. "Mary Ann has told me all about you." Bernette apparently thought this fact was cause for celebration, because she opened her arms and gave Dale a generous hug. She jiggled him like a birthday present, then retreated into the fold of her family, who had been poised patiently with fixed smiles. So many white teeth, so much blond hair. It was riveting.

"This is my husband, Barry. Barry . . . Mary Ann and Mr. Portwit."

Nods all around, then a sudden, bold step forward, and extension of the hand from Barry to Dale. Dale shook the hand. It dwarfed his own.

"And these are my daughters, Lauren and Hyperbole," Bernette summarized.

"Hyperbole!" exclaimed Mr. Portwit, smiling until his face felt strained at the girl in bubble-gum-pink shorts and SpongeBob SquarePants T-shirt, whose hairdo looked like Bernette's in miniature. Mr. Portwit lowered himself into a position usually struck for crapping in the woods and announced, "That is undoubtedly the most amazingly stupendous arrangement of letters ever to be devised by mortal man!" He turned his gaze on Lauren. "And *Lauren's* not bad either!"

A mixture of polite and sincere laughter, indistinguishable from each other, followed. The party adjourned to the dining room.

"I've told Bernette before, but I haven't had a chance to tell you . . . I love your house," Mary Ann said to Barry. She unfolded a yin-yang-patterned cloth napkin and slid it into the imperceptible space between her belly and the table.

Barry did not respond, though, because every eye was magnetized toward Bernette, who entered the dining room pushing a silver cart bearing three covered silver platters.

As Mr. Portwit studied the back of his wife's head (straight hair, dirty blond or dishwater, always *just, just* touching her shoulders), Mr. Portwit fell back (it wasn't so far) into the *conquering* mood that had possessed him during their mad months of courtship. Mary Ann had been like a stately and distant elk, one he needed to fell. Like Mrs. Brandmal, come to think of it. Although he never "had" Mrs. Brandmal in a sexual way, he did indeed have her as a friend. Those lunches were private moments, clandestine meetings—at least in his mind, since they coincided with the librarian's lunch break and since the blinds could be pulled to keep would-be playground peepers from fogging up the glass. He and Mrs. Brandmal were all alone, and she looked him in the eyes, and he felt like he mattered. If Mary Ann had gotten away, if she had rejected him, she would have become the mental image that brands a man, compels him to use blended scotch for the rest of his days and die by his own hand near the smell of frying meat.

Mary Ann had been—and still was—unaware of this power in herself. She was lonely and fearful. She couldn't conceive that her opinions "might possibly" (a redundancy she loved to say) be valued, or that her looks might possibly be attractive. She had feared Mr. Portwit for his intensity, and although fear was something he had deserved for a long time but never received, he wished it hadn't come from her. To scare a woman into marriage seemed disappointing.

Bernette unveiled the lunch. No smoke cloud mushroomed from beneath the lid. Instead, paper-thin green seaweed and slices of raw salmon, halibut, squid, and cooked shrimp were revealed. "Ooohhh, it's so pretty," marveled Hyperbole. The next tray: a pile of washed lettuce, columnar cuts of cucumber, a green mound of wasabi. No plume of smoke accompanied the final unveiling. It was a bowl of cold rice. Sushi rice.

"The real name is 'tay-ma-key-zoo-shee,'" Barry said in a Speak-and-Spell voice. "But we call them Japanese tacos."

"That's exactly what they are," Bernette said. "You load them up with what you want, fold the nori—that's these seaweed squares here—and eat up!"

"Why are we having sushi *again?*" dragged out Lauren with grand, tilting-head gestures of irritation. It was a beautiful display of the id-piloted child; Mr. Portwit envied her in this situation, because she embodied the goal he had set for himself after his failed suicide: to say and do whatever he wanted. Instead, like every good citizen, he'd found the inside of his cheek, and had learned how to chew it. In the real world, a person who said everything he wanted would be institutionalized, murdered, or given a talk radio show.

The Straws went to work, passing and grabbing and placing and stuffing and folding and biting and chewing and mmmm-ing.

"That green stuff burns out your brain," said Hyperbole, pointing a chopstick.

"I've never had this before," said Mary Ann, eyes watery. She had gobbed on too much wasabi. "You *have* to give me the recipe," she added.

She didn't know why she said it. Maybe she'd always wanted to say it. Her mother used to say it at Thanksgivings, family reunions, Fargas dinners, bridal showers. But it wasn't as if her mother ever *made* the recipes she collected. She just enjoyed forcing people to give her things.

Mother (with murderous sincerity): "You have to give me the recipe."

Bernette offered to write down the ingredients and volunteered to drive with Mary Ann to the Asian market on Westnedge. Barry talked about the Chicago Bears, which made Mary

93

Ann cringe sideways at Dale, who mercifully refrained from scorn and even, surprisingly, offered a *very normal* segue story of his father taking him to Detroit Tigers games in the 1960s. This evolved into conversation about bread makers, wedding presents, video games, street magicians, and, finally, Barry's job.

Since Bernette and Barry were the worldly ones—the travelers and success stories and cultured, progressive parents—Mary Ann couldn't help but suspect that while their faces showed teeth, internally they were in agony because the Portwits were utter dullards. (Dale was no dullard, of course, not on his own terms, but Mary Ann had drilled into him as preparation for this visit the need to *be civil*, which to him translated as *boring*.) Surely the Straws' neighborhood friends discussed literature and political theory and world history and modern painting over hot sake.

The zinfandel. Mary Ann pursed her lips, touched her forehead. With all the effort it had taken to get the recliner into the trunk, they'd forgotten the wine. She pictured the bottle on the shelf in the dark refrigerator. There was no way to get it now, no matter how vividly she imagined backing out of the driveway and suddenly yelling, "Dale, stop! The Inglenook!"

Who came to a dinner party without a gift for the hosts? She concentrated on taking slow, regular breaths.

With her fingers trembling (she hoped not visibly), Mary Ann excused herself from the table. She closed the bathroom door behind her. She washed her face with cold water.

Mary Ann and Bernette had been separated too long. As adults they knew too much; they were too old and too mannerly and too tentative to recapture either the excited back-and-forths or comfortable silences of childhood. Still, Mary Ann wanted to believe it was possible to regain those qualities, or at least to create a new version of them. After all, wasn't that the essence of growing old? Fashioning new versions of things you'd already done? Wasn't this the way to hold onto the past without becoming a slave to it?

Her neck was sweating. She ripped a handful of toilet paper from the roll, wadded it, and dabbed her skin. She needed to calm down.

Visions flooded her mind, of driving down Westnedge in Bernette's new VW Bug (would Mary Ann fit?), of the Straws coming to the Portwit house for dinner and drinks (after a major cleaning and a battery of repairs, which *who* would do?), of Barry and Dale finding common ground (surely it was possible). Lauren and Hyperbole would be her surrogate nieces.

From the drawer under the sink, Mary Ann retrieved the bottle of Librium. She swallowed two tablets with a palmful of water. The *Qty: 100* bottle was dated one year ago, yet was nearly full. Maybe Bernette had graduated to stronger medication, or gotten over whatever had been troubling her. Barry worked at a pharmaceutical company, for pity's sake! He could probably bring home a vat of whatever active ingredient was in these things. She stuffed the bottle into her purse.

Lunch ended without incident. Hype and Lauren, who had been quiet while eating, became energized. They squirmed. They bit their nails. They wanted to run away; running away was their privilege; they seemed to understand that in a few years they would have to stay at the table no matter the circumstances. Bernette excused them, and they exploded out of their chairs. It reminded Mary Ann of herself and Bernette Fargas after those incredibly long dinners. It had always been a relief to hear the magic words: "You girls can go."

"So, Mister Portwit," Barry said, entering the back porch loafered and khakied, fleece-sweatered. His dress, gait, and vocal inflections screamed, *I am comfortable!* From the corner-mounted speakers, bongos and marimbas intoned a cool, squanchy rhythm that Mr. Portwit recognized as a Cuban jazz piece made popular in a MasterCard commercial.

Barry seated his golden body on the empty Adirondack beside Mr. Portwit. He fluffed the longish curls behind his neck. He raised his Heineken bottle, lipped it, tipped it. His neck showed signs of a future wattle. Smile lines creased the corners of his eyes. Other than these minor defects, Mr. Portwit couldn't locate any physical indicators that this guy had been alive more than twenty-five years.

"Mary Ann tells us you don't like to be called by your first name," Barry said, in the tone of a person noting the color of a fire engine.

"That's correct, Mr. Straw. I prefer to go by my surname."

"Call me Barry. Please." He laughed with a forcefulness obviously effective in the pharmaceutical world. "On the weekends, I'm Barry. You come and work for me, you can call me Mr. Straw all you want!"

Mr. Portwit was about to issue his "the use of first names is not a right" speech, but frankly, he was tired of it—tired, quite suddenly, of explaining anything to anyone—and besides, he'd promised to behave. He was determined, this once, to abide by his word. "My surname is Portwit," he said finally, sipping his Kahlua and cream and avoiding eye contact. "You can say it *port wit*, which could imply the humor of the port. You know, wisecracks by dockworkers and longshoremen, that sort of thing. Or it might suggest wit enhanced by fortified wine. Or—"

"You could also say *poor twit*, couldn't you?" Barry said, erupting in a self-satisfied hyena laugh, his golden face succumbing to the red invasion.

"That's true," Mr. Portwit said. The *poor twit* thing had been scheduled as his next point. He was going to show that words were essentially playthings, like dollhouses and army men. Good for the imagination, but—

"So what do you make of my name?"

A challenge. It wouldn't do, given Mary Ann's instructions, to say "Straw, comma, ordinary as. A bland, blond substance under which molds fester and rodents make their nests."

"Straw," Mr. Portwit intoned pensively, massaging his hairless chin like a fortune-teller with a crystal ball. "Let's see . . . You're doomed to be blown apart by the Big Bad Wolf. Unless, of course, you manage to spin yourself into gold. But wait. Now that I look more closely, you do resemble St. Raw, the patron saint of uncooked meat. Or maybe Mr. Wolf won't bother you, on account of your WARTS, which I'm sure you know is your name backwards."

Barry laughed more loudly than the *tink-tink rhumba tink* from the speakers. Mr. Portwit found himself joining in. The laugh sounded strange coming from his mouth, like someone had dropped an alarm clock down his throat and at last it was beeping. He'd forgotten what his own laugh sounded like. He was drunk, and it was two in the afternoon. Bless the Japanese and their sake, he thought, while out of his mouth came the revelation, "And your first name is Barry, as in a strawberry, so I suppose you could be WART'S BERRY."

"An excellent band name," choked out Warts. His eyes were glistening. The Cuban horns *blam-blammed*, paused, *blam-blammed* from the speakers.

Why was this world-traveled yuppie idiot so goddamned funny?

Bernette Straw's ass came into the room. It was relatively attractive, thought Mr. Portwit, glancing up from his drink. Ordinary as an umbrella. But still, the type of ass a man could love. It ticktocked in the doorway, moving in careful increments toward them. The rest of her body followed. She was dragging the recliner, Mary Ann's favorite, the one they had brought in the Escort's trunk. Mary Ann appeared on the other end of the chair, her stubby arms at her sides, huffing for air, sweat drops parachuting onto her lavender shirt collar. She was so fucking huge. Mr. Portwit wanted to yell this conclusion to her, but he didn't. Perhaps someday he would make it to that plateau. He stirred his drink with his pinky as Barry leapt from his chair.

"What the heck is this?" Barry asked, emboldened by the imported beer and the imported bespectacled stranger in their Adirondack. He shooed his wife and Mary Ann to a safe distance, then squatted and gripped the recliner, cheeks puffing like a power lifter. "Where do you want it?" he demanded. He was up now, erect, arms bearing heaviness and joy.

"Geez, I don't know," Bernette protested. "You took it before we were ready. We were managing fine on our own." She looked to Mary Ann from her own lidded, tipsy eyes. "Weren't we, honey? These men have to butt into everything." She laughed, which gave Mary Ann permission to laugh, and then Barry made a big show of lurching here and there with the recliner in his arms, eliciting a playful double scream by nearly ramming into the shelf of colorful wooden Oaxacan figures to the left of Mr. Portwit.

So this is domestic life, thought Mr. Portwit. Teaming with another couple, comprised of one part distant or immediate connection, a few dashes of ignored differences, a handful of alcohol-fueled jokes. This was the way couples measured themselves. It was the litmus test for normalcy, for happiness; it provided something to talk about in bed, a "them" to unite against, or for, whichever the case might be.

Mr. Portwit threw Mary Ann a jumbo smile, a smile he hoped would match the size of her heart, that overworked red fist hidden beneath the tent of her shirt, the pillow of her bosom, and the cage of her ribs, the physical but also the metaphorical heart, because both had a place, and each was a different entity. He wanted, right then and there, to make love to her, to lead her into the living room and rip off her clothes, plunge inside, make her scream the way she loved to scream, his insignificant, wiry self suddenly the cause of her unbridled pleasure, his ass gripped by her desperate hands, the David atop the Goliath, the boy swallowed by the woman, boy as slave, as tool, as breathing means to an untamable end.

7

Happy. Retarded children were happy. Dogs. The paperboy was happy when his mid-pedal, Frisbee-esque release sent the rubber-banded bone of news hurtling end over end to its eventual *slap*, *slide*, and *stop* on the targeted porch. A pedaling paperboy: that was a happy person. But "happy" was no word to describe a fifty-year-old scientist, and so it did not bother Mr. Portwit that he could not think of himself that way.

Mary Ann was unhappy too, it seemed to Dale. She was overwhelmed by her job, by all the petty after-school activities that dominated the life of an elementary teacher. "Fun Nights" and "Family Bingos," technology meetings, staff meetings, school board meetings, mandatory "Super-Fests," "Uno Rodeos," prayer sessions for Mr. Foster—all things that "no self-respecting teacher who loves her job would miss" (Principal Jennings). The one place Mary Ann enjoyed going was the Straws', and she went nearly every day, yet the time and energy she spent dressing and applying makeup in preparation for her "casual visits" suggested that even this was a tenuous joy.

She'd bought an entirely new wardrobe. Dipping into a sizable savings that had accrued through years of frugality, Mary Ann knew that for most women, a shopping spree like this would be a joyous experience. But she felt little pleasure. She'd crossed the hump from 22W to 24W, and when she wasn't teaching, P.R.-ing, list writing, or sleeping, she emptied bags of Lane Bryant clothes onto the bed for imminent hanging. She stood pigeon-toed before the closet, tossing shirts, skirts, slacks, blouses, panties, bras, and dresses to the floor, where they lay for days in wrinkled piles like shed skin. She complained of pain. Her body was stretching. Most of her blouses, when they reached the washing machine, were splotched. Her stomach prevented her from leaning over her plate, and the food on her fork had to travel that much farther than a thin person's to get to her mouth.

Elkhart Elementary and Middle School had been the home base of their relationship, the defining context. It was where they'd met, where they'd learned each other. They were teachers who'd gotten married, not married people who taught. Now, as the days came and went without this common bond, they—like all couples, they figured—treated each other as signposts. *Stop. Yield. One Way. Caution.*

Dale pored over Mary Ann's lists while she was out. He sat on the cement of the basement's back room with a throw pillow under his butt, sipping hot cinnamon tea as Frank Sinatra echoed down the vents. There was a great deal of history in these three-ringed pages. It awed Mr. Portwit that Mary Ann had this link to her past. He could see the evolution of her handwriting as it moved from the hopeful lassoes of a high-schooler to the more conservative but elegant style that refrained from ballooning (except in the case of the 'D's, which resembled proud robins thrusting out their chests).

He read her most recent lists first. His curiosity was too strong to resist, though always the mantra "These are meaningless, these are meaningless" ran through his head. He prepared himself for criticism (after all, these were her innermost thoughts—they *had* to show the acidic Mary Ann), but at once this preparation seemed to indicate a weakness of his character. Shouldn't the professed (by him) meaninglessness of the lists mandate *not* worrying about their meaning, or even their potential for meaning?

His fears and metafears were for naught. Mary Ann recorded fond ideas about her husband. Her language was simple, but the effects were complex.

Five Things I Love about Mr. Portwit

5. His regal brow
4. How he looks into my eyes when he smiles
3. His classy walk, like a strong woman or a carefree man
2. His vigor (!)
1. The way he sees me

Five Questions I Would Like to Ask Mr. Portwit

5. What do you get out of this relationship?

4. Do you really like to watch me eat?
3. Was your childhood a happy one?
2. Why did it take you three years to talk to me?
1. What are you afraid of?

Other lists were about her health:

Six Foods I Should Learn to Love

6. Tomatoes
5. Granola
4. Lentils
3. Beets
2. Tofu
1. SlimFast

One list, dated two days before their first date, caught Mr. Portwit's attention:

Three Wishes for Me

3. To say good-bye to my dad one more time
2. To remove fifty pounds from my body
1. To have a man fall in love with me

The wording, especially on her Number One answer, seemed to tap into Mary Ann's deepest, most unconscious, feelings: It implied that it was easy to fall in love with other people—the tricky part was getting them to love you. Had she succeeded in her Number One wish? (Obviously, Numbers Two and Three were less likely . . .)

There were so many lists.

Four Terrible Sentences Mrs. Jennings Said to Me Today, Eleven Mistakes Mrs. Jennings Has Made as Interim Principal, Twelve Problems with Being Severely Obese, Five Benefits to Being the Size I Am, Seven Memories of Mother, Seven Questions I'd Like to Ask Mother, Five Sets of Parents I'd Like to Dropkick, Eight Sets of Parents I'd Like to Hug, Four Possible Reasons That I Have No Friends at Elkhart . . .

Thanksgiving was this Thursday. Two days from now. Here. At this house, the filthiest on the block. Dale's parents would be in attendance—a frightening prospect. Mary Ann had met them only once, at the wedding, their interactions consisting of one ten-minute talk during dinner and the dance with Oscar.

Her impression of Oscar Portwit was that the elderly man was sturdier than the middle-aged son. Photographs from the '60s and '70s gave the impression that Oscar had not so much aged as ossified. The difference between present-day Oscar and Oscar in his fifties was that he now looked cast in concrete. His head was completely bald. His white eyebrows were unruly, like overgrown houseplants, and they partially shrouded his deep-set green eyes. His nose was hooked and slender—Dale wore his mother's knobby nose—and Oscar's lips looked like a drawstring purse that had been cinched. The old man walked with hands tightly balled at his sides, in a slight lean that gave the appearance not of a stoop, as might be the case with others his age, but of a man intent upon cleaving anything that stepped into his path, including the air. Whereas Dale's manic energy came off as nervousness, Oscar communicated a destructive tendency held at bay (barely) by his stoic countenance. It wasn't that Mary Ann hadn't seen him smile—he had smiled a few times that night, flashing his teeth the way a lion does when it yawns—but for the most part, Oscar's main mode was wordless, contented grumpiness.

Dale's mother had made scant impression upon Mary Ann. Adeline's hand had wilted under the introductory shake, and then she engaged herself in conversation through the simple act of tilting her pleasant face toward Oscar each time he uttered a sound. Adeline spoke no more than a dozen words all night. Her makeup was as garishly applied as a teenager's, and her hair had been coiffed into a gray tornado. While they were superficially nice people, Mary Ann's general impression was that neither Oscar nor Adeline especially cared that their son had gotten married.

The Portwits would soon be seated at this dining room table (Whom was she kidding? It was a card table) with wide eyes roaming the adjoining living room and surveying with disgust the wrappers, tissues, books, folders, binders, potted dirt without plants, socks without feet, magazines without racks, and broken pretzel rods.

Mary Ann gobbled two Librium at the bathroom sink, then located Mr. Portwit in the living room and told him he was in charge of cleaning.

"Even though this is your mother's idea," he said.

"Why does it matter whose idea it was? It was my idea, as a matter of fact. And it's happening. We need to make it happen right."

"I'm prepared. I just don't think we should do it."

"It's TOO LATE. Accept it. And start cleaning the house."

"I can't vouch for my parents. I can't vouch for what *they* might say, or what they may hear *you* say that you didn't actually say."

"They were fine at the wedding. Your dad was a good dancer."

"Beautiful busty babe rides on cock."

"We need to clean."

"It's a phrase I used to love to see. Back in my pornography phase, when I looked at magazines and videos and the Internet. I was compulsive. And repulsive. And expulsive. *A beautiful phrase, from my pornography phase*," he crooned, taking up her hands, dancing her in a gentle waltz through the dust-filled sunlight shafts.

"Sweetheart, that's great, but we need to start cleaning. Really. Like now. We have so much to do. I need to shop and cook. And before that I need to look at recipes. Please understand this. I need you to clean. Now. Please."

He set to work, thinking of Mrs. Brandmal. He fluffed the couch cushions, although he had never done so before; no cushions, anywhere, had ever been fluffed by his hands. He was pleased to do it, and he stepped back, once he had finished, to regard his fluffing. He plugged in the vacuum, hummed in the key of D or whatever its whine was tuned to, rolled the machine back and forth over the living room carpet. A new memory had come to him just last night, as he drifted into sleep.

Age eleven, wasn't it? It had to be so. He was awake past bedtime, was outside. On tiptoes, peering through a bedroom window— tickled on the top of his head by tree leaves, screened from view of the street by a waist-high bush. Yet this cover wouldn't hold much longer. It was autumn, and already he could smell charred leaves from the season's first fires. A radio from a neighbor's house, distant but intimate, playing only for him Frankie Valli and the Four Seasons' "Big Girls Don't Cry." The slats of the blinds a bit more askew than usual.

He scooted the sofa from the wall, vacuum still screaming. He vacuumed the pale, flattened carpet there, which looked like the skin of a forearm after six months in a cast. Careful massages with the suctioning air brought the forearm back to life.

Mrs. Brandmal—really, actually Mrs. Brandmal!—caught in a rare band of gray moonlight, was topless. Her breasts were too perfect; on her back, on a bed, face shadowed, her breasts also shadowed, but too round and bold to be blanketed by blanket of wool or blanket of darkness, and he could see dark nipples atop the mounds; in his pants the monster strained, dying to be touched and touched and touched; could she feel him? Separated by only the thinnest window glass and the skewed blinds, could she feel the heat from his body? Then glory of glories, a hand, a man's hand, as if a phantom extension of Dale's mind, reached over and rubbed, began to rub, stopped, then rubbed again and rubbed even more the huge, soft perfections so perfectly framed by perfectly imperfect blinds. It was her husband; kisses were occurring; he was going to ravish her, like men did and were supposed to do behind the most-closed of closed doors, unless one boy across town was smart enough to climb through his bedroom window, drop silently to the ground, wheel his bicycle through the back gate, pedal across the empty field between the tire shop and the pond, drift from island of streetlight to island of streetlight until reaching Denner Court, smartly drop the bike at the corner, run along chain-link fences and backyards where he hoped dogs didn't lurk in black shadows, and finally, panting, overheated, thrilled, arrive at the window of the Brandmal house for the fourth (it might have been the fourth—this was a good, significant number, anyway) time in two months.

Dale stepped on the button, killing the vacuum. Its lung bag shriveled. He looked up to see Mary Ann speed-walking out of the kitchen with a book—*How to Cook Everything*—open in her hands. She had changed from her nightgown into one of the new Lane Bryant slacks-and-blouse combos that followed the advice of the fashion gurus: her oval-shaped figure, which included her "fuller" bustline and less-defined waist, "demanded" that her clothing redirect the eye to her face or legs. Shoulder pads were supposed to create the illusion of a small waist. Her blouse was vertically striped. She was avoiding high heels with short hemlines and tight waistlines.

Mary Ann clearly had no time to look at Mr. Portwit as she picked up the cordless phone and dialed her mother. "Mom!" she exclaimed, already reexiting the living room with a dull rumble of socked feet. "I have no idea how to make stuffing!"

Mr. Portwit couldn't help but be charmed. It was Mary Ann's moment to shine. And how often had she even gotten such a chance?

Despite his initial suspicion to the contrary, she had gotten under his skin, in a serious way. He respected her as he'd never respected anyone. His friendships, professional alliances, family—his postal carriers—had always left him wanting more. Relationships confused, frustrated, and disappointed him. And he confused himself, too: frustrated himself, disappointed himself. Deep down, most people were driven by the need to satisfy their egos. But Mary Ann was selfless. She cared for him and asked for only the same. She was no Pollyanna—she possessed a bullshit meter, and she didn't hesitate to let him know when he set it ticking—but her engine was fueled not by solipsism but by something else. What was the word for it? He didn't know.

She'd been an experiment, hadn't she? Like humiliating Rick Fletcher, or exploring the world of pornographic videos, or hanging himself, or, predating them all, becoming a teacher. Marriage was the latest in a series of experiments designed to help him re-see, even redirect, his life. Marriage was a fundamental human instinct—he'd rationalized—and besides, what else should an over-the-hill failed suicide do with the rest of his life? Find a bride or get professional help: these were the options. Marriage was so much cheaper! With less social stigma! Sexually gratifying, too!

Coming out of his near-fatal funk had been like waking from a sleep, and when he'd awoken, Mary Ann had been there, rosy-cheeked, chewing a lemon fruit pie at the teacher's-lounge table without a hint of irony or entitlement. Here was a slap to the faces of the superficial busybodies of Elkhart. Here was the ideal accomplice to his new life of noncensored thoughts and speech. Here was the perfect project and, truth be told, perfect body type. Here was the ugly duckling, the Cinderella shunned by her stepsisters. Here was the Plain Jane to whom no man gave a second glance, whose big weekend plans were to help her mother can peaches and to sit in a recliner writing lists in front of a *Sheriff Lobo* marathon.

Watching her then, in the lounge, as her jaw worked in quiet tremors at deconstructing the glazed pastry shell, hadn't he noted her similarity—not so much physical but, what was it, sensual?—to Mrs. Brandmal? He'd been in the presence (visually, aurally, odoriferously) of a buxom middle-aged woman teacher, eating to her heart's content, and once again hadn't he been overwhelmed by the desire to make her his own?

Mr. Portwit kick-started the vacuum cleaner, and below its insistent *wheeeeeeeeee* muttered the words he had recited to Mary Ann's face with rote affection so many times over the past several months: "I love you. I love you."

Thanksgiving happened. It happened despite the fact that Dale went to the Green Top the night before and downed an entire bottle of bubbly. It happened despite Mary Ann's tearful breakdown two hours before the guests were to arrive. (Mr. Portwit entered the kitchen and saw her seated in front of the open oven, the turkey baster poised and dripping on the linoleum. Mary Ann managed to get herself into the bathroom and swallow four tablets of Librium.)

It happened despite Dale's parents' confusion in locating their home.

"We ended up at the Crandalls' house," said Adeline, offering her cheek to Dale's lips. "You gave us the wrong directions, but those Crandalls were such wonderful people. They even gave us a little plate of turkey to take home."

Dale gripped his father's hand, taking pleasure in the fact that it felt like a soaked sponge. This was only the second time he'd seen his parents this year. He searched his father's eyes for signs of the senility his mother had described at the wedding, but found only a bemused affection. Adeline had said that one morning she heard cursing in the bathroom and discovered Oscar standing in the shower, fully clothed and drenched in the running water. His excuse was that he'd stepped into the tub to examine the dripping faucet. Over breakfast a few weeks later, Oscar insisted that the grapefruit she'd served him tasted like gasoline. He hurled it against the wall, then proceeded to eat Adeline's grapefruit.

"Did Mom take a wrong turn?" Dale said into his father's aided right ear. "I never give wrong directions. You know that."

"Nice to see you again, Tweety," said Oscar, struggling to free his arm from his coat sleeve. "This house looks smaller on the inside than it does on the outside."

"Tweety" had been Dale's nickname forty-some years ago. The other Cub Scouts had bestowed it on him because of his somewhat obsessive fondness for bird-watching. The tag was not meant affectionately, but it lasted only one year, which is how long Dale stayed in the Scouts. An obscure reference, to be sure. But this, even combined with his mother's stories, still wasn't enough to convince Dale that his father's mind was doing anything but concocting increasingly oblique bullying methods to satisfy its fancy.

"We're just glad you made it," Mary Ann said. She hugged the Portwits in succession. Dale took their coats. In the living room, Mary Ann reintroduced them to her mother. "You remember Martha, from the wedding. And this gentleman is her friend Hakim."

"Hockey?" Oscar Portwit said to Adeline, whose smile had continued unabated for six minutes now.

"Ha-*keem*!" Adeline enunciated into Oscar's ear.

"Okay," Oscar agreed, jaw working his cheek innards like a cow. He looked at, and then shook, the hand in front of him. It was Hakim's hand.

Dinner ensued, taking place on two adjoined card tables draped with one recently purchased bone-colored tablecloth. Seats were filled. Cloth napkins were unfolded and lap-placed. Dale sat at what he had labeled the "foot" of the table(s); Mary Ann's empty chair stood at the "head," which was the end nearest the kitchen. Dale felt it important that his father see that in this house typical gender roles did not apply. Unfortunately, upon seating himself, Dale remembered that his father had no idea which end was which. Mentioning the designations now, apropos of nothing, would seem provocative and juvenile. And in fact, couldn't this arrangement—with Mary Ann's end adjoining the kitchen from which she'd be serving the meal—be construed as just a more efficient way to enforce stereotypical roles? He tightened his lips and told himself he had nothing to prove.

Mrs. Tucker's beau, Hakim, sat smiling on one side, Dale's parents on the other. The overhead 100-watt soft-light bulbs worked their magic. Everyone and everything was visible. No one talked. They all found places to point their stares, like strangers in a waiting room with no magazines.

The meal was brought in by Mary Ann and Mrs. Tucker. First came the sweet potatoes, the mashed potatoes, the cranberry sauce, the stuffing, the salad, and the green beans (each dish had been covered, then quickly microwaved upon the Portwits' late arrival). The second trip brought a round porcelain tray divided into sections for whole olives (pimentoed green and pitted black), pickles (dill and butter), carrots (baby), celery (babied), mushroom slices (white), and in the middle, a lifeless mound of onion dip. With slow, careful steps, Mary Ann brought forth the turkey. Dale, seeing her strain, rose from his chair to help. Together, they centered the platter. Oscar and Adeline and Martha and Hakim applauded, whistled, and *ahhh*-ed. It looked beautiful, they announced. It looked delicious, they added, nods abounding.

"Smells heavenly," whispered Hakim.

"Succulent!" overpowered Oscar, with aggressive volume aimed into Adeline's ear, before a bite had even entered his mouth.

Mary Ann ate, but did not enjoy the food. Too much was at stake. It felt like her reputation as a homemaker, wife, cook, woman, adult daughter, fat person, hostess, and human being hung in the balance. Her senses were occupied; she had no capacity left for taste. Numbly, she chewed. She observed the guests as the lips smacked and the jaws tensed and the throats bobbed up and down. She joined the conversations with half her brain, which was more than enough for her to feel disturbed. This fucking Librium, she thought. For the first fifteen doses it had worked, had made her happy, excessively happy, but lately its effects had been spotty, inconsistent, so she'd upped the dosage to four pills four times a day, and still she felt this nervousness in her teeth, this out-of-body distance from everything, this urgent fascination with tiny details. The conversation proceeded.

Martha Tucker, straight ahead to Adeline Portwit: "Dale tells us you live in Oshtemo."

Dale, diagonally to Martha Tucker: "That's not true, exactly. *I* never told you. It was Mary Ann who told you."

Adeline Portwit, diagonally to Dale: "It doesn't matter who said it. It's true, is all that matters."

Adeline Portwit, straight to Martha Tucker: "Oshtemo is a lovely little community. Have you been there? They have a brand new Meijer store just up the street from us."

Hakim, diagonally to Mary Ann: "This cranberry sauce is so delightful."

Mary Ann, diagonally to Hakim: "Thank you."

Oscar, downward to the pickle in his fingers: "What do you call this kind of pickle here?"

Dale, straight to Mary Ann: "Would you pass the green beans, please?"

Martha, to her plate: "I have never been to Oshtemo. This gravy tastes like something . . . what the heck is it?"

Mary Ann, diagonally to Martha: "It might be the rosemary?"

Martha, to her plate: "Oh? So you didn't use my recipe, I guess."

Adeline, to everyone: "Dale used to love to cook, even though it's tough to believe when you see him now. But he used to help me in the kitchen with the cakes and cookies and desserts. He loved desserts, that one. Made a scrumptious peanut butter pie one year."

Oscar, to anyone: "What kind of pickle is this? It tastes like candy."

Dale, to his bean-bearing fork: "Why is it tough to believe, Mom? Why is it tough to believe, when you see me now, that I used to be helpful? I'm curious."

Everyone, to everyone: "——————"

Oscar, to Adeline: "Did anyone answer me yet?"

Adeline, in a slow, left-to-right pan (Mary Ann, Martha, Hakim, Dale, and finally Oscar): "It's just that he's so professional now. A science teacher, you know. In his argyle sweater and everything. We always said he could go to Harvard, didn't we?"

Oscar, to no one: "Who?"

Adeline, to Oscar: "Dale, darling."

Oscar, to no one: "Harvard? He didn't have the grades, I don't think. Christ, that was a long goddamn time ago."

Dale, to Adeline: "I've been a teacher for more than twenty years. Why say, 'Now,' like I just turned this way?"

Martha, panning everyone: "Who would, anyway? Go to Harvard? So much work. And such snobby sorts of people, if you ask me."

Everyone to everyone: "————————"

Martha, belatedly: "I hope no one here went to Harvard."

Hakim, to Dale: "This is a fine turkey."

Dale, to Hakim: "Mary Ann picked it out. She didn't raise it, though, so you can't credit her for that. Or blame her, as the case might have been."

Martha, Hakim, and Mary Ann: "Ha ha ha ha."

Oscar, to Adeline: "Did I park on the street or in the driveway? I need my blue medication. I have to take it with food."

Dale, to Oscar: "*You* didn't park anywhere, Dad. Mom drives."

Adeline, to Oscar: "The car's in the driveway, sweetheart. Let me get your pills for you."

Mary Ann, to Adeline: "I'll get his pills, Mrs. Portwit. You stay put."

Adeline, to Mary Ann: "Don't be silly, dear. I know just where they are."

Mary Ann, to Adeline: "You can tell me where they are. I'll get them."

Dale, to Mary Ann and Adeline: "You can *both* get his pills. Together."

Hakim, to Adeline: "*I'll* get his blue pills. Truly, ma'am. I am going right now to get his pills. Just tell me where the keys are and where in the car the pills are kept."

Martha, to Mary Ann: "Isn't he a sweetheart?"

Adeline, to Hakim: "The keys are in my handbag. Right here. There you go. And the pills are in the glovebox. The fat bottle. Oh, I'm sorry I didn't mean to say that. The bigger bottle. Not the little one. Thank you."

Everyone to everyone: "————————"

Dale to Adeline, after Hakim's exit: "Very smooth, Mom."

Adeline, to her glass of milk: "What's smooth?"

Oscar, to Adeline's ear: "Where did that Arabian fellow go?"

Dale, to Adeline: "You can't help it, can you?"

Martha, to Oscar: "Hakim went to the car to get your blue medicine! He'll be right back! He's from Detroit, actually. His parents are from India, but now they're in Benton Harbor."

Adeline, to everyone: "It's a funny thing about Dale. When he was a boy, he never wanted sympathy. Not even from me! Not even from his mother. Most boys cut their pinkies and show it to their mommies and have little teary eyes. They want to hear their mommy tell them what a strong boy they are. How brave and strong. Dale never did that. He put on his own Band-Aids, this one."

Dale, to Adeline and Oscar, with finger-pointing divided equally between them: "Here's a fact for both of you. You can chew on it right along with your turkey"; then to Mary Ann: "which tastes better than any I have ever had, by the bye."

Oscar, to Adeline and Mary Ann and Dale and everyone and anyone: "Is that fella going to *my* car?"

Dale, to Adeline and Oscar: "Mom and Dad? I have a quote that you should take to heart, with regards to my beautiful wife, Mary Ann. 'A sweet temper and a bony woman never dwell under the same roof.'"

Oscar, to the air in front of his face: "I left my change belt and wallet in there. I hope he's only getting the pills."

Martha, to Oscar: "Mister Portwit, really. I've known Hakim for more than a year. He would never take—"

Dale, to Oscar and Adeline: "It's an old axiom, Mom and Dad. 'A sweet temper and a bony woman never dwell under the same roof.' Victorian scientists—respected scientists, and others—believed that *fat cells* are *crucial* to a well-balanced personality. Fat cells! Crucial! Italics mine! Therefore, thin people are naturally *quarrelsome* and *unhappy*. Explains a lot of things about *me*, I should say."

Everyone to everyone: "——————————————————
————————————————————————————————————
———————————————————————————————————
————————————————."

Mary Ann, feeling like a leaking balloon, set her fork onto her plate and stood from her chair, her head filled only with the pleasant goal of arriving safely in the bathroom. She took one lunging step, then crumpled to the ground, collapsing into a seated, cross-legged position, as if forced by fainting into a meditation session. Her face was whiter than an egg, pupils pointed toward the ceiling of her skull, exposing additional whites for all to see. For a moment, her torso wavered but remained erect, and she resembled a swami in the throes of religious ecstasy.

Then—in front of Oscar, Adeline, and her mother—Mary Ann's

body tipped, tipped, tipped onto its side, so that she looked like a 280-pound fetus curled upon the carpet. She was motionless, and her eyes were closed as if she had decided to sleep now, in spite of the plaintive shrieks from her mother, the oblivious, belligerent insistence by Dale that his mother and father *listen* for a minute, and the door opening and Hakim exclaiming to the room with triumphant joy, "I have your pills, sir! I have the blue pills!"

8

It was like stirring manure with a shovel: it was bound to raise a stench, attract flies, send a person gagging and stumbling for fresh air. He never should have started poking around in there.

Now it was too late. He had spent too much time away from Elkhart—from the Rick Fletcher dramas, the teacher's-lounge battles, and the hospitalized-principal tragedy. Too much time alone, like the old days. For over a month, he'd lived from bedroom to barroom. He slept, ate, jerked off, and drank like a goddamn Viking, while internally he shoveled and flipped sections of the manure heap until, one day, a vivid picture formed.

Yes, he'd gone to lunch with Mrs. Brandmal. In the school library. Regularly, because he was the winner of her games. Mrs. Brandmal had sat near him and chewed, the air thick with flowery perfume and salty braunschweiger. Yes, she had masticated her sandwich and adjusted her glasses and told him he was one of the best students—one of the very, very brightest—that she'd ever taught.

Yes, he had sneaked to her house at night. Once. Twice. Three times. Four. It was so easy. He had circled, tiptoeing, peering through blinds and curtains, always through layer upon layer, squinting into darkness and half-light for insignificant rewards: a flash of movement; a walking body unidentifiable as either man or woman; the back of a man's head as he talked on the telephone; a leg in a skirt, a moving leg, gone faster than his latest heartbeat.

Nothing to see, until that one night when Dale went much later than usual. His parents were always asleep by 10:30, and Dale was normally out the window at 10:35. This time, Dale waited until midnight—the witching hour. Witchy things would be transpiring, and these were what he wanted. And he got it—the deed, or at least the beginning of the deed—the iridescent flesh, those breasts stained blue by the moonlight, and the head moving, the kissing, and the husband's hand on the ripe, round, amazing, blue-stained, what-does-that-feel-like, and then . . .

He was gripped on the ear. Pinched and twisted until he cried out like a puppy. A man—it was his father—hissed, "Not on my watch, mister." Dale was pulled by the ear along the sidewalk, was slapped on the face and called a perverted pervert. Had his father actually said that? Dad was not a linguist by nature. He opened his mouth mostly to eat or to yell at the neighbors or at Mom.

It had taken weeks, but Dale had finally flipped the manure pile. What was the impetus? Mary Ann's fainting spell, caused by the Thanksgiving dinner during which his dad had smacked his lips and slurped at his own saliva, was a possibility. Or maybe the string of binge-drinking nights at the Green Top.

Most likely, though, it was the afternoon Dale stumbled from his bed, tried to step into one of his socks, tipped, bumped into his dresser, and knocked Rufus's framed photograph onto the floor. When he repositioned the picture atop the dresser, he looked at it—and had the distinct feeling that this was the first time he was truly seeing the man with the blurry face. The face wore a magnificent smile. An overjoyed smile. A smile that could melt frozen water pipes. The eyes twinkled like gems in the broad, benevolent dough-face. It was an intimate, caring glance, frozen in time, and it reminded Dale of another intimate glance he used to see on a regular basis before it vanished without a trace.

Dale, as he stood at the mirror an hour later, sliding a razor over his lathered cheek, had recalled a terrible piece of information, information that formed a dark coagulation beside the undigested turkey sandwich in his gut: he remembered that he had gone back to Mrs. Brandmal's house two more times after getting caught that first time—and had succeeded only in getting caught again, and then again.

The second time Oscar apprehended him, he slapped Dale once on each cheek, dragged him by the hair to the car, at home made him suck on a bar of soap for an hour in front of the mirror. For the duration of the Salisbury steak dinner the following evening, he taped Dale's eyelids shut. "He needs to learn what eyes are for," his dad said. "We don't take them for granted in this house."

The third time Dale was caught, Oscar threw Dale to the ground and punched him in the face until Jessie Brandmal ran outside in his bathrobe and pulled Oscar off the bleeding boy.

It was 1962. Boys beat each other up all the time, and fathers smacked their sons on occasion. Mom didn't make a big deal out of it. She *tsk*-ed as she scorched Dale's cut eyebrow with an iodine-soaked cotton ball. She staunched the nosebleed by twisting toilet tissue into his nostrils. She kissed him on the forehead and fed him two aspirin with a tall glass of Ovaltine. "Your father is pretty disappointed." She rustled his hair with her palm. "Dale, Dale, Dale," she incanted.

Like his mother, Dale never blamed his dad.

After being caught once, Dale had done it again and again. If a dog pissed on your shoes, you swatted it with the rolled newspaper. If he did it three times, you graduated from swat to pummel and from rolled newspaper to steel-toed work boot. A child needed limits. "Once, shame on *you*," explained Oscar, leaning against the bathroom door frame while Adeline tended to Dale's wounds. "Twice, shame on *me*."

It was for his own good, his father explained, and it didn't mean they didn't love him. It meant, actually, the opposite of not loving him, which was loving him. They loved him enough to protect him from himself, because people, especially children of a certain age, had a tendency to lose control, and peeping once might have stemmed from natural curiosity, which was quite normal and helpful to our society, but more than once became a reflection on Mom and Dad and the type of household they were running.

Dale had hated the pain, but much more than this, he'd hated the sight of scrawny, pale, shorter-than-everyone-else's-dad Dad straddling him. He'd hated Dad's lopsided glasses and the unseeing, rage-filled eyes. This simple man, brought to violence in the bushes beside his son's teacher's home. Even as he whaled on Dale's face and head with clenched fists, Oscar looked like a fool, a weak fool. Dale cried out, begged him to stop. Porch lights snapped on, neighbors emerged. Now, Dale tapped the razor against the bottom of the sink to dislodge the whiskers and remembered the oath he had made to himself as his father beat him—that he would never let his emotions control him; instead, he would be their master.

This incident had been troubling. If this had been the entire story, Dale would no doubt have suffered years of anger, would have been scarred. But scarring a child is a parent's job, ultimately, and even if they do it literally and bloodily on a public sidewalk, it's not a big deal, it's not something you don't get over. No, what made things really bad—what had, now that he looked back on it, ruined everything, had made his life an irredeemable wreck—was when Mrs. Brandmal stepped in.

She—the unflappable Goddess of the Classroom, the Teacher, the Sex Object—gasped when Dale entered Room 15 the following day. She knew abstractly what had happened, but she had remained inside, telephone in hand, poised to dial the police; she had spared herself the details. Seeing Dale's crooked nose, red-veined eyeball, and purple cheek the next morning . . . it was too much. She intervened. She stirred up her own mound of manure, and that mound was named Oscar Portwit.

She had emotions about this boy. She couldn't hide it. Maybe she loved him. Upon seeing the marks of Dale's punishment, her eyes watered and her face sagged in a vision of despair. She left the room. Dale's classmates giggled. They surrounded him and examined his bumps and bruises. When Mrs. Brandmal returned, she pulled him from class and escorted him to the office, offering him the worst kind of assurance: "*You* aren't in any trouble." Her manner was distant and professional. All the way down the hall, she didn't touch him. No hand on his shoulder. No pat on the head.

Thirty minutes later, his father was there. Mom was there, too, and Principal Maitner. The door clicked shut. Principal Maitner told Dale to "have a seat." The towering trees of adults swayed stiffly above his head. Dale was the center of it all, surrounded and unable to move. Up there at the tops of the adult trees, the shifts in vocal inflections were a Bugs Bunny cartoon, an Abbott and Costello routine: anger and rage, pity and perplexity, polite laughter and polite condolences. Rain and shine. Darkness and light. A flashlight on and off, on and off. Dale remembered two things about that meeting: that he could barely breathe because of his broken nose, and that he hated Mrs. Brandmal, hated her because she was destroying his life. From this low angle she had no face, was only a shelf of breasts. Or not a shelf—her face was a roof made invisible by the intervening eaves of her breasts. And if the eaves dropped now into his hands, what would he do with them? Punch, knead, take them into his mouth? No, no—he *could* do that, but he wouldn't. The eaves wouldn't drop, and he wouldn't eavesdrop. He was frozen and tiny, sheltering beneath the roofs of these bickering adults under clouds under outer space. In his smallness, he could do nothing but quiver in his clothes and ache.

The meeting ended without any apparent conclusion, but within four days, Mrs. Brandmal had quit. She couldn't work at school—"this" school—anymore, couldn't even finish out the year once it was decided that no punishment could or should be imposed on Oscar Portwit, once it was established that trespassing and peeping tom-ism were criminal offenses and that Dale was lucky, in the long run, to have escaped a juvenile record. Mrs. Brandmal announced to the fifth-grade class, with a puffy face, that she needed and would take a "long vacation." The following Monday, she was gone from Dale's life. He recalled hearing that she moved to Saginaw to be closer to her family.

These details, circumstances, occurrences, facts; these whats, wheres, whys, hows, and whos—these were inspiration enough for Mr. Portwit to determine that the very salve his life needed—*needed*—right now, more than anything, more than a job or a cuddle with his wife or a reconciliation with his super-old, abusive, very possibly dotty father, was the death (or confirmation of death) of the beloved and hated and mentally fucked though never quite fully remembered fifth-grade teacher, Mrs. What's Her First Name? Brandmal (and, if necessary, her husband too).

⟨♥⟩

Mary Ann made an appointment with Doctor Jackoby. Her Thanksgiving fainting spell had been the second in a month. She called Elkhart and told them she would be in after lunch. Then she popped four Librium with her orange juice and went to the bedroom to watch Dale sleep.

Bernette was kind enough to drive. Her VW Bug rolled into the driveway at 10 a.m. Mary Ann had instructed her not to come up to the house, but just to toot her horn. She tooted. Mary Ann didn't want Dale to know about the appointment. He would overanalyze its significance; he might worry that the doctor would order her to drop fifty pounds. She didn't enjoy lying to Dale, so she scheduled the visit for the morning, when he was normally asleep.

Dale was more than asleep. He was comatose. He had come to bed at 5:30 a.m., and now, as Mary Ann leaned in to kiss his cheek, she noticed a red, splotchy rash on his neck. With her cheek by his mouth, she could feel his furnace breath. He was alive. Stinkingly alive.

As she prepared to leave, she looked into the dining room at the six empty Labatt's Blue bottles on the table. He would pay for drinking beer; she wondered what had inspired him to do it. She opened the mouth of her purse, checked inside for something—what exactly was she checking for? She didn't know. She'd already taken her pills. She gave up. She zipped the purse and went out the door.

In the Kalamazoo Family Health waiting room, the walls were a shade of green that reminded Mary Ann of the car her dad had been killed in. Bullfrog green. Creature from the Black Lagoon green.

Two framed paintings—one a ram poised atop a mountain, one a long, ugly walrus lying across the ice to kiss its pup—hung side by side on the opposite wall.

"That's an animal you don't see paintings of every day," Mary Ann said.

"I've seen ram paintings before," Bernette said. She paused, realizing. "I guess you mean the walrus. I can be dense."

"Dense? What is wrong with 'dense,' Bernette?" Mary Ann said, mimicking Mr. Portwit's cadences. "If I said this slice of cake was dense, would that be an insult? Or this bank vault door? A dense novel is considered a wonderful thing. In certain circles."

The women laughed.

"Is it a Down on Dale Day?"

"He drank beer last night. He'll be sick for forty-eight hours. God, Bernette." She inhaled and discovered that her lungs fluttered. She lowered her voice. "A couple of weeks ago he threw up in the bed. He cleaned it while I was at school. We haven't acknowledged it."

Bernette moved her eyes to the carpet. She needed to think about this, but Mary Ann didn't want her to think about it.

"He's fine from five until seven. We eat dinner, pretty much like a normal couple, except neither of us can cook. Then he disappears into the basement until I go to bed. He reads my lists and leaves the binders all over the floor. Nothing is cleaned in our house, ever. The wastebasket in the bathroom, it's overflowing with tissues; our bedroom is knee-deep in clothes. That's why we never ask you over. It's embarrassing." She was crying now, overwhelmed. "I mean, I can't get *too* mad at him. He's depressed, I guess. I think he misses school more than he lets on."

As Mary Ann talked, the door opened. A man with a gray beard stepped into the waiting room. He removed his winter hat and coat and hung them on a wall peg beside Mary Ann's coat. The man was lean and wiry. His puffy beard, full of body, looked like a cat clinging to his face. The man noticed Mary Ann watching him. He saw her tears, and the face beneath the beard formed a smile that was less "happy" than "encouraging." His eyes were blue and kind. He strolled briskly, in baggy brown slacks, to the counter. He signed the register.

"Who is your appointment with?" the receptionist asked.

"It sounds like he's depressed," Bernette finally agreed, having thought over Mary Ann's situation and chosen the right—at least the safe—words.

The receptionist, not bothering to look at the clipboard in front of her, asked, "Which doctor?"

"Forrester," answered the man.

Then, ignoring the fact that he'd written it on a piece of paper no more than twelve inches from her nose, she asked, "Your name?"

His voice was sonorous and clear, and his words, in a distinct Yooper accent, curled at their ends like a handlebar mustache: "Rufus Moore."

"What if you brought him by the house again?" Bernette suggested. "He got along with Barry. And the girls thought he was funny."

"Are you a new patient?" the receptionist asked.

"No ma'am."

It couldn't be. But it was. Of course it was. Each day, his framed photograph was the first thing to greet Mary Ann when she awoke, the last thing she saw before clicking off the lamp. She'd seen his face so many times it had lost meaning, had ceased to be a face, like a word repeated over and over until it is only a sound.

Yet now that Rufus Moore was here, alive, unblurred, lowering his three-dimensional butt into a chair beneath the walrus painting, it could not have been clearer. His beard was whiter, the lines around his eyes were deeper, but it was Rufus. It felt like a sign. A sign of good things. The little old postman was the olive branch after the flood, the penny on the pavement ("Find a penny, pick it up, all day long I'll have good luck"), the rainbow after the storm.

"Sorry Bernette, I need a moment," Mary Ann said. She placed the *Marie Claire* in the rack. She sucked in a breath, held it, and walked across the room.

"Excuse me, did you say your name was Rufus Moore?" she asked.

"You heard correctly," he said. He proffered an "engaging" smile, then extended his hand, which was equally engaging. His grip was warm, assured, and it broadcast pleasant vibrations into Mary Ann's arm.

"My name is Mary Ann Portwit. Does that last name ring a bell? Portwit?"

He considered the question. Then he shrugged. "I'd love to tell you it did, ma'am. I've heard a lot of names in my life. I'm a mailman. Been delivering for twenty-eight years, twelve different routes. Did I deliver to you? I think I'd recall your face if I had."

"No, Mr. Moore—"

"Call me Rufus."

"No, Rufus. I was thinking you might remember my husband. Dale Portwit? Bald on top? Glasses? Skinny guy, about your build. Five foot six, in heels." She shot a laugh from her mouth.

"The name does sound sort of familiar." Apparently immune to jokes, he tugged stoically at his cat. "I really have delivered to a lot of people over the years."

"You don't remember *Mister* Portwit? I'm sorry if I sound surprised, but I was under the impression that you two were close. Friends, in fact? Outside of the mail. He speaks highly of you."

"Oh yes!" Rufus's eyes flashed in the overhead light. "I do remember a Dale Portwit. Sure. Yes. Dale Portwit. He liked to talk. Talked me silly whenever he caught me. Quite a fellow, I think. He's your husband?"

"Dale would love to hear from you." Mary Ann sat down sideways in the chair beside Rufus, noticing as she did so that his face lost some of its enthusiasm. He'd entangled himself in something, but he wasn't sure yet what it was. Mary Ann continued, "Mr. Portwit has hinted, *sort of*—nothing obvious, but we're married, you know, so I pick up on even the tiny things—he has *hinted* that maybe, I don't know, he's slightly *disappointed* that you two lost touch? And that you, you know, he wishes you would've kept in touch after you went to another route. That's all. I think he'd love to see you again."

Rufus took a moment. He appeared to be collecting himself. He directed quizzical expressions at various spots in the room, as if telepathically interrogating the furniture and potted plants for their opinions on the matter. Meanwhile he stroked, yanked, and twisted his beard. At last, with a sigh, he said, "Ma'am, I don't know what you're talking about."

"You said you knew my husband."

A door opened somewhere behind Mary Ann, somewhere on the other side of the globe.

"Mary Ann Portwit," the nurse said. "Mary Ann, you can come on back."

"That's you, isn't it?" said Rufus. "Mary Ann?" He looked at Mary Ann helplessly, apologetically, as if he wanted nothing more than to have been actual friends with Dale Portwit, to have done anything other than tolerate Dale's unsolicited diatribes for as long as possible before waving and saying, "Gotta run!" and jogging away to the next house, cursing under his breath the hazards of positioning oneself in the crosshairs of the general public.

"You two weren't really friends," Mary Ann whispered. It was a quiet, nearly inaudible realization, full of fury so tiny it sounded more like apathy.

Bernette called, "Mary Ann, the doctor is ready for you. Everything OK?"

"He seemed nice enough," lied Rufus. Then, truthfully, he added, "I never really got to know him, though." Finally, strangely, he said, "But you can say hello for me, if he would like that."

Mary Ann was weighed and measured. She was five feet, four inches tall. She weighed 292 pounds. Her blood pressure was high. Not deadly high, but the kind of high that kept doctors in business.

"167 over 108," said the nurse, writing on the clipboard with what Mary Ann considered to be an inappropriate level of excitement. "That puts you in what we call Stage 2 Hypertension. We'll make sure to let Dr. Jackoby know."

Mary Ann was ushered to the examination room, told to have a seat. The door clicked shut. Mary Ann couldn't lift herself enough to get onto the examination table, and the chair looked too flimsy. So she stood. She stood for eleven minutes, until the doctor arrived.

"Mary Ann *Portwit*?" Doctor Jackoby said, nose pointed at his clipboard. He was an old man, past retirement age but not retired. He'd been Mary Ann's doctor for twenty years. "How are you doing? You aren't Mary Ann *Tucker* anymore! What happened?" He whinnied like a horse and finally looked at Mary Ann. He tried, without success, to disguise his astonishment as a facial itch when he witnessed what the past year had done to her. He scratched the corner of his left eye.

"I got married not too long ago," Mary Ann said. People's reactions didn't bother her anymore. She'd gotten defiant toward them, angry at them, numb to them.

Coming from Doctor Jackoby, though, it made her feel . . . what was the word? *Diseased?*

There was that heavy heartbeat again, rattling her ribs.

Doctor Jackoby helped her onto the padded table. His hands were tender and his movements graceful. The paper crushed and crinkled beneath her.

"Congratulations on the marriage," he said. "Still teaching?"

"Oh yes."

"Glad to hear it. We need people like you on the front lines. Now it says here that you've had a couple of fainting spells." He produced a pen-sized flashlight and a tongue depressor and said, "Open."

She opened her mouth. He shined the light inside.

"Ahhh," he said.

"Ahhhhhhh," she said.

He turned off the light. He felt her neck with fingers as warm as oven-fresh breadsticks. "Glands feel tiptop. So your husband: what does he do?"

"He's a teacher, too. Science. Like you," she added.

"Cough for me," Doctor Jackoby instructed. He pressed a stethoscope against her back. Its pressure had always felt urgent and sexual.

Mary Ann coughed a fake cough.

"Again." He moved the stethoscope to another spot on her back.

She coughed a second fake cough. This one, to her, sounder faker than the first.

"Once more." He moved the stethoscope.

She coughed the fakest of the fake coughs.

"Oh, I'm not a scientist," Doctor Jackoby said, removing the stethoscope. "I'm a maintenance man. I help people maintain themselves. Real science—that takes patience. In my business, you don't want to fail. Scientists, though—they learn from failure. You have to *want* to fail, to be a scientist. Nope, I'm just a maintenance man."

He was now poking the flashlight into her ear. In her peripheral vision she saw him squinting to see into her head. He walked to her right side and penetrated the other ear. He removed the plastic tip from the light, tossed it in the trash can, walked to the counter, sat in the chair, put the clipboard in his lap, scrawled something, then faced Mary Ann.

"Everything looks fine," he said. "Now it says here your blood pressure is fairly high. Not off the charts, but it's something we need to keep an eye on. You've always been a bit higher than normal, but it has gone up since your last visit, which was . . ." he flipped a page, "more than a year ago."

Doctor Jackoby was showing signs of age. Liver spots speckled his hairline, which was still, technically, a line, but more like a shoreline surrounding a lagoon of baldness. The skin on his face was loose and folded, and his fingers trembled when he wrote. A family of hairs had moved into his nostrils. He still had the same deep brown eyes, kind and uncynical, young eyes trapped in a deteriorating body. She was glad, upon seeing him, that her father had been spared the inelegance of aging.

He stood to deliver the verdict. "I don't want to rush into any treatment. Fainting spells could be caused by any number of things. If you have high stress, or anxiety? Or it could be an inner ear issue, which doesn't appear to be the case. Also the possibility of low blood sugar. Of course there's the off chance that it's something more serious, something neurological or the like. We'll have the nurse take a blood sample, and we'll run some tests. Get plenty of sleep, try to do some light aerobic exercise. Watch what you eat." He cleared his throat. His cough sounded as fake as her third had. "Now Mary Ann, be honest." He regarded her over his glasses. "You've put on some weight."

Why had he done that? She had trusted him for twenty years. Twenty years! It was like a marriage where you only saw the husband when you didn't feel well and the husband's only job was to fix you. It was an important job! Doctor Jackoby had always been generous with his time, careful with his descriptions and diagnoses, personable and soothing with his company. With that one phrase, he had undone twenty years of trust.

Bernette shifted the VW's gears, gripped the steering wheel, talked to Mary Ann's left ear about Hyperbole's piano teacher and Barry's ingrown toenail. Her voice was background noise, like the '80s rock station ("Everybody Have Fun Tonight").

How could he be so phony? He was a *doctor*, for pity's sake! Doctors weren't supposed to tiptoe—they were paid to STOMP! Her weight was written there, on his clipboard, in official black ink on official pink goddamn paper! This wasn't psychology!

And his attitude—his stupid pretense of not having *noticed*— "What?" his attitude said, "You mean you gained more than one hundred pounds in a year?! I am perplexed and stupefied!" Somehow, in her mind, he'd assumed a German accent. Behind and above his head, she saw a black bird perched atop one of the examination-room cabinets, squawking, "Coy! Coy! The Colonel of Coy!"

Mary Ann started to cry, and her face felt overheated, so Bernette pulled off at the South Westnedge exit (living in the suburbs meant that going *anywhere* required the expressway) and parked in a Bob Evans lot. Mary Ann explained how she felt betrayed by Doctor Jackoby because he had tiptoed, and how she felt betrayed by Dale too, because she'd met Rufus Moore in the waiting room, a man supposedly Dale's good friend but in fact, it turned out, nothing but Dale's postal carrier. She felt, quite suddenly, afraid to go home. She articulated this, and even as it came out of her mouth it sounded inaccurate, but she didn't know how to fix it.

"You don't think he's dangerous, do you?" Bernette asked, checking her lipstick in the rearview. Her tone was rhetorical. Its intent was to keep the conversation moving.

Mary Ann shook her head.

Bernette sighed. She turned toward the red Bob Evans barn that filled her window. She talked to the barn, or possibly to the window. "It seems like you've got a lot on your mind. A helluva lot." Bernette glanced, ever so secretly, at her wristwatch. Then she scratched her forearm through her blouse. Mary Ann could see she was distracted. She needed to get home to her girls. She didn't say this out loud, but she liked to imply it. Parenthood was an admirable obligation for a person to possess; it was an excuse for all seasons.

In part to relieve the pressure on Bernette, but also to give recognition to the factual in a way that Doctor Jackoby hadn't/couldn't/ wouldn't, Mary Ann said it aloud: "You need to get home to your girls."

"Will you open the glove compartment?" Bernette asked.

"Why do we still call it that?" Mary Ann sniffled. "Nobody wears driving gloves anymore." She smiled though she didn't find her comment funny in the least—it was the sort of thing Dale said all the time. *For better or worse*, she thought. She popped open the plastic box.

Bernette held up her own gloved fingers and wiggled them like cockroach legs. "Well, they *should*," she answered, flashing a smile. Irritated? Condescending? Who could tell? "Will you grab that tube of medicine for me?" she said.

Mary Ann had only known this person as a child. Bernette Fargas was Bernette Straw now. Mary Ann would have failed if handed a phone book and told, "Find Bernette Fargas." Half of Bernette's name, and thus half of her identity, was different now. Half of Mary Ann's name was different, too. Didn't two halves make a whole? Wasn't a whole person missing from their relationship? Not to mention the Adult Deception Factor, or ADF (she'd absorbed the lessons of learning-disorder naming). It was a wonder adults could accomplish intimacy on any level, Mary Ann thought, and she regretted bringing this woman, this stranger, along for such an intimate task as a doctor's appointment.

Mary Ann handed Bernette the tube. "I'm sorry," Mary Ann said, then realized that her apology could be interpreted as being for the glove comment, for the psoriasis, or for any number of things. She herself didn't know what she was apologizing for. Nothing was going right today. She wished she would've stayed in bed with her ill husband. She thought of Dale, her other half, with his eyes closed, dreaming away, dead to the world. He might well be awake and vomiting now. She could cradle his head, wipe his chin with a cooling rag.

Bernette peeled off her pleather driving gloves. Respectfully, as one would treat $100 bills, she stacked and straightened them in her lap. She unbuttoned her cuffs and rolled up her sleeves, revealing forearms spotted with pink, scaly, painful-looking psoriasis. She squirted a translucent glob of ointment into her palm, spread it over her left arm. "You have no idea how good that feels," Bernette sighed, eyes closed. Then she did the other arm. She asked for the Handi Wipes, which Mary Ann gave her.

She was right. Mary Ann had no idea.

"You need to get home to your girls," Mary Ann said. She buckled her seatbelt and prepared for the ride by facing forward.

9

Mr. Portwit drove. His Escort hit the expressway chugging. He gunned the engine and merged with oncoming traffic. South Westnedge Avenue, and all of Portage, fell away behind him. In his hands, the steering wheel came to life and vibrated, as if the nerves of the car were as overstimulated as he.

What had he done? What kind of mess had he left back there? He pushed it from his mind. He wouldn't think about it.

To his right, on the passenger seat, the atlas displayed Michigan in all its mittened glory. The corners of the page lifted now and then at the prompting of the frigid wind that poured through the driver's-side window.

Beside the atlas lay a bottle of Pepto-Bismol, a box of Sudafed Non-Drowsy, and a thermos of tomato soup. On the floor in front of the passenger seat, a bottle of prescription pills rolled around noisily every time he touched the brakes or accelerated. Mr. Portwit made a mental note on his mental notepad to relocate that bottle, whenever and wherever he made his first stop.

The day wasn't sunny—there was *no* sun (or actually there was, according to what he thought he knew about the world). More accurately, gray clouds formed a completed puzzle that left none of the sky in sight.

He felt like shit. His neck was blotchy. He was feverish. His stomach roiled and raged. The air in the car swirled—loud, ice-making air, the same volume as a 747 preparing for takeoff, the same temperature as, well, *zero*, on the Celsius scale. The temperature was nothing, literally. He was shivering in the horrible chill of *nothing*, and yet he was still in Michigan.

The Escort's radio didn't catch signals anymore, nor did the heater catch heat. The parking brake couldn't catch a brake, the air conditioner couldn't catch cold, and the cigarette lighter was in the dark. As for the windshield wipers, Mr. Portwit's only hope was that nothing, liquid or solid, would fall from the sky ever again.

To entertain himself, he composed songs and sang them in whatever key the wind, engine rumble, and pavement vibrations combined to make. His first song was a waltz-tempo sea chantey:

> If the lake were just nearer and I weren't such a fearer
> I'd leave for the Erie coastline tonight.
> 'Neath the yellow moonbeams, I'd play out my dreams
> And drown you 'til you're bloated and white!
> For I was a loser, a scientistical man,
> With my big bloated Mary I could be quite scary,
> So I needed to comprise . . . compose . . . a plan!
> I just try to shit like thunder . . .
> That might just be . . . my blunder . . .

Damn. It had begun with such promise. It even rhymed, back there at the beginning. He made up more songs. He crooned them the way he thought all songs should be crooned: in the Bing Crosby way. Old times, that name suggested. Old times at home, sucking on a candy cane, sitting in a too-big armchair, staring at his socked feet, hoping that Santa wouldn't leave a handful of coal in his stocking (a real possibility in his house). Christmas lights in red, green, and blue, the smell of pine needles, a fat tree poised in front of the bay window. Dad was a Bing Crosby man, Mom a Bing Crosby woman. Dale had often wished his own name was Bing. Or Elvis. Or Albert. Anything but *Dale*. Dale, according to his Webster's unabridged, meant "valley." A low point. Also, "a tube, trough, or pipe, esp. from a ship's pump." The lower intestine—the colon!—of a boat. Less than inspirational.

He drove due east, toward a sun he couldn't see but that he knew, sort of knew—of course knew! ha ha!—was there. *Sun, sun, sun . . . here it comes*, he Bing-ed, then immediately felt dirty for doing it. He decided to perform an absolution on himself, so in a strong voice, while the engine *hrrrrrrr-ed* and the wind *wwww-www-ed*, he recited aloud Newton's first law of motion.

Index finger plumbed, he became an old-fashioned taskmaster, mastering tasks. "Commonly known," he intoned, "as the law of inertia: an object at rest tends to stay at rest, and an object in motion tends to stay in motion with the same speed and in the same direction unless acted upon by an unbalanced force."

Mr. Portwit's bare head felt cold and itchy. He scratched it, then viewed the fingertips of his gloves, which were damp. Even in this speeding icebox, he was sweating.

He improvised an addition to the Newtonian law: "I, Dale Portwit, have been acted upon by an unbalanced force. And by the commutative property of unbalanced forces, I have been made, myself, into an unbalanced force."

His job now was to end the inertia of others.

Gripping the steering wheel with his knees, he reached for the thermos and the Sudafed. A green sign, approximating the distance to Flint to be 101 miles, approached, and Mr. Portwit medicated himself for the fourth time that day by washing down a pair of pills with a swig of warm tomato soup. It was two minutes past noon.

Mary Ann had to be home by now, had to be opening the door and finding what he'd left for her.

He turned his mind to an article he'd just read—was it last night? The beer haze was difficult to penetrate. Propped on his elbows in front of the computer screen, eyelids up and down, up and down. Had he actually taken a hacksaw to Mary Ann's computer monitor? He had, it seemed, sawed into the plastic, and nothing dramatic, no sparks or fireworks of any kind, had resulted.

Ah, yes. Two black holes were about to collide. Somewhere far away. "We can see it," the Internet report had read. Even though it was 400 million miles away, they could see it. The astronomers were calling it a "merger." A black hole merger.

As part of his cross-state driving entertainment, Mr. Portwit reconstructed the report that he'd seen, or thought he'd seen, or read, or spent some time with, on the Internet last night, after maybe the fifth beer and with the hacksaw lodged firmly in the top of the monitor.

ASTRONOMERS SEE BLACK HOLE MERGER

The dance, the circling dance, of two black holes—each the mass of the sun multiplied by millions!—in a pirouette. One hundred million years old, this dance of space bodies.

"They wanted to merge. They merged," said a guy with a long

name. "When they blended into the merger, the galaxies merged into a single, bright, extraordinarily bright, brighter than what we would ever call 'bright,' singular galaxy known as NGC6240. Because of its distance from us, from our planet, from our eyes and our mechanical eyes, the image the astronomers are now seeing is 400 million years old."

We are seeing our own future in the faraway merger of the past. The Milky Way, its sun and its planets, has a black hole at its center. It would/will/did/could/should happen here. Spew. Radiation and gravitational waves spat across the universe onto everybody's plates: 671 million miles an hour will spew the spewed radiation and gravity waves.

The merger of holes would/did/could/will do the following: warp the fabric of space, warp it like (think about it this way, children) water warped by a tossed pebble, galaxies and planets the floating leaves in that pond. Rise and fall, rise and fall.

"Such a giant warp that a *planet* could pulsate in the path of that spew," said Talker Longname. "A whole planet could be squeezed by an inch or so every few minutes, depending on its proximity to the merger." Satellites will jiggle, wobble, jiggled, wobbled. The two black holes have enormous appetites. Each minute they suck in mass equal to the mass of the sun. A black hole is a point in space so dense with matter that its gravitational field will not let anything—not even light—escape. So don't even try. (UP) Unified Press

Mr. Portwit pulled into a rest area. The Escort sputtered as it decelerated. He parked. He killed the engine, then hoped immediately that it would be resurrectable.

He stepped out of the car feverish, head throbbing. He lurched along the sidewalk in his socks toward the one-story brick building where a bathroom awaited.

He sat on a toilet and latched the stall, then promptly fell asleep. He slept for two hours. When he awoke, his neck was stiff. His hands were red and aching, and when the reason for his sore, puffy hands entered his mind, he pushed it aside, concentrating instead on the fact that his head was now a low-level sprinkler, dribbling sweat over his face and into his ears.

He barely managed to unbuckle and yank down his pants before the diarrhea came. It was symphonic, alternating between airy clarinet, wet cello, and sepulchral tuba. He was sick. Last night, walking through the Green Top door, feeling overjoyed with his new terrible memories, he'd been ready to get drunk with Biggs— or, accurately, *in front of* Biggs. His plan was to continue whatever conversation they'd had the last time Mr. Portwit was in (Biggs would remember, wouldn't he?).

Biggs was a good friend, someone who knew when to talk, when to listen, when and how to laugh. This time, Mr. Portwit had even been prepared to stick around until closing, maybe help with wiping down tables or tallying the evening's earnings. He would buy Biggs a Bass Ale, and for the first time they would step out of their merchant/patron roles and become equals. They would sit as a pair, two backs, two figures hunched over the bar, two longtime friends with a history, sipping cold ones at the end of a night.

It was Mr. Portwit's misfortune that his Biggs plan had unfolded on November 29.

November 29 had been Monday Night Football, regardless of how much Mr. Portwit wished it hadn't been. One couldn't change the past! Ha ha.

Mr. Portwit tore a length of tissue from the dispenser, folded it into a thick pad, and dried his pate. He tucked the pad between his legs, into the bowl.

Biggs—fuck Biggs. He was a fake. Buy a bottle of champagne from him on an off night, and he'll point his toothpick at you, give you a wink. Catch him alone and he'll talk your *ear* off, let *you* talk *his* ear off, offer you his *other* ear, ask for *your* ear again!

But with a crowd of Cattle Kens filling the bar, he won't even remember your name. Fuck Biggs. That's what Mr. Portwit had wanted to scream after Biggs looked up distractedly from the slow-filling pitcher of Natural Lite to shout, "What can I get for you, bud?"

It had been too loud in there, too loud for Dale to waste his breath. Too loud and too cold. Yes, cold. "There's an adjective for you, Biggs—COLD!" He should've said that instead of nothing.

He flushed the toilet, then discovered that he couldn't stand. His energy had abandoned him. He studied his feet, half-expecting to see his energy scurrying, mammal-like, over the floor. He read the scarred stall, into which people had carved names, dates, and wisdom like *Natcho Dick*, *Cyanide*, and *This realy hurts*.

That was another point against Biggs. Mr. Portwit's graffiti,

Some come to sit and wonder / I come to shit like thunder, had been painted over. What was the point of being somewhere if you couldn't leave your mark? It had to have been Biggs, commanding some twenty-two-year-old stoner to repaint the stall in exchange for a six-pack of Goebel's in cans.

Mr. Portwit was just at the point of using his car key to gouge his message into the rest area stall when he heard the men's room door swing open, followed by the click of numerous boots. The boots stopped in front of him. A sharp rapping on the stall door, possibly from a nightstick, followed. Mr. Portwit jerked upright, but didn't say anything.

A man's voice: "Everything OK in there?"

"Yes," Mr. Portwit said. "I have plenty of paper."

"Step out here for a minute, guy."

"Sure thing. Just allow me to make myself presentable."

He stood, buttoned, re-pocketed his keys, tucked, zipped, buckled, coughed, flushed. He relaxed himself by pretending he was chewing gum. He came out of the stall. There were three men: two police officers and a man in a green jumpsuit.

One thing was clear: They didn't like Mr. Portwit. They hadn't liked him when he'd been a pair of feet in the stall, and now that he was out, they *really* didn't like him. This was obvious by their probing eyes, eyes so deep in their skulls that an ice cream scoop couldn't dig them out.

"You better not be doing anything nasty in there," warned the maintenance man, wagging a crooked finger. He was the antsiest of the three because whatever happened, *he* would have to clean it up.

Mr. Portwit reasoned, "I can't be doing anything in there. I'm not in the stall anymore."

"Take it easy," the head policeman advised no one in particular. The head policeman was a barrel-chested, flat-topped, cone-headed country boy. He chewed real gum. Minty real. His uniform was shockingly starched. A person could slice a tomato on those creases. The gold name plate above his right pectoral muscle read, "Officer Dan Witport."

Mr. Portwit burst into laughter. "That's not possible."

"Sir, are you under the influence of any controlled substances?" asked Officer Witport, his nightstick pointing like a flashlight toward the darkness of Dale. Even in the wake of humor, this officer was humorless.

The other officer, a tubbier, shorter version of Officer Witport, kept one hand poised near the nightstick attached to his belt. He fashioned his face into a noiseless growl. He didn't want Witport to be the only menacing one.

"No," said Mr. Portwit, swallowing his amazement, reminding himself that full cooperation was in his best interest. "No controlled substances, Officer."

"Can you tell us what you've been doing in there for the past hour?"

"*Two* hours," corrected the maintenance man.

"I fell asleep," Mr. Portwit said.

"Smells like more than sleeping," Officer Witport remarked, with a crinkled nose.

Mr. Portwit nodded. "Just overexerted myself. I'll be on my way."

The officers escorted Mr. Portwit out of the bathroom, into the lobby. The maintenance man glared while disappearing behind an unmarked door, presumably to maintain a few more things. Outside, the sun poked through the clouds. Officer Witport took Mr. Portwit's driver's license, studied it, studied Mr. Portwit, then handed the license to his silent, tubby partner, who wobbled toward the squad car parked behind Dale's Escort. Officer Witport pointed and asked, "Is that your car?" Mr. Portwit agreed that it was. Officer Witport remained expressionlessly perturbed.

Dale couldn't help himself. "Did you notice anything about my license? Or, really, more accurately, about my name?"

"No sir, I did not. Would you please step back? I was merely verifying that the license was valid and that you were the correct owner of the license. Please sit tight, sir."

"My name is *Portwit*," said Dale, unable to control the squeak in his voice. "*Portwit*." It felt important that the officer come up with the answer on his own.

"Please step back," insisted Officer Witport. He stabbed a stiff finger in Dale's direction but kept his eyes on his partner, who now climbed out of the cruiser with some struggle and began hustling stiffly toward them, checking left and right with a stern visage, daring any oncoming cars to just try and run him over.

"His license is clean," Tubby reported to Witport. Tubby's chest swelled and shrank, swelled and shrank. His journey had left him exhausted.

"You ought to buy yourself some handkerchiefs," Witport said to Portwit. He pointed at Dale's forehead. "That sweat can impair your vision."

"Yes sir," said Mr. Portwit, wiping his brow with his forearm. "At the next department store." He couldn't help but feel disappointed. The guy wasn't getting it. Presented with the perfect opportunity to meet his own doppelgänger, he was too asleep to notice. Oh well. You couldn't force the negative to see the photograph, the shadow to see the . . . shadower?

Mr. Portwit waved good-bye to his brain-dead opposite, stepped into his Escort, and closed the door. The cops remained rooted, cross-armed, watching and waiting as Dale drove backward, braked, shifted into first gear, then accelerated toward Saginaw to murder Mrs. Brandmal.

At five minutes before noon, Mary Ann climbed out of Bernette's car. She collected her breathing and stooped to say good-bye.

"Let me know if you need anything," Bernette said cheerily.

"Sure thing," Mary Ann answered. She hoped her facetiousness wasn't obvious enough to cause pain, just obvious enough to be suspected.

Bernette drove away, tooting. Mary Ann stood in front of the closed garage. It had been open when she left. So Mr. Portwit had gotten out of bed? As she walked, digging her fingers into her purse for the keys, Mary Ann felt embarrassed. She'd become so clingy, so needy. Visiting Bernette every other day, complaining all the time about Mr. Portwit, Elkhart, her mother, and her weight. No wonder Bernette treated her like a charity case.

Mary Ann's keys slipped from her hand and hit the cement porch with a noise like a set of chimes being put out of its misery. She bent to pick them up. Damn Doctor Jackoby, and damn Bernette Straw. Mother had always wanted Mary Ann to be helpless, and now it had come true, so damn Mother, too. Bending to reach her keys was a struggle. Mary Ann pitied whoever happened to glance this way.

Standing erect, she located the house key. Oh yes, and damn Mr. Portwit too. What would she say to him? She didn't know whether to be angry, sad, or frightened by the Rufus encounter. One thing felt certain: Rufus hadn't been lying. He had no reason to lie. The key was in. The knob turned. And the toast at the wedding? The "Best Man" enshrined in a cheap frame on the dresser? What in God's name was wrong with Dale?

The door opened.

Her first thought was that it had snowed. Inside their living room. The dusting on the lawn was nothing compared to this. White everywhere. But a dirty white, because good grief, those are torn sheets of paper, covering everything—the entryway, the sofa, the carpet, the end tables, the coffee table, the bookshelf, the dining room table, the throw rug at her feet. She removed her hat, her coat—no need to panic—and hung them on a wall hook. Her heart rattled away, shaking her rib cage. She talked to her heart, quietly, as one would a child, while she stooped to examine the remnants at her feet. "Now there there, let's stay calm. Let's not worry about this. Obviously *somebody* went a little cuckoo, but that's what garbage bags are for." She gathered a handful of paper.

"Dale!" she called, hoping to hear his voice from the bedroom, half-expecting him to step out of the kitchen with a camera in his hand, saying, "Surprise!"

"Mr. Portwit, honey?"

No answer. Mary Ann examined one of the scraps. One side was blank, the other had handwritten text. *Three Wishes for Me*, it read.

Overwhelmed, confused, sickened, Mary Ann scanned the room. The guts of her life were piled everywhere, ripped apart and strewn methodically over every inch. Was this an elaborate prank? "Ha ha!" she exclaimed, feeling very funny, like tingly funny, in her hands and legs. "Ha ha ha!" She walked ahead, to the confluence of living room, dining room, and hallway. She stopped, surrounded by the loose-leaf abortion. She beat her left breastbone with her fist, felt tears spill out of her eyes, and screamed at everyone—Mr. Portwit, Mother, Father, Bernette, Barry, Mrs. Passinault, Principal Foster, Principal Jennings—all of them flashed through her mind as she thumped her chest with a needling fist, her knees unsteady, and she massacred the air with the most incredible "FFUUUCCKKYYOOUU!!!!" she could summon.

She stomped into the kitchen and flung open every possible

door: cupboard, refrigerator, and freezer. She opened each drawer and canister. She opened anything that might hide an edible good. She threw items onto the counter: mayonnaise, mustard, ketchup, bread, milk, cheese, yogurt, Spaghetti-Os, sausage ravioli, canned soups, Hostess fruit pies and Zingers, leftover gravy, cranberry sauce, stuffing, sweet potatoes, black olives, a half-stripped turkey carcass, ginger snaps and chocolate chip cookies, popsicles and egg rolls, corn chips, potato chips, nacho chips, and chocolate chips. Once everything was on the counter, or in the sink, or rolling and dropping with a series of thunks to the floor, Mary Ann set to ripping and tearing and can-opening and unwrapping. She stuffed whatever she could into her mouth—great, goopy handfuls of cottage cheese, whole Twinkies, stacks of Pringles, sticky balls of ground bologna. Her teeth pulverized unmercifully, her throat convulsed. Her mouth could not catch everything her hand fed it, but what dropped out sometimes managed to land on the hand that bore the next load, thus making it inside. She was a shark; she would not get full. Handfuls of mayonnaise, a pair of raw hot dogs, a clump of white-bread stuffing, hard taco shells, slices of oatmeal bread, a raw egg (why not?), sunflower seeds, Froot Loops straight from the box. She would defeat this food. She would kill it. She would leave nothing for anyone. She would take and take and take.

She didn't know how much time had passed when she began to slow down. A knife blade had been stuck between rib #4 and rib #5. Intense pain on her left side. She looked down and saw that her red sweater was coated with half-chewed mash. The air felt pasty and unfriendly; the kitchen was 110 degrees. She fanned her face with her hand, belching like an automobile backfiring. She spun, expecting Mr. Portwit to be in the doorway, leaning on the frame, arms crossed, saying, "Mary Ann, you certainly look stunning when you gorge yourself." Then she lost consciousness and crashed to the floor.

THREE

10

Mr. Portwit's Escort was parked on the side of the expressway. As cars and trucks buzzed past like two-ton bees (*hhhhhhowww, hhhowwwhhhaowww, hhhaowww*), he wept. The Escort's engine, though not exactly purring, did not disturb Mr. Portwit's blubbering cry. He finally accepted what he had done this morning.

He'd been driven by noble, if manic, intentions. It had taken one solid hour of dedicated ripping. He'd sworn to sever Mary Ann's umbilical cord to the past. She needed to be free! To live each day as new! He himself was proof of the harm of looking back. It was a dangerous business, this remembering, best left to biographers and mental patients.

How could he have done it? He prided himself on his precisely calibrated mind, and in retrospect, tearing up her lists seemed . . . inaccurate. It would be misinterpreted. She would think he hated her lists, that he thought them petty, insignificant. She might (might?!) think he was lashing out at her. It would be read all wrong. He hadn't even left a note, to ensure clarity of purpose. He cried some more, until it felt as if all his tears were in his hands.

Then he wiped his hands on his pants, waited for an opening in traffic, and maneuvered back onto the expressway. The surrounding fields gave way to equally bare, low-lying parking lots. A flurry of snow and billboards crowded the sky. Traffic became dense, more aggressive. Sports cars threw slush in all directions as they sizzled past. His watch showed five minutes until 5 p.m. Daylight was fleeing to the corners of the sky. The signs said Saginaw was eleven miles away.

He didn't know where he was going, exactly. At the exit for *Downtown Saginaw*, he split from the expressway. He turned left at the end of the ramp. For fifteen minutes he drove through avenues named after presidents, circling short blocks of worn, huddled buildings. There were pawnshops and Checks Cashed shops. Beneath banners that advertised *Gold Teeth—$29.95* leaned prostitutes in miniskirts and winter jackets who kissed their cigarettes and eyeballed the passing cars. On corners, clusters of young black men, cloaked in long, puffy, cocoonlike coats, postured for the world with angry, impervious eyes. Such confidence and swagger, mixed with apathy. How did they do it?

Mr. Portwit parked in front of a brick building with boards for windows. A weathered, hand-painted placard read *Jinx's Recording Studio*. He cut the engine, stepped out into the lightly falling snow, and stretched his arms above his head. He yawned. His muscles tensed like a rubber band. The group of four teenage boys who stood below the placard broke into a cacophony of laughter.

"How you doing, man?" one boy asked.

"I'm troubled," Dale said, to the group.

"Yeah, me too," said another boy, and he smacked his fist against another boy's fist.

"You ain't a queer, are you?" a third boy asked. "That shit's down Jefferson."

A squeal of delight from another boy.

"Not in the homosexual sense," answered Mr. Portwit. The breeze massaged and freshened his pate. "I'm on the trail of a woman, as a matter of fact."

This revelation was hilarious to the four boys, who dipped and swiveled, clapped their hands, and hollered. Mr. Portwit figured they were imagining this pasty geezer in an untucked, wrinkled T-shirt doing the deed with one of the beautiful ladies positioned along Gratiot Avenue. Mr. Portwit laughed with them. He wanted to tell them that in the past he *had* dallied with women like that, women who gave and received oral sex and vaginal sex and anal sex and hand sex and once even foot sex. He wanted to tell them that he knew why they were laughing, and that it was probably in part because they were uncomfortable. He wanted to tell them that sex with strangers had ephemeral benefits, but that ultimately it made a person feel like he was worth nothing, in the cosmic sense.

"Man, your asshh can't even afford the crack hoesshh," said the fattest boy, who had an unfortunate lateral lisp.

"I don't need *any* hoes anymore," promised Mr. Portwit. "I'm looking for an ex-teacher of mine. From elementary school."

"You a cop, motherfucker?" asked the first boy, who puffed on a cigarette and stared out from his hood cave.

"Neither," said Mr. Portwit. "I just need a convenience store."

The fat boy pointed vaguely west and said, "Bunch of shit that way."

Dale tipped an invisible hat, said good luck and good-bye, and got back into his car.

He headed west until he spotted a 7-Eleven. He went to the pay phone bolted to the brick wall out front. He tried to call Mary Ann collect. A computerized woman's voice told Dale to state his name after the tone. "Your husband," he said at the prompt. He waited. He imagined the ring echoing through their house. He saw Mary Ann hustling from the kitchen, drying her hands with a dish towel, shuffling toward the cradle where the cordless receiver, cartoon-like, jumped and shook with each RING! He imagined Mary Ann saying, "Hold your horses, I'm coming."

Instead, the prerecorded voice returned. "No one is answering. Please hang up and try again at a later time."

Mr. Portwit hung up. He stood, shivering. The sky above the houses was now the color of a poorly erased blackboard. For as far as he could see, streetlights threw dim yellow patches onto the road and sidewalk. Mr. Portwit took into his arms the tethered telephone book. He opened to the Bs, flipped a few pages, and found Brandmal. He tore out the page, folded it into a square the size of a coaster, and tucked it into his front pocket.

Just then, a woman wearing a green-trimmed uniform leaned out the door. Spotted across her torso, like measles, were hundreds of tiny red 7-Eleven logos.

"You ripped out one of them pages!" she said, wagging a finger. Her thick, magnifying eyeglasses stood dangerously close to toppling from her nose. "You get on in here! We're gonna call up our manager, and he can tell us how much you need to pay for that, because that book ain't there for people to rip up whenever they want to!"

The woman was round, short, brown-skinned, and sexy, shaped like a Christmas bulb—nearly as fat as Mary Ann. Her most prominent features were an aggressive set of long white teeth and inhumanly prodigious breasts. In Mr. Portwit's hasty estimation, these weighed twenty pounds apiece.

Mr. Portwit didn't want any trouble. He envisioned, briefly, a carnal interlude, the woman bent over the counter reading a *People* magazine and grimacing with delight every few seconds. This mental picture was jarring, and it temporarily disabled his senses, but he gradually became aware that time had continued, and that the 7-Eleven woman was still waiting, more suspicious with each passing second, for a response.

He assembled a hasty sentence. "Let's not get carried away," he suggested, employing what he considered to be a pleasant tonal cocktail of humility, imperative, and condescension, perfected over two decades of teaching preteens. Next he leaned forward as if to take a drink from an invisible fountain, squinted, and read "*Loretta*" aloud from her name tag. As he did this he casually, very casually, reached toward his back pocket.

Loretta saw his moving hand. Her eyelids opened until it appeared her orbs would drop out onto the pavement. She darted into the store, hollering, "Nine-one-one! Nine-one-one! He's got a gun! He's got a gun!"

She repeated this singsong rhyme as Mr. Portwit realized his error, his terrible error, and hurried to his Escort. He'd only been reaching for his wallet to pay for the phone book.

He drove with no sense of where he might end up. Except for the regular interruption of red signs and red lights, he drove without stopping. Some streets were narrow, bleak, and lifeless; snow collected on parked cars like volcanic ash. Others were wide, optimistic, well-lit avenues where people transacted business at gas stations and fast food restaurants. Mr. Portwit rubbed the windshield with his coat sleeve every two minutes to keep it from frosting over. Near his elbow, the heater kicked out a lukewarm breeze.

He turned whenever he wanted, wherever he wanted. At each new intersection, he expected to see lights flashing, police cars barreling toward him. But why would they arrest him? On what charges? The longer he drove, the calmer he became. What evidence did they have? A torn page from a phone book? Good heavens, he was a vandal! A thief who had filched a sheet of paper! The cops would question Loretta, ask if she'd actually *seen* a gun in the suspect's hands, and she would have to admit that she hadn't. Even if Loretta swore on her children and her husband and her minimum-wage job that the bald stranger had been packing a Magnum in his slacks—even if Loretta swore to this, the cops would simply take one long, skeptical look at her enormous glasses, teeth, and breasts, pretend to write a report, and head to the nearest Krispy Kreme for an hour-long pastry debriefing. People with enormous *anythings* were never taken seriously.

Still, it was a bad way to begin a murder. He'd been seen by too many people: Officer Witport and friends at the rest area, the boys on the corner, now Loretta. He blamed his carelessness on the beer allergy that even now held his body temperature above normal—101.5, he guessed—and sent him into fits of intense teeth chattering. Last evening, the sickness had stripped away any hope of restful sleep, had, in effect, *erased* last night and part of this morning from his memory.

Hunched over the wheel, forearm wiping the windshield when needed, teeth Morse-coding some elaborate message in his skull, Mr. Portwit haunted the streets until he located an expressway—any one would do. He drove for fifteen minutes, until glowing hotel signs hovered in the night sky. He pulled in at a Super 8.

As he walked to the office to book a room, he imagined his post-murder, postcapture television news report. (He couldn't envision getting away with it. It had come to this: even in fantasy, he was a failure.) CUT TO:

Joshua Riggs reporting LIVE in front of the Portwits' suburban home. "He was a lonely man, police say, prone to fits of what one colleague called 'laser-sharp anger.' He attempted suicide only a year ago, after a bout of depression brought on by what Mr. Portwit was heard to call 'the vertiginous downward spiral of everyday existence.' It's a quote that has many people here in Portage, as well as around the world, perplexed and intrigued. This reporter included, Suzanne."

"What about his teaching?" Suzanne asked, finger in her ear, split-screened now to the left, with trenchcoated Joshua on the right. "I understand he was a science teacher?"

"Let me put it to you this way, Suzanne," Joshua said. "I spoke to one student today, a seventh-grade boy, who told me . . ." Joshua unfolded a sheet of paper and read, "'Mr. Portwit was the most perfect human being I have ever known. He made me understand so many things. He was always telling us that the world runs on certain natural laws, like Newton's laws of gravity and stuff. And that even things like friendship and love and parent/child relations are bound by these natural laws, laws that are 'second-tier' natural because they come from *us*, *we* make them, yet because *we* are natural creatures, it follows that the rules that we create *must*'—and there's an emphasis on that word, Suzanne—'MUST, in some second-tier way, initiate in nature. *A* creates *B*, then *B* creates *C*, thus *A* creates *C*. And yet our evolution now allows us to make our *own* rules, rules of a social sort, distinct from the laws of the natural world *(how a man should treat his wife* or *how often a person should phone his eighty-year-old parents* vs. *how often a person must defecate* or *which genetic strain is bound to show itself in his offspring)*. The end result is that we become the gods of these so-called 'third-tier' rules. We have the power to make or break them, to obey or to chuck them. This free will leads to all sorts of deviations from nature because inevitably we *do* break the rules that our biology has established, and people stab one another and grow tumors and freak out and explode in one way or another.' Suzanne, this little boy wraps up his statement with one of the most heartbreakingly simple sentences I've ever read: 'Mr. Portwit was a savior to me.' That's what one student had to say about this fantastically complex person. This is Josh Riggs, Channel 8 news, reporting live from Portage."

Once inside his room, Mr. Portwit ordered a twelve-inch pizza from a nearby Domino's. He paid with MasterCard. It was too late now for concealing evidence—that chance had been squandered. Trying to cover one's tracks was an affront to science—it was impossible, after all, given today's tools of detection—and, more important, would violate the spirit of Mr. Portwit's quest. He was not a "criminal" to be harassed and condescended to by cops who would think they'd outwitted him. No, his mission was an act of cosmic retribution, the end product of a lifetime of righteous struggle, and it was important that he leave his spoor. Otherwise, the world would be one big toilet bowl, swirling our identities out to sea in a rush of blue disinfectant water. Mr. Portwit signed the slip for the delivery kid, adding a one-dollar tip to the total.

In theory, none of the *Brandmal* entries could be crossed out right away. Mr. Portwit chewed the ham and double cheese pizza, sipped his carbonated lemon-lime beverage through a straw, and read the hijacked telephone book page that lay unfolded on the bed. Even an entry like *Brandmal Bart and Trudy 1128 Gratiot 432-0934*, names and numbers that to Dale's knowledge had nothing to do with the Mrs. Brandmal he knew, could not be discounted. Mrs. Miranda Brandmal (he'd remembered her first name while imagining his arrest, the cops reading him his rights) might be mother and mother-in-law, respectively, residing as an unlisted invalid in Bart and Trudy's home. Since there were only eighteen, Mr. Portwit decided to call every Brandmal in the Saginaw area.

"Good evening," he said. He'd selected this opening after careful thought. He didn't give the person on the other end much time to reply (two seconds, max) before adding, "I'm an old friend of Miranda Brandmal, from school. May I speak with her?"

"She didn't go to any school that I know of."

"She was a teacher," Mr. Portwit said. He'd unintentionally adopted a deeper, slower, and thus more mature-sounding voice. "She was an elementary school teacher for many years, from 1960 until maybe only a few years ago."

"My Miranda wasn't *born* in 1960," the man said. In the background, a baby began to cry. "She's still in diapers." The line clicked.

"Good evening. I need to speak with Miranda Brandmal. I'm an old friend of hers, from school."

A woman: "Who-zat?"

"Miranda Brandmal?"

"Marvin? There ain't no Marvin."

"Mir . . . an . . . duh. Miranda Brandmal, please."

"I can't understand what this motherfucker . . ."

Pause. Jostling. Thumping.

A not-too-happy man's voice: "Hello?"

"Is this the Brandmal residence?"

"Some kine bithin frrr . . . asshole . . ." Jostle. Click.

Mr. Portwit felt antsy. He turned on the television and pressed a series of buttons on the remote control, at one point drawing his MasterCard from his billfold once again to enter in the digits. *Ranch Hand Job* arrived quickly at a naked part. A veiny penis emerged from a pair of jeans. A blond woman in a cowboy hat grabbed it. He muted the volume.

"Good evening. I need to speak with Miranda Brandmal. I'm an old friend, from school."

"Sorry. You have the wrong number."

"Sorry."

"God bless."

"Bye."

He hadn't cared about girls after Mrs. Brandmal left him. Her departure had redirected his life. During his adolescence, *sex* took a backseat to *text*. The idea of getting near girls, being seduced by their Chinese Osmanthus odors, their milky necklines and false promises . . . it angered him that this temptation even existed, because it was a threat to the only thing he could count on: dispassionate rationality.

So he diverted his sexual instincts, snipped the cable that connected his brain to his privates. During the one period of his life when it was excusable, if not expected, to behave like a rabbit in a teddy bear factory, he'd spent Friday nights straining his eyes on Darwin's theories and practicing stern faces in the mirror. He guessed that this, as much as anything, was at the heart of his discontent: his biological urges had been nullified by a stupid childhood act, by his own lack of self-control. It made him feel like something other than human.

He couldn't hate his father. His father was too stupid to hate. Oh, certainly, he was clever when it came to hooking a wife, getting her pregnant, laying off employees to balance payroll, buying a house, whacking his son's naked bottom with a brush, living past the age of eighty, changing spark plugs, and criticizing pound cake, but not much else. His father's was a phony intelligence; his adeptness at manipulating and controlling other people masked a deficiency in understanding himself or the world he inhabited.

Dale received his high-school diploma, along with salutatorian honors, thicker glasses, and shaggy (though already thinning) hair. In college he dated, but lazily. He found conversation with most people, especially women, to be a chore. He was only interested in experiencing the sexual act, and he resented the notion that he should love the woman he screwed. In fact, he didn't see the point in men and women interacting on any level other than sexual, at least until each was ready to give up his or her individuality and get married. The campus was crawling with students unable to complete their homework assignments, zombified by grief or ecstasy caused by false feelings of love.

Still, he wasn't a complete boor, and two willing girls with ordinary builds (wide hips, upside-down-bowling-pin legs, thighs pocked with cellulite before they called it cellulite, sexy misshapen teeth, mild halitosis) liked Dale enough to spend the night with him. They never cared about him, nor he about them.

He never called for second dates, no hearts were involved, and while nothing was gained, nothing was lost. Everyone broke even.

In middle age, after an unplanned eighteen-year moratorium on woman, only days after his belt proved its impotence (he even remembered where and what and how and why; it was at the Kalamazoo Art Fair, sipping booth-bought lemonade from a straw while watching a young, hippy wife in a loose shirt bend to hand her daughter a bag of caramel corn, and seeing, as if for the first time, a complete breast as smooth and pale as a scoop of vanilla ice cream), Mr. Portwit had decided he would, what the hell, give pornography a shot. After all, he was still alive, right? He approached it as he would a science experiment. As a man, he was supposed to get off on this stuff, wasn't he?

In his attic apartment, with Wayne's Tumor rocking violently two floors down, he spent hours each day and night envying the Porn Star Men with their unstoppable boners, their high-speed thrusts, and their scrotums like tight little purses. They knew how to make women pant and moan and bounce bounce bounce. Mr. Portwit envied the Porn Star Men until he himself began renting hookers, graduating after five months to gorgeous but vain and near-frigid $200 escorts, and realized that in real life, sex could never live in the same way it did in his mind. Porn Star Man appeared to have the perfect job, but after a long day at work, while driving home in his closed car, Porn Star Man could smell himself. Olfactory! The most objective of the senses. Hard to argue with odor. Leaning toward the mirror in the bathroom of a pricey Bay Area restaurant, one week after munching on a not even particularly hirsute vagina, Porn Star Man still found pubic hairs between his teeth. Once the stage lights died, *yes!*ing Porn Star Girl smacked Dentyne, talked nasally on a cell phone in non sequiturs to her cocaine dealer, and grew an unexpected second chin.

"Good evening. I need to speak with Miranda Brandmal. I'm an old friend, from school."

Was there a scientific basis for Murphy's Law? Mr. Portwit pondered making this Irishman's Law the subject of a future, formal study. What other factor could account for the *final* of eighteen phone book entries being the right one?

The listing was *Brandmal, Zachary*. The blonde woman on the television was saluting Porn Star Man's flagpole.

"Yes, I know Miranda Brandmal," said the elderly man who answered the phone. "I don't know if she's the one you're looking for."

"Really? I mean, I don't know if she's the one, either," stammered Mr. Portwit, fumbling with the remote to kill the picture.

"What's your name?"

"Mr. Portwit. Dale Portwit. I was a student of Mrs. Brandmal's."

"Well, the Miranda I know hasn't taught for some years now."

"This would have been in the early 1960s."

"She was an elementary school teacher over the west side of the state, long time ago."

"That's right," Mr. Portwit said. "That's exactly right. Is she at home now?"

"She don't live here," the man managed to articulate, amid a rattly cough. "She's up to the home in Davison. Her husband, my brother, passed on five years ago. She doesn't take care of herself anymore."

"I'm sorry to hear that," Mr. Portwit said, though he was relieved to hear of the husband's passing. He imagined Mrs. Brandmal in a ratty nightgown, her pink skull visible through a web of wispy white hair, shuffling down an empty, fluorescently flickering hallway, mouth agape, eyes black. "What was the name of that home again?" Mr. Portwit asked.

"Oh, she's up at Whispering Valley," the old man said, with what might have been a tinge of pride. "You ought to visit her. She's real sick. In fact, she's just about out of options, if you want to know the truth. She's in awful pain most of the day." The old man seemed to have gotten sidetracked, as his voice died down, then became brighter. "But she loves company. I'll give you directions. Go visit her, see for yourself. You say you're a student of hers? That's wonderful. I'm glad you called. She was a wonderful teacher, wasn't she?"

"That's right."

"Heck, I'm sure you know. She deserves the best."

"I don't disagree."

"You won't ever hear her complain, but the woman is suffering."

"Mm."

"Terribly."

148

"Maybe it'll make her feel better," Mr. Portwit ventured, "to have a visitor."

"Yes. Definitely. She needs help, for sure. She asks for it, too. Darling woman."

Mr. Portwit felt uneasy. He wanted to get off the phone. "I appreciate your help."

"Hang on. Let me tell you how to get there."

"That's OK. I know where it is," Mr. Portwit lied. Zachary Brandmal's eagerness was disconcerting. "You have a good night, now."

"Why don't you give me a call when you're finished visiting with her. We'll talk."

Mr. Portwit had no answer to this unorthodox proposal, and even if he had, it wouldn't have done any good: Zachary had hung up.

The digital clock read 9:32 p.m. Dale went to the window and parted the heavy drapes, just enough to peek his head through.

The parking lot two floors below showed its white lines, its nonverbal instructions telling people where they were allowed to place themselves. Dale looked beyond to the grid work of city lights stretching toward Lake Erie, then Canada, then, eventually, to the ocean. Somewhere in those lights, or in a grid work exactly like them but in the opposite direction—he didn't have any idea where Davison was—Mrs. Miranda Brandmal waited, possibly working her gums with a soft-bristled brush or swabbing her ear with a Q-tip, unaware that she was about to die. He thought about the fish heads; if they were here right now he would splash them across the bed, strip to his underwear, and have a feast. He'd show how many he could devour.

He thought of Mary Ann. She would be worried. By now, she would have phoned the Green Top, and his parents, and—whom else? There was no one else. He attempted to call home. He sat on the bed with the receiver pressed to his ear. The answering machine did not activate. Each ring was the same tone, the same cycle length—2.0 seconds on, 4.0 seconds off, a delicate *purrrrr*—yet this sameness somehow gained intensity with each repetition. After about the forty-third *purrrr*, he hung up. He waited 2.0 seconds, then lifted the receiver and tried again. No luck. There were 2.0 possible reasons that the answering machine did not engage: Either it had been turned off, or the tape inside was full.

Mr. Portwit put the back of his hand against his forehead. It

149

felt like touching a sidewalk in June. The beer reaction, still alive, temporarily unnoticed because of his mission concentration, now reasserted itself. He removed his T-shirt, dropped it to the floor, and stood before the mirror. A red blade of rash was imprinted from his Adam's apple to the center of his chest, obscured in the tangle of hairs there. He went into the bathroom and stripped. He ran cold water in the tub, and when it was full, he stepped in with one foot. It was frigid, bit his skin. He brought his other foot over the rim. Nearly in tears, remembering how when he was a child his mother plunged him into an ice bath to lower a 104 fever, he levered and braced the tub sides with his spindly arms, clenched his teeth, lowering himself gaspingly into—*Holy shit is that cold!* Then the ass and jewels. Oh no. Wow. Pull out, take a couple deep breaths. Try again. Ass and jewels revisiting, not as painful as the first time. Then the backsides of thighs, lower back, belly, all in, all in, teeth chattering with hollow clacks, thinking *Got to lower this fever, set my head on straight, get a good night's rest, grind up the pills, find Mrs. Brandmal, feed her, get home to Mary Ann.*

11

Diving dream, under deep water. The surface only a suggestion, an illumination, far, far above. Schools of fish zig-zag-zip as one undulating unit, in foreground and background, then vanish, revealing, in the distance, still clouded in darkness, a cluster of familiar faces, a school of detached human heads: Mrs. Passinault, Ramone the custodian, Mrs. Farfalinga, Mrs. Jennings, Mrs. Ogilvie, Principal Foster, and Mr. Portwit. In formation they swim, propelled by unknown forces, easy-paced, mouths opening and closing to catch invisible prey. It's a sad, sickening bunch, veins dangling from their jagged neck stumps. Hair billows, puffs, and extends like octopus tentacles behind the women's heads. Mr. Portwit's glasses drift away from his face. He furrows his brow and watches them plummet. "Those glasses were nothing more than an adjective," he rationalizes. "A physical adjective, modifying *me*. Who needs them?" The Principal Foster head, pulling up the rear, smiles wistfully, then coughs out a batch of bubbles. His eyes are downturned. The school of school heads disappears behind a bank of coral. Mary Ann lowers her chin to look at her body. She is a shark. A famished shark. Her gut spasms in anger and hunger. Kicking her tail fin, she cuts through the water, gaining. So hungry! Her stomach sounds like an idling lawn mower, blade spinning, motor churning. Up ahead, such zombies, without life, merely floating, mouths taking whatever invisible food is in front of them, eyeballs bugging out and fraying a little. Mrs. Passinault gums the threads trailing from Mrs. Ogilvie's sockets and swallows them, but as she lacks a stomach, the threads simply pass through her neck hole. Mary Ann opens her complicated mouth, her explosive, many-hinged jaw with five rows of teeth. The heads are getting larger and larger as she approaches, and now her mouth is open to its limit, and the first head, Principal Foster, collides with her, breaking off a few teeth, but what the hell does it matter since she's got three hundred of them, and her jaws SNAP! Again and again and again. The head is pulverized; the water clouds red. Now the other heads are panicked, eyes wide, lips going *glob glob glob*, unable to turn or maneuver too well. Mrs. Passinault bumps into Mr. Portwit, Mrs. Ogilvie knocks Ramone, Ramone turns and rams Mr. Portwit. Knock. Knock. "Excuse me." Knock. "Look out, please." They are uncoordinated in their terror. Mary Ann creates a bloodbath. She makes mush of Mrs. Passinault, Mrs. Farfalinga, and Ramone, all at once. Weightless in the water, she dives lower, mawful of awful pointed teeth spread like a bear trap, inhaling Mrs. Jennings, who screams on her way inside, "No, Mary Ann! I bought you a special chair!" Mrs. Ogilvie comes next, swimming right up, resignedly accepting her role in the food chain. She is gobbled and swallowed. Then Mary Ann feels nauseated. She has eaten too much. But no—a shark is always hungry. "A shark is always hungry," agrees Mr. Portwit, floating ten yards away, beside a stalk of coral. "I'm not hungry anymore," Mary Ann insists, burping; an ear propellers out of her mouth. She turns like a blimp in the sky, begins swimming away. "You *must* be hungry," asserts Mr. Portwit, following at a safe distance. "You're a shark. Your appetite is endless. It's what makes you the king of the sea. You can't deny your biological impulses. It would be *unnatural*." Mary Ann spins, faces him. Mr. Portwit shrinks back, smiles uneasily. "So you think I should eat you?" Mary Ann asks, displaying her teeth. There is no other food in sight; the ocean is murky, vast, mostly unseeable. There is only Mr. Portwit's softly bobbing head, neck veins like spaghetti noodles beneath him. "I'm saying that if I were you, I'd eat me," he offers, squinting without his glasses. "Even if I'm full?" "*Full* is a relative term." "No, Dale. It's not. I. AM. FULL. Period." "I don't believe you." He swims a few feet closer, testing boundaries. She catches his scent. Her stomach growls. Mr. Portwit smiles. "See?" he says. Mary Ann thinks a moment. She swims closer, nudges him with her nose. He tilts and wobbles in the buoyant salt water. "I guess I *could* have dessert," she says, shyly. "That's my girl," Mr. Portwit says, sidling up to her face. He kisses her on the snout. She opens up. He lowers the head, the head that is him, and enters the mouth cavern. "One request," he says. "Don't digest me next to Mrs. Passinault. Put me with Ramone or something." He laughs, adding, "I know you don't have much control over that. But try, sweetheart!" VOOSH! He is sucked into her stomach.

Satisfied, she swims onward. The ocean is dark. It's easy to become disoriented. She swims in circles. Up becomes down. Right is up. Left is down. Underneath is above. Her stomach pulsates, resists. So many skulls in her belly, so many bones. There is nobody left. Bernette. Bernette must be here, somewhere. Bernette or Mother. "Mother!" she yells, but it is bubble-speak, incomprehensible. This stomach pain is like a fire. She swallows water to douse it, but the water gags her. She gurgles, upchucks. She expels clumps of hair, Mrs. Passinault's lips, a confetti spray of teeth, a boomeranging tongue, blood in great clouds. Mary Ann is engulfed in a red soup. Bitter backwash is all she tastes.

12

The hour-long bath in fifty-degree water succeeded in lowering his temperature. Despite having fingertips that resembled the abdomens of dead insects, Mr. Portwit, as he dried himself with the Super 8 towel, felt almost normal again. The tub drain sucked at the water noisily, thirstily. Naked before the mirror, he hunched into a bodybuilder pose and flexed his arms like two pincers. It was nearing midnight. He crawled into bed and called Mary Ann. He fell asleep somewhere around the fifty-eighth ring. Every 4.0 seconds.

A woman: "That's the thing. This is what I've been afraid of for a long time."
A woman: "I hope he's OK. I mean, I hope he didn't do anything crazy."
A man: "How's she doing?"
A woman: "Oh, I don't know."
A woman: "Wait, hey. Did you see that? Look at her eyelids."
A man: "She's coming back to us . . . Mary Ann? Mary Ann, can you hear me?"
    Mary Ann made every muscle push. Pushed, pushed, let soft lumination in. Squares. Off-yellow squares. Three heads of shadow leaned together, three heads looking down at her. One, Bernette. The second, Mother. The man said, "Good morning," and shone a blinding light in her eye.

A harsh knocking. Mr. Portwit sat upright. The room was black. Thick curtains. "Housekeeping!" said a muffle. The clock: 1:30. He picked up the clock. P.M. ?! He'd slept for more than thirteen hours. Missed checkout time.
    "Come back later!" he yelled, mouth full of glue.

He stepped into yesterday's pants, packed his duffel, threw on a shirt, and headed out the door. He had work to do.

◇

A hand touched her arm. It was a warm hand, attached to her mother.

"Mary Ann, can you hear me?"

Mary Ann tried to nod, wasn't sure if she succeeded.

"I think she's saying yes," said the man. He was a doctor, or a dentist. He was in a white coat. "Don't try to move," he instructed. Now *his* hand was on her *other* forearm.

So comfortable with eyes closed.

◇

He drove to the nearest gas station, filled the tank, bought three bottles of apple juice, a box of miniature powdered doughnuts, and a map. He parked the Escort beside the gas station. Meticulously, without enjoyment, Mr. Portwit devoured all twenty-four miniature doughnuts. He drank his apple juice. The powder on his fingertips made him think about Mary Ann. He walked to a wall-mounted telephone, just like the one at the 7-Eleven, and called. She didn't answer.

◇

"Wey . . ." Mary Ann managed to whisper.

"You're at Bronson Hospital," Bernette said.

"We're with you," added her mother, stating the obvious. Her mother's eyes were luggage.

"You're very lucky to be alive," said the doctor.

"We're here with you," repeated her mother.

"Mary Ann, if you can hear me, say 'Mmm-hmm,'" instructed the doctor.

"I c'n . . . ear," gasped Mary Ann. Her throat burned. Other than that, she felt decent. Rested. Sort of floaty. She blinked, yawned. There were tubes sticking out of her nostrils.

"Don't overexert yourself," said the doctor. "Speaking might wear you out."

"Mary Ann, there's something I need to tell you," her mother said. Her eyes began filling with tears.

"Not yet," Bernette tried to slip in, under the radar.

155

Mother looked at doctor. Doctor at Mother, doctor at Bernette. Bernette at doctor, Bernette at Mary Ann. Weak smile from Bernette. Tears rolling out. Poor Bernette. No smile from Mother. No smile from doctor. Where was Mr. Portwit? Was this about those Librium pills?

"Mmm?" asked Mary Ann.

※

Mr. Portwit wondered, as his eyes and fingers roved the lap map. Mr. Portwit wondered, seated in the driver's seat; he wondered, idling beside the Mobil wall.

His fingers, meanwhile, located Davison County.

※

Her words breaking apart, Mother stuttered, "I do n't w a nt y ou t o pa ni c, Mar y A nn."

Then, like Mother's words, Bernette broke apart. A gasp escaped her mouth. She squeezed her eyes. She hurried from the room.

"Whaaa-iiiisss iiii-?" Mary Ann managed.

With trembling hand, Mother blubbered. Maybe she was being electrocuted. "They had to, to re-, they had, had to, they, removed, they, removed, your leg. Oh, I'm so sorry, sweetheart."

"Maaa . . . lehhh? Whaa aboww maa lehh?"

"She's hyperventilating," said a cotton-haired nurse who emerged from behind the doctor.

"Boost the morphine," the doctor said.

※

Whispering Valley: a "Living Community" of red brick houses, one story tall, exactly fifteen feet per side, each identical to the next, previous, first, and last. Any order you saw them in would yield the same result, Mr. Portwit mused. An interesting way to defeat the myth of causality was to make everything the same. He stepped from the car, slung the duffel onto his shoulder, and wiped his mouth with his coat sleeve to remove any remaining powdered sugar. The main office, named *The Center*, was not, Mr. Portwit noted, in the center of anything. It was the building nearest the road; this was its only distinction from the others.

He opened the flimsy screen door. It let out a metallic scream. Soft carpeting the color of honey greeted his feet and eyes as he

156

entered. He inhaled the spicy perfume of ointment. Maybe Ben-Gay. Or Aspercreme. Just like the olden days, like *Travelling Stan's Miracle Cream*, or *Benson and Son's Whipped Copperhead Lipids: for nongastric relief of stomach cramps.* Geezers loved their liniments. His dad's medicine cabinet had always been full of wrinkled tubes with scabbed-over mouths, and his dad gazed upon those tubes three times a day, in order to experience a feeling that approximated happiness. He didn't need to *use* what was in the tubes; he just wanted the tubes to be there. Like a crucifix to a Christian.

Mr. Portwit removed his jacket, laid it over his forearm, and emerged from the entryway into the lobby. There was a counter, a window, and a receptionist. The receptionist slid the window open.

"Are you family, sir?"

"Yes."

"Which one?"

"Which family?"

"Which resident?"

"Brandmal, comma, Miranda."

The secretary, a late-middle-aged woman who had a nice plump body like Mary Ann's, but not as pretty a face, and hair that could have been fashioned into a dozen serviceable hunks of steel wool, rolled her chair backward to read her computer screen. Even with her pink-painted, three-quarter-inch claws, she managed to click out a few characters on the keyboard. From speakers embedded in the ceiling came the mellow strains of an instrumental version of Stevie Wonder's "I Just Called to Say I Love You." The secretary, who would herself undoubtedly be a resident of this place in ten years, studied the contents of the screen, then regarded Mr. Portwit with an in-your-face apathy.

"Name," she said. Her voice was like a three-day-old crust of toast. The thought of killing this woman instead of Mrs. Brandmal flashed in Mr. Portwit's mind. *And I mean it from the bottom of my heart.*

"Mr. Portwit," he answered.

"Poor . . . twit," she said slowly, typing slowly. "P-O-R-E . . . How do you spell that?"

"By arranging the proper letters in their proper sequence."

Her sense of humor had not come to work with her today. She cast a mauve-shadowed eye upon Mr. Portwit's powder-and-sauce-smeared shirt, his perspiring head, and the duffel-bag burrito under his arm. He sneezed. Three times. Into his hand. A web of snot was left between his fingers. "Do you have any tissue back there?" he asked. He hoped this gesture to propriety would prove he wasn't a complete savage.

The secretary handed a box of Kleenex through the sliding window. "You say you are family of Miranda Brandmal?" she asked, returning her now-skeptical gaze to the computer screen. Flags had been hoisted in her mind.

"I've had a long night," Mr. Portwit said, transforming his tone into the auditory equivalent of a chocolate-chip cookie direct from the oven: melty and squishy and irresistible. "I realize I don't look my best. The truth is I had an allergic reaction from something—a liquid, specifically. Fever, sharp headaches, dull headaches, a rash. In fact, let me . . ." He pulled the neck hole of his shirt, hoping the redness was still visible.

The secretary was unimpressed. "Sir, are you family or not?"

"Not blood family, no," answered Mr. Portwit.

"An in-law?"

"Not . . . not . . . no."

"Are you a friend, then?"

"Yes, I am."

Her hard stare softened. Her tone became gentle. "OK, sir. I'm going to need to confirm who you are. Can I see your driver's license?"

So his cookie hadn't worked after all. Her newfound pleasantness was actually born of sadism: She thought she would catch him in a lie, and then, wouldn't he be sorry.

Well, he had nothing to hide. Mr. Portwit dug his wallet from his back pocket and fished out his license. Gleefully, she typed in his name and address. Handing back his ID with a smile, she asked if Mrs. Brandmal was expecting him.

"Don't you need more information off of here?" he said, tapping the plastic card on the counter. "It's got height, weight, date of birth, corrective lens information. All kinds of good stuff. Say . . . why don't you Xerox it while I've got it out? I'll wait."

The secretary was unfazed. "Is Mrs. Brandmal expecting you?"

He said he didn't know. He put away his license. The secretary picked up a telephone. She dialed a three-digit number and waited, her eyes falling to the fingernails of her left hand, which she arranged in a fan shape, like peacock plumage, before her face. "Mrs.

Brandmal?" she said. "There's a gentleman here to see you. His name is Dale Poor Twit. Are you expecting him?"

Mr. Portwit waved his hand and whispered, "When you said 'expecting,' I didn't—"

The secretary laid her index finger on her lips to hush him. "OK, honey," she said into the phone. "Can you hold for one second? I'll be right back. Hold for a sec, sweetie." The secretary pushed a button on the phone's face. "She says she isn't expecting you and she doesn't know who you are."

Mr. Portwit chuckled, as if to say that this was just what he'd planned for. "Tell her Zachary asked me to drop by. I'm an old student of hers."

The secretary pressed the hold button. "Honey?" she said. "The gentleman says he's a friend of Zachary's." He hadn't said that, exactly, but he didn't correct her. "Should I send him back?" She nodded. She nodded again. Mr. Portwit wondered if the secretary had considered that Mrs. Brandmal might not be able to see her nods. "OK, sweetie," she said at last. "I'll tell him."

She hung up. "You can go on back." Her manner was business-like, nonjudgmental, neither warm nor cold, as she produced a clip-board and pen. "House number 14," she said. "Down the sidewalk, take a right at the third walk. We give the sidewalks names here. You want to turn right on Golden Glen. Second house on your left. Print and sign at the bottom, and estimate the length of your visit."

Mr. Portwit printed and signed his name. He estimated an hour.

"We'll need you to come back here and sign out when you're through. You can use the bathroom down the hall, if you want to clean up," the secretary said. She managed to assemble a paltry, but nearly pleasant, smile.

"Mrs. Brandmal won't mind my appearance," Mr. Portwit said, returning the pen to the secretary's hand. "I'm not staying long."

Dale gave the secretary a thumbs-up. He spun on his heel, nod-ded to the empty lobby seats that had listened so carefully to their verbal transaction, and departed amidst the screech of hinges.

For the first time in her life, Mary Ann couldn't eat. The nurse wheeled in a Salisbury steak dinner, but upon smelling it, Mary Ann vomited into the bedpan.

Mary Ann elevated the head of the bed until she sat like a person in a recliner. From this vantage, she was able to study the flattened section of sheet at the end of the eight-inch stump. She placed her hand upon the spot where her right leg used to be and felt a tingle in her lower back.

"You should be hungry," her mother said. Her fingers worked knitting needles into a strip of red fabric. The silent hobby. Her mother was convinced that if Mary Ann wore a bright red scarf from now on ("It could be your trademark, like Michael Jackson's glove!"), it would draw the visual emphasis away from the leg. She kept referring to it as "the leg"—but it wasn't "the leg," it was the "non-leg," the "stump," the "residual limb." Any of these would've been honest, but honesty had never been Mother's highest priority. She took it upon herself to dial Mary Ann's home every half hour, cursing ("God blessit") when Mr. Portwit didn't answer. She offered to sew up the right legs of all Mary Ann's slacks, to inquire at PayLess about buying shoes "on a singular basis," and to research the Internet to find the most "user-friendly" prosthetic they could afford, as well as the best wheelchair for the off times. As a finale, Mother proposed hiring a good therapist who knew how to deal with the psychological trauma caused by "phantom limbs."

Why wouldn't Mom look at herself? Mom's handling of Dad's phantom was hardly a blueprint for success. Her perky optimism was a mask; deep down, she was a terrified woman, unable since her husband's death to do anything but sit at home and live off the life insurance. To the present day, she maintained her phony friendship with the Fargas family for the sole purpose of getting invited to their monthly dinners and receiving their lavish Christmas gifts. She emerged from the security of her two-thousand-square-foot East Grand Rapids home only for holidays, car washes, pedicures, and, apparently, amputations.

But then again, whom was Mary Ann kidding? Hate Mom? No. Mary Ann couldn't hate anyone. It was all fine. A few minutes earlier, she'd pushed the remote button for the PCA (Patient-Controlled Analgesia) machine. From behind the morphine buffer, Mary Ann knew that she was *supposed* to be feeling a number of things—fear for her husband's safety, horror and despair at being crippled, gratitude that she hadn't died on the kitchen floor wearing a shirt covered in Ho-Ho crumbs and cottage cheese—and yet, here in the hospital bed in the early evening of the day of her rescue and emergency amputation, Mary Ann was able to feel only one: resigned to the fact that she was supposed to feel a number of things that she wasn't actually feeling.

This morphine was strong. The sky was elephant skin beyond the window. Mary Ann wanted to lick it. Darkness was forming, and soon the elephant skin would be gone.

"You've got to simply *not worry* about going back to school. Not yet," her mother said. "I'm sure they'll get a nice, smart, enthusiastic young woman to take good care of your students. Principal Jennings said they were all praying for you."

"I don't think you should talk so loudly," Mary Ann said.

Her mother continued knitting.

"The school is falling apart," Mary Ann said. Her words were butterflies, launched delicately from her lips, fluttering away. "Principal Foster, Mr. Portwit, me. There's nobody left." This idea struck her as funny. She grinned, but mustering a laugh was out of the question.

She drifted to sleep. As soon as Mary Ann's eyes were closed, closed, closed . . . as soon as lids were lowered and latched . . . Mother was going to stand up . . . stretch her arms like a fairy godmother . . . yawn as if just woken from the most beautiful dream . . . drape the blood-red scarf over the back of her chair . . . pull a hacksaw from her purse . . . saw off Mary Ann's other leg.

The door swung open. Behind the screen stood Mrs. Brandmal.

By some miracle of nature she was alive, or at least gave the impression of life, although this would not last much longer with or without his intervention, Mr. Portwit realized with a mixture of relief and disappointment. Narrow tubes joined her nostrils to a wheeled oxygen tank that served as both cane and lung. Mrs. Brandmal's body—or perhaps more accurately, her skeleton—was wrapped in a bathrobe held closed by Velcro flaps. Wisps of white hair clung to her head with all the conviction of wet noodles. At first glance, she resembled any elderly woman ravaged by time and disease. She was quite short. Her earlobes were flabby, her head palsied. The stylish cat's-eye glasses had been replaced with thick, unwieldy trifocals. Was this the bugbear of his past? Was this the formidable temptress who had taken a bite of his psyche and thrown his core into the trash? He checked the number on the door to make sure this was the right residence, the right life-ruiner.

But the eyeballs were the same. Mr. Portwit experienced a moment of internal appreciation that eyes didn't wrinkle, sag, turn yellow, or fall out. Seeing them, recognizing them, Mr. Portwit could believe, with at least a measure of confidence, that his past had actually occurred. Staring into those eyes, he felt pity.

"Mrs. Brandmal," he said. There was a power in his youth now. Years ago, she'd had the power. For all of four seconds, he felt calm and confident. Then he stuck out his hand, immediately regretting the move but unable to back down. How could she shake it without pitching forward, tumbling onto the pavement? A wave of optimism rushed over him. Perhaps it would be that simple: murder by handshake.

But Mrs. Brandmal ignored his hand.

He stated in a clear, robust voice, "I'm Dale Portwit. Former student. From many years ago."

He was blowing it. What tone was he employing? Robot? He blamed lack of sleep, too much sleep, the beer, the mini-doughnuts, his wife who would be sending the cops out for him any minute. Why was he here? It was a school day, and all over the nation, at this very moment, children were swooning over their teachers. How many of these kids would become depressed, vengeance-seeking misfits? Few. He wondered fleetingly what Mary Ann was doing, which little boy was falling in love with her. Dale felt absurd. For as often as he had imagined this moment, for all the work it had taken to get here, he had achieved nothing. Thoughts were worthless. Words were impossible. And yet, as slave to Newtonian principles, he would not stop: He was in motion, and in motion he would stay until he collided with something.

Mrs. Brandmal's eyebrows remained elevated, expectant.

"I'M DALE PORTWIT," he repeated. His voice resounded through the claustrophobic brick neighborhood. "I WAS A STUDENT OF YOURS IN GRAND RAPIDS? FORTY YEARS AGO?" He lowered his voice, suddenly exhausted. "You must remember me."

Very old people were capable of poker faces that younger people could never emulate. *The weight of the wrinkles*, Mr. Portwit thought. Heaving a portentous sigh, Mrs. Brandmal unlatched the door and retreated into the shadows, dragging her obedient oxygen tank. Mr. Portwit followed her to the living room. The fingers of his right hand, buried in his pants pocket, massaged the loose palmful of Librium tablets he'd shaken out of the jar as he made the solemn journey up Golden Glen Way. He counted them as he walked.

Mrs. Brandmal sat on the covered sofa. She patted the plastic within arm's reach, directing him. She nestled the tank between her knees.

Twenty-eight pills. Mr. Portwit sat on the spot Mrs. Brandmal had patted. He surveyed the room. Furnishings were sparse: glass coffee table, iron desk lamp on the end table, empty magazine rack, a television no larger than a toolbox poised atop an anemically stocked bookshelf. Every wall was virgin white, free of penetrations of any kind.

"So Zachary sent you," she said.

Mr. Portwit didn't have time to decide how to answer this, so he simply said, "Yes."

"And he explained everything?" Her breathing was deep and measured, almost nerve-racking in its calmness. "And you're fine with it?"

"He told me about your health problems." Mr. Portwit felt the need to choose his words with care. "It's absolutely unfair, and upsetting."

"Oh, he's such a baby. Squeamish about every little thing." She stared accusingly at the coffee table, as if Zachary was hiding beneath it. "I wonder how in the world he found you." She looked up at him. "How did he find you?"

Her directness caught Mr. Portwit off guard, but he chuckled knowingly, treating her question as rhetorical. "Indeed," he said. When she continued staring, he shook his head, shrugged his shoulders, and whistled softly, hoping the barrage of gestures would make her forget her question.

She rubbed her knees and took a deep breath. "Well," she said, "I suppose we should talk."

"How about I fix us some tea?" Mr. Portwit asked. "Assuming you drink tea, of course."

She looked surprised. "Yes, yes. Certainly," she said, winking. Her eyes twinkled.

What did this mean? He chalked it up to dementia. "Wonderful," he answered, returning the wink.

"I was under the impression that we would just talk today," she said. "This is a nice surprise."

"We can talk," he answered, "and drink tea at the same time." His palms were moist. "I'm talented that way."

She appraised him soberly. "By all means, put on the water. Let's do this."

Mr. Portwit stood and gestured toward the kitchen. "That way, I assume?" When she nodded, he asked, "Unless you had other plans for this morning?"

Mrs. Brandmal laughed. "What a sense of humor."

He filled the teapot and put it on the burner, which he turned to high heat. His hands trembled, and he realized he still carried the duffel over his shoulder. Upon returning to the living room, he found Mrs. Brandmal with her eyes closed and her hands folded. Her lips moved in prayer. He remained standing and waited for her to finish.

"Most seniors in my condition would kill for a place like this," Mrs. Brandmal said, after crossing herself. "Even though it's not home and never will be. Everyone knows it's not home, but people like to fool themselves. Fake happiness beats no happiness, right? They bring my meals," she added, "even when I don't want them."

"Do you know who I am?" Mr. Portwit asked. He unslung his bag and placed it on the glass coffee table.

"Only little Dale Portwit would drop a dirty knapsack on a host's furniture," she mused, her mouth forming, incrementally, a smile. "You never cared what anybody thought of you. Glad to see you haven't changed. I suppose that's why there's a certain poetic inevitability to you being the one."

He was slightly amazed; but then, was it possible to be "slightly" amazed? He was confused, too. Slightly. But was it possible—oh, fuck it. Was she remembering him? Or forgetting him? "You're saying I didn't care what anybody thought of me? I'm Dale Portwit. It was . . . years ago."

"You went along, face forward, didn't give a damn what anyone said." Her tongue poked out and lubricated her lips. "I remember the time in the cafeteria when you told Principal Maitner that his toupee was crooked. You didn't understand the concept of tact. Everyone hated you." Her mouth squeaked rhythmically, like a person running up a mouse-covered staircase. This was her laugh; he had forgotten about her squeaky laugh. What else had he forgotten?

"I didn't remember that about myself," Mr. Portwit said. "I suppose that's enjoyable to hear. Not that I was hated, of course. But the other thing." He had always recalled himself as a meek kid, quiet and nervous in front of his peers, a child who wracked himself constantly with concerns about how the students and teachers viewed him, a kid who altered his behavior minute to minute based upon these views. If Mrs. Brandmal's story was correct, and he was so wrong, how could he fairly assess himself at any age?

The teapot whistled. Mr. Portwit volunteered to get it. Mrs. Brandmal told him where he would find the tea bags and mugs.

Once in the kitchen, he scarcely noticed his surroundings. He was focused as he set the mugs on the counter and poured the water. He reached into his pocket and pulled out the tablets. He needed to grind them into powder. His eyes shot around in search of a pulverizer of some sort. The counters, what little there were of them, were immaculate. Gently, Mr. Portwit opened drawers, keeping his eyes trained on the wall near the kitchen entrance, in search of an approaching shadow. The drawers were virtually empty: a small stack of baggies; a rubber spatula; a few wooden spoons; plastic dinnerware; plastic glasses and plates in the cupboards.

He would have to grind them on his own. He set to work, popping four pills into his mouth, chewing. He leaned over and deposited the powder into her mug. He repeated this procedure seven times. Between mouthfuls, he spat noiselessly into the sink, wiped his tongue with his fingers, then called out some innocuous comment to Mrs. Brandmal: "Such a pleasant color they chose for the cupboards in here," and, "I'm really flattered that you remembered me, out of all your students" (to which she answered, "You're the reason I gave up teaching, Dale!"), and "I'm going to let these steep for a moment before I bring them out!"

He came back to the living room with two steaming mugs and was shocked to find Mrs. Brandmal rifling through his bag.

"Where did you get these?" she asked. She held up the fat brown bottle of Librium. "Do they work?"

"Here's your tea," Mr. Portwit said. He set her mug on the coffee table, without a coaster. Let the trail of evidence lead to this little brick house. The weak sunlight coming through the gauzy curtains would stand witness.

Mrs. Brandmal leaned back into the couch, allowing Mr. Portwit to return to his seat beside her. His heart was in the middle of an extended drumroll. He sank into the cushion. He didn't feel good about himself; he felt like a low sneak. It was easy to be brazen in his thoughts, but he was too chicken to tell her what he was doing to her now, as recompense for what she'd done to him when she left. If he'd had the guts forty years ago to speak bluntly about his desires, maybe he wouldn't be here today.

"Why did you come?" Mrs. Brandmal asked. She quickly added, "I mean, how did Zachary find *you*, of all people? It's a surprise, I must say. Not that I'm not grateful."

"You were my most memorable teacher," Dale said. His mind flashed with an image of her white teeth penetrating the skin of an apple, her eyes behind the teardrop lenses of her glasses, fixed upon him.

Mrs. Brandmal said, simply, "I'm sick. Very sick."

Mr. Portwit's eyes met hers. They were the same eyes he'd photographed with his mind so many years ago, except now the face that housed them, if one were to use the standard that applied to fruit, had gone rotten.

"I have cancer," she said. "Of the lymph nodes. I start chemo in two days, though I don't want it. If you refuse something like that, they treat you like you're crazy. They took away my silverware, my aspirin, my good curtains. And now they're going to radiate me like a carrot. I'm very, very glad to see you." Gravity drew the tears from her sockets and pulled them down her cheeks.

"I didn't know they radiated carrots," Mr. Portwit said.

"The chemo isn't going to help. I'm sick everywhere."

Mr. Portwit wanted to say words that would help. He'd expected to feel something, anything, toward this woman, once he laid eyes on her again. But he was empty. Where was that store of pent-up anger with which he'd intended to murder her? He might as well have been sitting at a bus stop, talking with a stranger.

"Lots of things are gifts," Mrs. Brandmal continued. Her voice sounded airborne and speckled, like a grackle's. "My husband was a gift. Teaching was a gift. They both got taken from me. Your father . . ." Her head bobbled atop its neck post, a rung bell. "He was quite a man. Is he still alive?"

"Intensely," Mr. Portwit answered.

"He was older than me, wasn't he?"

"Still is."

"Quite a man," she repeated. "I never blamed you, Dale. You were a curious boy. A bit manic, but sweet. You won all those science bees. I suppose today they'd label you A.D.D. or something. See, my mind is sharp. That's the worst part."

"Arithmelympics," Dale corrected her. "There weren't any science bees." He sighed. "That whole situation made a mess of my life."

Mrs. Brandmal laughed sardonically. "*Your* life," she said. "Do you know that the rumor got around—to schools all over the state, mind you—that I had *told* you to come to my house? *Instructed* you to come and peek in my—cough cough cough—excuse me. My bedroom window? I couldn't get—cough cough cough. This was the early 1960s, mind you. I couldn't get a teaching job anywhere. Although I can tell you there were a number—a GREAT number—of male teachers and principals who kept their positions even after *proven* offenses."

Mr. Portwit's insides were gummed up and sticky feeling. He looked at the mug, at the steam issuing from it, at the stillness of the water into which he'd delivered the death dust. He imagined himself poised above the Bunsen burner in his classroom lab, goggles strapped to his face, announcing with gusto, "As you raise the temperature of the water, the leaving rate increases and the equilibrium shifts toward higher vapor density and less liquid water! By the time you reach 100° Celsius, the equilibrium vapor pressure is atmospheric pressure, which is why water boils at this temperature! Above this temperature, the equilibrium vapor pressure exceeds the atmospheric pressure! That is why we have this beautiful bouquet of steam!"

Mrs. Brandmal produced a handkerchief from inside her robe and hacked into it.

Mr. Portwit couldn't speak. Her robe. He was studying her robe, seeing it as if for the first time, and a horrid realization swept through him. What he'd mistaken earlier for a glimmer of life in her sparkling eyes was actually desperation for death. She'd probably tried a number of times already. Thus the dearth of metal kitchen utensils, the electric range, the flimsy curtains that would tear at the slightest pressure, the Velcro bathrobe with no removable belt. No belt. She was, after all, exactly like him. It was a heartbreaking discovery.

Killing Mrs. Brandmal would be all wrong. It would solve nothing.

"Do you suppose the tea is cool enough to drink?" she asked. "I think I'm ready."

He picked up the mugs and stood.

"Thank you," Mrs. Brandmal said, misunderstanding his gesture. She held out her hand. "I can hold it myself. I need to be the one to do it."

"I'm dumping these out," Mr. Portwit said.

"What now?"

He offered no explanation. He walked into the kitchen and poured the tea down the drain. Afterward, his heart felt light, his head clear, and his feet dry. He would drive, this moment, at top legal speed, back to Kalamazoo, to Mary Ann, to his students, to his science. This had been a fine and noble experiment; he would calculate the results when he got home. He might even consider apologizing to Rick Fletcher. It could save him a scene like this in his own dotage. As it turned out, what you did to your students wasn't your fault—they were the aggressors.

When he returned to the living room, he found Mrs. Brandmal dumping Librium into her palm. She saw Mr. Portwit in the doorway; she stuffed the pills into her mouth.

He stepped forward and swatted the bottle away. Tablets exploded into the air. The bottle whapped against the curtained front window, and the flimsy spring-loaded valances fell. With both hands, Dale fought to wrench her teeth open, but her jawbone was still strong. Her nostrils flared; both of her oxygen tubes detached. Her eyes peered up at him, pleading. They asked him to let her go. He recognized the dilated hunger in her eyes because he'd seen it in his own bathroom mirror, when he'd scrubbed his face for the last time so that he would leave an oil-free corpse. He had no right to stand in her way.

He released her. He stepped back. She worked her jaws. The tablets crunched and popped in her mouth like two dozen tiny knuckles. She had either a good dentist or good dentures. He sat on the couch beside her. With a wince and a contorting throat, she swallowed. She opened her mouth and showed her tongue, which was bright yellow.

"I wish I had that tea right about now," she said. She hadn't reinserted her tubes, and her breathing was labored.

"This entire episode has made me sad," Mr. Portwit said. His heart was the weight of his heart on Jupiter. He missed Mary Ann.

"You know what I always said about sad?" Mrs. Brandmal asked her former student. "If sad had three fewer letters, it wouldn't be a word at all."

"True enough."

"I don't mind that you chickened out," she said.

"Chickened out?"

"I told Zach I'd do it myself. *He* was the one who insisted that it be a third party." She chuckled dryly. "And with Kevorkian in the slammer, it makes things tough."

Mr. Portwit had nothing to say. His face, his hands, his eyes—no part of his body knew what to do.

"Really, honey," Mrs. Brandmal said. "I'm just glad you came. And I know Zach appreciates it, too. Don't worry. Take your bottle with you, pick up those pills that went everywhere, and go on back home. It'll be fine. You did the right thing."

Mrs. Brandmal's eyelids, too, became the weight of her eyelids on Jupiter. Mr. Portwit cleared a space on the couch, helped her to lie on her back. He fetched a pillow from her bedroom, which he fluffed before placing under her head.

"I never told you," he whispered, not wanting to interrupt her departure. "I became a teacher, myself."

She smiled faintly. Perhaps she'd heard. He pressed a hand onto Mrs. Brandmal's left breast—that big, beautiful, hilltop breast of so many young boys' fantasies, the breast of his first public erection, of his first self-inflicted orgasm, the breast that had driven him into fits of euphoria and senselessness, kept him awake deep into the night, the breast that ultimately warned him of the dangers of falling prey to his animal urges. Even today, this breast under his hand was formidable. But it had changed, had a new context. It wasn't a breast to be ogled, squeezed, or licked. It was now nothing more and nothing less than the softest possible cage for a woman's heart. He could feel the heart, way down inside, whumping away. At first it walked heavily, with persistence, like boots on a wooden staircase. Within the span of a minute, it slowed its steps, took off its boots. It became bare feet on carpet, then barefoot tiptoeing.

Mr. Portwit leaned to Mrs. Brandmal's mouth. No breath touched his ear. He felt her neck; no blood passed his thumb. Not in this body. Not unless someone tipped her upside-down.

He tidied the room. He rehung and closed the curtains and wondered if anyone walking past had glanced inside. He went to the telephone. He dialed 6-1 for the Center. He told the secretary that Mrs. Brandmal had committed suicide.

Then he walked to his car and drove home.

13

The morning brought Bernette. Perfectly arranged as ever stood her crown of natural blond hair. Her cotton-candy lipstick glistened. But Mary Ann knew that her woolen sweater sleeves covered flocks of psoriasis. Slacks hid the flocks on her legs and behind. No one could tell how damaged Bernette really was.

"I feel like this is my fault," Bernette said.

"I stole your pills. I took four times the recommended dose. I gorged myself until there was salsa coming out my nose—Bernette, *how could you*?!"

Bernette managed a tired laugh. "The girls want to make pizza, help clean the house. Whatever you need. They'll be your assistants. Hyperbole says you have the smartest heart in the world."

"You have GOT to try this morphine," Mary Ann said. "Makes Librium seem like Grape Nuts."

"You haven't eaten any of your breakfast."

"I drank some of it."

"You need to eat."

"I think I might have wished for this."

"For what, honey?"

"For *this*." Mary Ann gestured with a wave of her hand, but the breakfast tray was concealing her lap, so her point wasn't made. "I wished to lose fifty pounds from my body. I used those exact words. Right before Mr. Portwit asked me out the first time. I made three wishes for myself. I had never wished that before. My mom— where'd my mom go?"

"Out for a newspaper."

"She always said I never did anything nice for myself. I wrote on that list—'I wish to lose fifty pounds from my body.' I remember it clearly. 'Lose fifty pounds from my body.' What an unusual phrase. How much did my leg weigh?"

"Mary Ann," Bernette said.

"How much did it weigh?"

"We can ask the doctor if you really want," Bernette said. "I'll grab him. Say the word."

"It's not important right now," Mary Ann said. It was enough to know that Bernette was willing to help. "Those lists are gone. He destroyed them. What am I going to do?"

"Pretend it was a tornado or something. An act of God."

"He'd love the comparison."

"I should let you sleep," Bernette said. She stood.

"Please don't leave. I'm high. I'm embarrassed that I stole your medication. I'm in pieces." Mary Ann wanted to ask Bernette why she was so nice to her when she had a family, a network of friends. "It's the strangest thing," Mary Ann continued, staring at the bedsheet, "I still *feel* like I'm flexing my toes. There. Like that. I'm doing it, and I'm *feeling* the sensation. I can even bend my knee. Watch. I mean, you can't see it, of course. But it's weird. Is it happening or not?"

"It's going to be a long adjustment," Bernette said. "But you'll do it. You have lots of people who love you and can help you."

"Just you," Mary Ann said.

"Morphine."

"OK, morphine and you."

"That's not what I meant."

"My mother loves the idea of me being helpless."

"Morphine talking."

"Be quiet. Listen. I'm right where she wants me. And the teachers? I'm a three-hundred-pound conversation piece. Mr. Portwit? Screw *him*. Does *anyone* know where the hell he is? Is this a marriage? How would I know? I don't know what a marriage is. My dad died when I was seventeen. You and Barry, out of anyone, must be the ideal—I start thinking this, and then I find out that even *you*, even perfect Bernette Fargas, medicates herself. It's depressing. It's not your fault. The problem is the problem. The problem of *feeling* our problems is the problem. Not understanding how feelings *work*, and so then not being able to *stop* them when they get out of hand. That's why I stole your pills. I thought they might tell me how to feel. About my own husband. He's a mental case. There, I said it. A mental case."

The nurse poked her head into the room. "Everything OK in here?" she asked.

"We're fine," said Bernette.

"I don't think this button is working," Mary Ann said, dosing herself.

No one could find Mr. Portwit. Mary Ann lay in the hospital bed, marking time by the shadows that filled and fled the room. Mother was never gone for more than three hours at a stretch. Occasionally she brought Hakim, who conferred a single white rose each visit, which Mary Ann sniffed and stuck into the vase beside her bed.

Principal Jennings, Mrs. Ogilvie, "Bar-Far" Farfalinga, Ramone the custodian, and even Betty Passinault appeared on the first Saturday after the accident, Mary Ann's fifth day of one-leggedness. The guests arranged themselves in a semicircle at the foot of the bed.

Principal Jennings spoke: "On behalf of the teachers and students at Elkhart, let me say that you are in our thoughts and in our hearts. We are saying prayers for your speedy recovery. No, Mary Ann, you don't need to speak. Just listen. Listen to your students, who composed this beautiful poem under the supervision of Ms. Jessica Russert, your temporary replacement. It goes like this." Like a conductor, she positioned one hand in front of her face. At her hand's downbeat, the group recited in unison:

> Missus Portwit, you are nice.
> We loved it when you taught our class.
> We want to give you good advice.
> Please don't run too fast.

Principal Jennings bestowed an enormous 18 x 24 handmade greeting card upon Martha, who handed it to her daughter. "I agree that the last line is a little off-color," Principal Jennings said. "But we weren't going to censor them. Ms. Russert and I agreed that you wouldn't want them to be censored."

A paper plate with a smiley face drawn on it was glued to the front of the card. In crooked letters was written, "WE MISS YOU, MRS. PORTWIT!!!!!!!" On the inside, twenty-one signatures surrounded the poem. Reading each name, Mary Ann envisioned each child's distinguishing characteristic: gapped teeth, freckles, jagged haircut, silver boots, dirty socks, Powerpuff Girls backpack.

Betty Passinault's arms remained folded on her chest. She never said a word, but she seemed determined to engage Mary Ann with her eyes whenever possible, to display her premeditated empathy no matter what the context. When their eyes locked, three things happened to Mrs. Passinault's appearance: (1) her head tilted, (2) her eyebrows curled inward and upward, like two swans trying to kiss, and (3) her teeth gave a gentle, sympathetic bite to her red lips.

Mary Ann hated her, and she reveled in the hotness of the sudden, raw emotion. The lighter helpings of morphine, from which she was now being systematically weaned, left Mary Ann naked and vulnerable and unable to express herself. Her mind wandered through eloquent confrontations with Mrs. Passinault, but she was powerless to bring these into the real world, with real words. She needed Mr. Portwit for that. Instead, she listened to stories from her visitors until she could stand it no more; she pretended to be sleepy so they would leave. The one bright moment came as they were filing out the door. Ramone the custodian stepped to her bedside and gave her a hug. He said that a friend had lost his hand in a factory accident, but that his friend had trained himself to play the bass guitar with only one hand. "He slaps the strings on the neck, you know, with his left-hand fingers," he said, miming the action, "like bomp, bomp. Like that. He turns his amp really high, and it sounds great."

It was just before noon on Tuesday when Mary Ann had come home from Doctor Jackoby's, and discovered the list massacre. The eating frenzy, coupled with the Librium and the Stage 2 Hypertension, had sent all 292 pounds of her crashing to the kitchen floor. As on Thanksgiving, she didn't tip to the left or the right when she collapsed. This, her doctor said, signaled a rare condition. Some fainters tended to collapse straight down, the rear end finding its most direct and forceful route to the ground. Genetic factors like body type, leg-length differential, heel thickness—the doctor rattled off so many, and what did it matter?—contribute to the predisposition. There is even a name for it: *pattern medialcentral body collapse.*

The problem was, Mary Ann didn't fall *exactly* as she had on Thanksgiving. This time, her right leg bent underneath her. It snapped at the knee. Mary Ann would have bled to death if Mrs. Vugermann the Elkhart secretary hadn't become worried when Mary Ann didn't return after lunch and called her house for two straight hours, leaving messages until the machine was full. Principal Jennings then phoned Mary Ann's mother's cell (*Contact in case of emergency*). Mary Ann's mother (who was on Highway 57, halfway to the cottage) in turn called Bernette. Bernette drove to the house, pounded on the door, peered through the windows, shattered one, and crawled inside to discover the carnage.

Mary Ann had lost some blood, but not enough to die. The hemorrhage had been staunched, ironically, by the stiff pressure of the same weight that had demolished the leg in the first place. She was rushed into emergency surgery, but the severity of the breaks and blood loss meant that the leg was "no longer viable." It came off near the top of the thigh, an "AK" amputation, which, Mary Ann learned with disappointment, meant simply "above knee."

She slept until the following afternoon, Wednesday. Once awake, she pinballed between despair and euphoria. Mother and Bernette kept constant watch. Every hour on the hour, they called Mary Ann's house. They also telephoned Oscar and Adeline, who had not seen nor spoken with their son since Thanksgiving. "Honestly," Bernette said about Dale's parents, "his mother didn't seem to care where Dale might be. She did wish you 'Good luck with your recovery,' though. Ain't she sweet?"

On Thursday afternoon, the Portage police, persuaded at last that Mr. Portwit might not have simply run away, had agreed to accompany Mary Ann's mother to the residence. There was no answer when they knocked. Mr. Portwit's car wasn't in the driveway. Using Mary Ann's key, they went inside, searched and hollered and poked nightsticks into closets, but couldn't find Mr. Portwit. And he was not the only thing missing. His dresser and closet had been raided; his toiletries were gone. The final and most surprising missing item was the blizzard of torn-up lists. Miraculously, every scrap of paper (according to Mother, who had a radar for rogue scraps) had vanished. The house was spotless. The air, according to the police report, smelled of Resolve and Pine-Sol. Even the kitchen mess Mary Ann had made—which Bernette had described as looking and smelling like "rancid diarrhea"—had been purged. "Like it never happened," Mother marveled. Mary Ann concluded thusly: Dale was a tidy abandoner.

The evidence suggested Dale had left of his own accord. Being an adult, he was not considered a missing person. Nonetheless, a

Detective Simons gave Mary Ann his card and said he would post Dale's description and automobile information to the other Michigan departments. However, he said, Mary Ann shouldn't consider it an active investigation, and therefore shouldn't expect any fast results. He urged patience: "Usually," he said, "guys like Dale end up coming home with their tails between their legs."

By Monday, Mary Ann could, with minimal assistance, maneuver out of bed and into the wheelchair in under five minutes. Once seated, she had only to nudge a lever with her finger to zip up and down the hallways. Her strength had returned, as well as her appetite. Her spirits lifted when her doctor said that if she got down to 225 pounds—from her current 255—she could be fitted with a prosthetic leg. Mother and Bernette were also excited by this news, and each offered to help cover the approximate $5,000 price tag once her target weight was reached.

Exactly one week after her amputation, Mary Ann was taken home. Mother helped her inside. Mary Ann had gained enough upper-body strength to use a walker, which was easier to balance and less painful on her armpits than the crutches. With her stump beneath her, she lowered herself onto the sofa. Her eyes fell to the patch of empty carpet that had once held her recliner. That recliner had been with her twelve years; she'd bought it in 1990, her first piece of *real* furniture, for $285. Thinking about it now, it was disappointing that one of her few major purchases had been an item so slovenly, so repose-forcing. That recliner had contributed, at least in a small way, to her obesity. Anger rose inside her: how much life had she missed while her rear end ballooned on that pile of springs, wood, and cloth?

Then Mary Ann was visited by a new vision of herself in the recliner—on any given Friday night, over the course of many years, she had sipped decaf Mandarin Orange tea, a closed hardcover book upon her lap (*Gary the Gardener's Guide to Gardening* and *The Paintings of Andrew Wyeth* were among her favorites) serving as writing surface for her ballpoint. She'd written eight lists every Friday, but only the three best were saved. Such a deep groove she'd formed in that seat while her pen had worn grooves into those book covers. She envisioned leaping up and locating those books, tilting the covers to the light, translating the indentations to salvage even a few of her archives. It was a fleeting fantasy. There would be no leaping. Her leg was gone. Her lists were gone. Her recliner was now a bed for the Straws' Abby, who used it primarily as a scratching post.

Mary Ann had lived with that chair for twelve years. She'd been a teacher for fifteen years. She'd written lists for twenty-six years. She'd had her leg for forty years. She'd known Mr. Portwit (marking from their first conversation) for nine months. It filled her gut with fire, the vision of Mr. Portwit standing on this very floor, committing homicide, sheet by sheet. Rip! RIP! R.I.P.!

He'd been stifled in his fish-head feast; he'd had sex with one too many warmed hot dog buns between his wife's breasts; he'd shot a roll of photographs that revealed his own ineptness instead of any vandals; he'd lost his cool, he'd lost his job; he had no relationship with his parents; he'd forged a friendship with a mailman who scarcely knew his name. No wonder the guy needed a release. She had married a loser. But to be furious or heartbroken? This was the question.

Mary Ann opened her eyes to see the Tower of Mom, topped by a congenial face.

"Everything OK?" she asked.

"That's a dumb question," Mary Ann replied.

"I'm making your favorite casserole."

"Beef stroganoff?"

"You got it."

"You're sweet," Mary Ann said. "Would you mind bringing me the magazines?" It made sense that Dad had loved this woman, if only for her undying dedication to micromanagement. Love that made sense made sense. Did her and Mr. Portwit's love make sense?

Her mother retrieved the brown sack from the table. "Detective Simons said again today it's highly likely that Dale will come back on his own."

Mary Ann slid the latest *People* from the bag. The cover photo showed a dark-eyed actor shooting a sideways stare. He'd been dubbed "The Sexiest Man Alive." She thought of the way, many months ago, Mr. Portwit had reminded her of Jeremy Irons. She thought of the dips and dents on Mr. Portwit's cranium, the warmth of his thigh on her belly, his rages against religion and teenagers and the ring of the telephone on Sunday afternoons. She recalled the depth of his connubial stare, which often lingered until she felt an almost physical pressure, as if her heart had been squeezed.

"I know he will," Mary Ann said.

176

The first letter appeared the following day.

Inside the empty, unheated two-car garage, Mary Ann should have been cold. Despite the clouds issuing from her mouth, she perspired copiously. She lapped the perimeter of the garage—foot then walker, foot then walker, foot then walker—focusing on the black sweat tracks that dotted the cement floor. A CD of standard big-band tunes sung by Barry Manilow echoed from the box in the corner.

During one of her rounds, Mary Ann saw through the garage windows the postman's truck easing to a stop in front of their mailbox. She shuffled toward the bucket of cold water, pulled a washcloth from it, and squeezed the water onto her head and body. She toweled off, then pressed the green button to open the garage.

Outside, snowflakes hurled themselves at the ground, a million swirling suicides. Icy wind gnawed her exposed flesh. Her arms felt heavy, rubbery, her palms tender and sore. She eked her way down the driveway. Her mother had wanted to install a new mailbox beside the front door, but Mary Ann vetoed it. To date, her mother had already chosen (1) the support group (Amputees for Life), (2) the walker (the Ambulator 2000), (3) the surgeon who'd removed her leg (forgot his name), (4) the method of limb disposal (Mary Ann had been inclined toward standard hospital-provided cremation, but Mother had been horrified at the thought—the burial was to take place tomorrow); (5) last, her mother had grocery-shopped for Mary Ann's first eleven home meals, and had shortened and stitched each of Mary Ann's right pant legs (as promised). Mother also maintained contact with Elkhart Elementary and stayed abreast of Detective Simons's activities.

The mailbox would stay by the road. Period.

Mary Ann gathered the mail. Her face and fingers were already going numb. As she scaled the driveway's minuscule incline, she could feel her right foot pushing at the ground, working in tandem with the left, but when she looked down and saw the pinched pant leg and snowy space beneath her, she had to pause under a wave of lightheadedness.

Up ahead, Mother's shadow parted the living room curtains. As Mary Ann reached the front door, it was already opening. Mother swatted the snowflakes from Mary Ann's body as if they were live embers.

Next, the ordeal of getting into the tub: Mother cradling Mary Ann's naked, jiggling mass; both women huffing, grunting; the final "You sure you have what you need?"/ "Yes!" exchange; the click of the latch.

After her bath, Mary Ann ate a braunschweiger sandwich on wheat bread with a side of green grapes and Lo-Fat Salt and Vinegar potato chips. Mother updated Mary Ann on the latest of the latest, a mountain of nothing ("I've got some great ideas for scripture we can use at your Limb Memorial. I'll call the priest after lunch" and "Remind me to have you sign the thank you for the teachers").

It wasn't until 4 p.m. that Mary Ann settled onto the couch to open her mail. While she'd been in the hospital, Mother had taken it upon herself to handle the post ("You have so much else to worry about!"), so Mary Ann had made it a point to *insist* on the privilege from now on ("I need to feel *normalcy* again, if that's possible").

Under the energy bill, the *Have You Seen Me?* notice, the get-well card from her State Farm agent, and the sample packet of Pert stapled to a coupon waited a fat 9 x 12 manila envelope. It was addressed by hand to *Mary Ann (I hope you still are) Portwit*.

She tore it open. Inside, she found sheets of white paper as stiff as if they'd been laminated. The sheets had been ripped apart, then meticulously reassembled, like two-dimensional Franken-stein's monsters stitched by Scotch tape. Jagged edges didn't nest properly; missing fragments left holes; smudges from greasy fin-gers blurred the penmanship in spots—but Mary Ann recognized them as if they were her own children. She gasped. Ten of her lists. A random ten. She estimated three to be from the '90s, four from the '80s, the final three from this decade, which hadn't been named yet.

He was out there. He was thinking of her. He was fixing his mistake. She searched the envelope for clues. The postmark read *Kalamazoo* and was dated the previous day. No return address; no glyphs, ciphers, or codes. Nothing to help her know how to feel.

Mary Ann refolded the lists, stuffed them back inside, and slipped the envelope beneath the sofa. It was evidence. Detective Simons, Mother, Bernette—all of them would be supremely disap-pointed in her for hiding it.

She lay on her back. Her hand slid beneath the elastic of her sweatpants. In the kitchen, Mother clattered and clanged utensils. Mary Ann's first two fingers found the spot, nestled into place, and she rubbed herself to a quick, furious climax. Her face flushed. She drew breath and exhaled, drew and exhaled. She propped herself onto her elbows to look around—she was certain Mother had been watching, that she knew everything about her daughter's perversions, her son-in-law's mania, their marriage failures, about everything, whether shameful or normal or what-have-you.

Mary Ann resolved to get rid of her. As helpful as she had been—doing the laundry, cleaning the house, preparing meals, giving advice—Mother needed to scram. She stood in the way of the natural course of events. In his bizarre, misguided way, Mr. Portwit was communicating his love. If Mother found out, she would go to the detective, and this, Mary Ann was a bit surprised to learn, she did not want.

After a dinner of salmon loaf, green beans, applesauce, French bread, and a lemon meringue pie ("Mom, you really didn't need to go to the trouble."/ "But honey, I never get to cook for anyone. Hakim doesn't like American food unless it's covered in cheddar cheese"), Mary Ann lingered at the table, hands folded as if praying. Mother began clearing the dishes.

"Go watch TV," Mother said. "Relax."

"I need to talk to you," Mary Ann said. An unexpected curtness had invaded her tone. "Have a seat," she added.

A glint of suspicion drifted through Mother's eyes, a cloud over the sun. She didn't look at Mary Ann as she seated herself.

"Don't start it this way, Mom."

"Start what what way? I'm sitting down!"

"You know what I mean."

"I know that my back is sore from scrubbing the floors in that bathroom . . ."

"That's what I'm talking about!"

". . . mountain of dishes from lunch . . ."

"Mom, listen to me!"

"Don't you need your medicine? You're supposed to take it with your meal."

"I appreciate everything you've done for me. Really. Thank you."

Mother frowned. Her nails became fascinating red jewels at the tops of her fingers. Her bottom lip stiffened. "But?"

"But I need to learn to do things for myself. Wait a minute. I don't have to *learn* anything! I'm not a baby. I did twenty-four laps around that garage!"

"You're alone, and you just lost your leg," Mother said, then laughed caustically.

"I've been alone for a long time. I realize that this bothers you."

"It doesn't bother me!"

"I'm thankful for your help."

"And now you want me to leave." Another laugh, this one wetter.

"I can't imagine if you hadn't been there."

A bitter smile remained attached to Mother's face, but tears fell out of her eyes. "I have been nothing but helpful to you, and this is *so* unfair. So unfair."

"This is what it's always like."

"*Always*. Listen to you. Like I see you more than twice a *year*!"

"Twice a month!"

"Not for a long time now it hasn't been like that."

Mary Ann expulsed air from her nostrils, forcefully enough to blow out birthday candles. "I knew it," she said. "This is about Mr. Portwit."

"Who?" her mother asked. "WHO?? I don't see *anyone* by *that name*! I didn't see any *Mr. Portwit* at the hospital when the doctor was tying off your carotid artery so you wouldn't DIE!" Down came the hand, a mighty smash, upon the tabletop. The dining ware jumped, as did Mary Ann—a little lopsidedly, she couldn't help noticing.

A silence ensued, during which the SLAM! of the hand strike replayed again and again in Mary Ann's mind, immense at first but fading, like a shout from a canyon. Mary Ann touched her cheek and found she wasn't crying. It felt like a minor, but significant, victory.

"I won't trouble you any longer," Mother said. Adhering to a formality they'd never practiced, she excused herself. On her way to the bedroom (where she had pitched a sleeping bag on the floor), she paused to ask the air, "Unless you would prefer to mail my clothes to me?"

Mary Ann hadn't wanted it to come to this, but deep down she'd known it would. Deep down, she also knew that Mother would be over it within a few hours.

The next day was the scheduled funeral and burial, at St. Alphonso's Cemetery. Mary Ann awoke in the morning thinking about her leg. What did it look like now? Had the mortician fixed it up, painted its nails, performed a post-amputation liposuction? Would there be a shoe on it? Would there be a headstone, and if so, how would it read? What coffin size would they use? Mary Ann had inquired at the hospital, and was informed that, in total, her leg and foot had weighed in at 39 pounds, 10 ounces. Probably a toddler coffin.

It was likely that Mother had made all these decisions. To be fair, Mary Ann hadn't shown any interest in the funeral, so it was understandable that Mother had taken charge. Now, though, on the day her leg—her leg!—was slated to go into the ground forever, the idea of Mother helming its sendoff sat in Mary Ann's gut like curdled milk.

At noon, one hour before the service, Mary Ann's mother phoned to ask, in as clinical a tone as she could manage, whether Mary Ann would like to be picked up? With a matching clinical tone, Mary Ann answered, "No." She steeled herself against the inevitable backlash, then added, "Because there isn't going to be any funeral. Not today."

❦

Dressing, brushing her teeth, taking a bath, answering the phone, hunting through the refrigerator, washing dishes—these took longer than before, but nothing, it turned out, was impossible. Well, jumping jacks were impossible, but she'd never done those anyway. She could order pizza, slap together a peanut-butter-and-jelly sandwich, and heat up a can of soup with the best of them, exactly as she had done for twenty years as a single woman. Her walker became her best friend.

Her mother had given her a book, *Where Did It Go?: A Guide to Coping with Limb Loss*, which helped Mary Ann to see herself as "a person with limb loss" rather than an amputee. She also learned to refer to her residual limb as her "short leg," an appellation Mother was instantly more comfortable with. The physical pain had subsided, for the most part. So much so that often Mary Ann forgot her leg had been amputated, and would stand up from the couch before realizing, in the midst of nearly toppling sideways, that half the equation was missing.

When this happened, it reminded her of the half of the other equation that was missing.

Stitched lists arrived each day. Sometimes there were five in an envelope. Sometimes ten. Sometimes two or three envelopes clogged the box simultaneously. There was never a note, never a return address. The only evidence that Mr. Portwit was behind the mailings was the penciled address in his distinct handwriting, capital letters as angled and precarious as old outhouses.

Mr. Portwit's checking account had been drained, and all the envelopes were postmarked in Kalamazoo. These facts (none of which Mary Ann shared with Detective Simons) meant that Dale, driven madder than usual by guilt and regret, had holed up in a motel, carrying with him a pair of bulging trash bags of shredded lists. A smaller bag (most likely from the Walgreen's pharmacy where, he insisted, "one can find the best deals on office supplies"), held twenty rolls of Scotch tape, a box of envelopes, books upon books of stamps, and a pair of ballpoint pens (black).

With violent fingers, Mary Ann ripped into each envelope. She read every list as if it'd been written by someone other than herself. It was a remarkable act of reseeing, an opportunity to reread her own life, in random order, through the mail.

Ten Worst Traits of Betty Passinault, the Librarian (2002)

10. Her shoulder pads
9. The smell of her granola bars
8. Her smudged lipstick
7. The way she sucks her fingertips when eating
6. Her mint-blue 2001 Jeep Explorer
5. The backs of her knees
4. Her phony smile
3. The yellow tooth in the center of her phony smile
2. Her slow blinking eyes
1. The panty line

She'd written this on the Friday before the Monday in the teacher's lounge when Mr. Portwit had leaned to her ear, with a half-chewed apple wedge in his mouth, and said, "A lot of people think that sharks can blink. It's a myth." It was the first thing he'd ever said to her, other than "You dropped your gum eraser, miss."

Four Random Fantasies (1978)

4. Graham St. Finn, the tallest boy in the sophomore class, carries me down the hallway and out the front doors, into the spring air.
3. Graham St. Finn finds and returns one of my barrettes, between classes. He smiles.
2. I open my bedroom closet and find Bernette inside it, folding my clothes.
1. Graham St. Finn taps on my window in the middle of the night, waking me.

Graham St. Finn: the hours and hours she'd wasted daydreaming about that star center, the money she'd squandered on tickets to his basketball games. He had consumed her for two solid years before he transferred out of the city with no knowledge that a person named Mary Ann Tucker had ever been born, let alone stayed awake on weeknights crying over his yearbook photo. Now, she could scarcely recall his face.

She got to know her mailman. Every morning at 11:30 she bundled up in a coat, hat, mittens, and scarf, and embarked on the driveway journey. Postal Carrier Clayton Barbasol was consistent; within two days, Mary Ann had it timed so that she never had to wait more than fifteen minutes for his arrival. He was a sharp-nosed, gangly man, the thinnest person Mary Ann had ever known to warrant the title "jolly." Married, the father of three daughters (six, three, and eighteen months), he played on an intramural hockey team at the YMCA and enjoyed hunting pheasants with his uncle. He loved Phil Collins, Peter Gabriel, and Mike and the Mechanics, but hated Genesis. She learned every one of these tidbits during their daily two-minute chats. He always reminded Mary Ann to "Take care now" as he rumbled away in his truck with the steering wheel on the wrong side.

If Clayton Barbasol were asked two years from now, "Do you remember Mary Ann Portwit?" chances were slim that he would answer, "Yes. She was my friend." This was the trap of any public-service job. Mary Ann herself had had numerous past students (Bilson Bitters only last year, in fact) approach her in a shopping mall and exclaim, "Mrs. Tucker! You were my favorite teacher! You helped me so much with my times tables." Mary Ann had grinned, felt a gush of pride, and for the life of her couldn't remember who this person was.

Yes, Mr. Portwit's exaggeration of the Rufus relationship was sad and certainly spoke to how lonely he had been. It was also weird, unusual, and unorthodox (Mary Ann had begun to side with Mr. Portwit on the issue of adjectives; how could they be trusted?), but it no longer indicated that her husband was psychotic. Now, whenever she spoke to Clayton Barbasol, Mary Ann felt a vicarious closeness to Mr. Portwit.

She called Detective Simons and told him to call off the investigation.

"Well, there never was what we'd call an active investigation, Mrs. Portwit."

"Good. Then it should be easy to stop."

"Did he come home?"

"No."

"You don't want to find him anymore?"

"Close enough."

"Why don't you tell me what's going on?" Detective Simons said.

She pictured the detective standing beside his desk (she'd never been to the station, but he had disclosed that sitting for too long made his feet swell).

"I'm not worried anymore," she continued. "I think Mr. Portwit's going through some personal issues, and I'm positive that he'll be back soon."

There was a long enough silence on the other end for Mary Ann to think they'd been disconnected. "Hello?" she said.

"You aren't the only one who wants to find him," Simons said, finally.

"I'll talk to his parents," Mary Ann was quick to add. "They'll understand."

"I don't want to alarm you," Simons said, "but I've come across some information that might link your husband to a suspicious death. I'm not allowed to say more than that."

Mary Ann braced herself against the sofa arm; though she was seated, she wanted to make sure she didn't faint again. "He murdered somebody?"

"I didn't *say* that," insisted Detective Simons. His irritation irritated Mary Ann. This was a petulant man, a man who had resisted the case from the beginning. He had patronized Mother for two days before even deigning to send the police to the house to check things out. Now he was fabricating stories to make the "inactive investigation" worth his time.

"I demand to know what is going on!" Mary Ann exclaimed, losing her temper and loving it, "or I will speak with your supervisor, and I will have satisfaction!"

Simons shrank under the vague threat. His voice came out with all the thunder of a leaky balloon. "Mrs. Portwit, calm down. Officers in Saginaw have placed your husband at a number of locations in the area. Let's see . . . he was spotted at a rest stop, suspiciously inhabiting a bathroom stall. Later he turned up at a 7-Eleven, where one employee reported seeing him with a firearm —"

"He would never have a gun! Get me your supervisor! You cannot make up lies."

The leaky balloon began to whine. "I'm telling you what was told to me, Mrs. Portwit. If you must know, another employee says he *didn't* have a gun. So it's possible that you are correct. He later checked into a Super 8 motel and made a series of phone calls, all to residents with a particular surname. The next day, Mr. Portwit visited a resident of a convalescence home in Davison County, a resident with the same surname as those people he had called. Later, this resident was found dead."

"He didn't know any rest-home people. Who was it?"

"I'm not at liberty to say."

"How? Dead how?"

"Overdose of a Benzodiazepine that *hadn't* been prescribed. By all accounts, it appears to be a suicide."

"A Benzo what?"

"A Ben-zo-di-a-ze-pine, ma'am. A prescription narcotic that is lethal in large doses."

"He wasn't taking any medicine."

"No, and this prescription wasn't for him, either. That's all I'm at liberty to say."

Oops. He was referring to the Librium—how could she have been so stupid? She changed her argument: "You can't arrest him for a suicide!"

"I never said anything about arresting anyone. I am telling you that the search for your husband has turned up certain circumstances, and that *I must investigate these circumstances*. The Saginaw police department is asking for my help! They want to ask Dale a few questions. Now if you have any information, any at all, with regards to Mr. Portwit's whereabouts, I advise you to inform me of it *now*, rather than jeopardizing any future—"

"Can't help you," Mary Ann said, and hung up.

She gathered the envelopes from beneath the sofa, held them under her arm. With the walker, she carted herself around the house, looking for a place to hide them. In a drawer of menus, she buried the evidence. It was curious, the story Detective Simons had told. The Librium was missing from the house; there was no denying it. But she was sure that there was an explanation. Mr. Portwit would never harm anybody.

And even though he was innocent, her own little Dale was a fugitive. She wished he would knock on the door this instant, eyes peering from beneath a hooded sweatshirt. She would hide him in the basement, and he would sneak into the bedroom during the middle of the night to make bandit love to her.

14

"Hey, Dale! You need to wake up!"

Then, later: "Up! Up! Come ON!"

Then, later: "Sonofabitch, I'm serious! Get. Your. Ass. Up."

The shouting. The noise. Why wouldn't it stop? It was endless. Sounds of construction: hammering, *beepbeepbeepbeep* of a backing truck, *rhuttattatatatatatata* of a jackhammer. Birds. Bus engines. Bicycle bells. Now the quivering. Dammit.

"I'm up," Mr. Portwit said. "Stop shaking the bed."

"My girlfriend's coming over for dinner, remember? With her folks. I need to clean. You need to go *somewhere*."

The door slammed. Mr. Portwit opened his eyes. Sun poured through the curtainless windows. He turned onto his back, licked his lips. The mattress felt like a giant slice of day-old bread. His eyeballs burned, his head throbbed. By summoning all his energy, he managed to prop himself onto his elbows. A vacuum cleaner *wheeeeeed* to life outside the door.

What day was it? He wasn't sure. Biggs didn't have to work tonight, so it must be . . . Sunday? It was impossible to keep straight. Although, yes. It was Sunday. Which was why he couldn't send any lists today, and why he had gotten so drunk last night.

Mr. Portwit squinted at the clock. The numbers came into focus: 12:23. Five hours of sleep. Not bad. He stepped into the same clothes he'd worn yesterday, and the day before, and the day before that, and probably . . . blah blah blah . . . what were days anyway? The green button-up shirt smelled no worse than certain gourmet cheeses. He couldn't bring himself to sift through his duffel bag for a new one. It was too much trouble. He put his arms through the sleeves.

He walked down the hallway, which Biggs was vacuuming. Mr. Portwit nodded. Biggs didn't nod back. In the kitchen, Mr. Portwit poured a cup of coffee (smelled on the burnt side) and took an apple fritter from the box on the counter. He sat upon a secondhand barstool and looked out into Biggs's newly vacuumed living room. Into his mouth the fritter went, sweet and flaky. Bless Biggs. A good man. A real friend. Biggs had stepped up to the plate, put his mouth where Mr. Portwit's money was, had accepted $200 to let Mr. Portwit stay for "a little while" at his apartment above the Green Top.

For eighteen days now, he and Biggs had been roommates. Each day, after delivering ornate, bombastic reassurances to Biggs that this was a project of noble and not criminal intentions, Mr. Portwit dumped the garbage bags of near-confetti-sized paper scraps onto the bed and performed his work. From 9 a.m. until 3 a.m. the following morning, Mr. Portwit hunkered in the back room (a compact space with no closet that would have served as a den, had Biggs had any need for such a thing), emerging only to mail lists, buy newspapers, and grab olive burgers at the Hot 'n' Now (all within walking distance). Each day, Mr. Portwit murdered his lower back by sitting Indian-style on the uncarpeted floor, and was close to destroying his eyes with the endless arranging, stacking, piecing, and taping, while around him the sunlight threw shadows, exposed dust particles, and then died in a golden, regal display that convinced him, every time, of his own body's ugliness and insignificance.

He fought off the constant urge to call Mary Ann, disclose his location, reassure her of his sanity, and reveal his mission. Her voice would break like a tree branch in an ice storm. He would rush home and sing an impromptu song about his foibles and her pretty smile, then let her carry him into the bedroom for a food-free bout of lovemaking that would wake the neighbors.

The vacuum spiraled into silence. Biggs yanked the cord from the wall, wrapped it, and rolled the machine into a living-room closet.

"You look rushed," Mr. Portwit said.

Biggs closed the closet and scurried around the room. Four itty-bitty squares of bloody toilet paper stuck to his neck and his jaw. "Shit," he said, bending to pick up stray copies of *Bar Owner* magazine, a pair of dirty socks, and a Doritos bag from the floor. "They're going to be here in an hour."

"Should I be M-I-A when they arrive?" asked Mr. Portwit. "I could be out for a few hours, no problem."

Biggs rounded the corner into the kitchen, opened the cupboard below the sink, and dropped the magazines and Doritos bag into the trash. He handed the socks to Mr. Portwit, who stuffed them into his shirt pocket. "That's the thing, Dale," Biggs said, his voice dipping into a somber whisper. Biggs only called Dale "Dale" when he wanted a favor. "I know we agreed on three or four weeks, but I can't do it. You understand. I'll give you forty bucks back, but I need you to pack up today."

"I've got nowhere to go."

"Sorry, my man. Judy's folks decided to spend the night."

"I'll come back tomorrow."

"Well, you know," Biggs stammered. "They might end up staying a few more nights. You know how it is."

Mr. Portwit was tired. His joints ached, his tongue was furry, his head had been splitting for 432 hours. The elation he'd felt moments before, inspired by the goodness of this individual in a pink tank top that read *Captain Jack's Bahama Squeeze '97*, melted away.

He decided it didn't matter. When he'd first come to Biggs's apartment more than two weeks ago, his mind was whirling from a mad session of housecleaning that included mopping a pool of blood from the Armageddoned kitchen floor. Mary Ann had quite possibly gorged herself on food and then slit her wrists. It terrified him to think that catastrophe had befallen her, but with the image of Mrs. Brandmal's lifeless body and the rest-area policemen and the 7-Eleven clerk haunting him, he couldn't bring himself to call anyone, local hospitals included, to find out her fate. It was too risky.

To distract him from any darker possibilities, he'd charged himself with a sacred mission: bandage the lists and get them into her hands. He'd convinced himself that she was fine. She had probably, justifiably, gotten P.O.-ed at her destroyed lists, and had lashed out at the thing that best represented him—namely, every food item in the house. Sometime during her rampage, while opening a stubborn packet of hot dogs, for instance, she'd cut herself, pretty seriously, with a knife. This explained the blood. If she had died, the house would've been cordoned off and surrounded by cops when he'd arrived. Once assured that this scenario was the truth, he told himself he could win her back if he just buckled down and did this thing.

However, the difficulty of his task hadn't been clear. Some lists were torn so that the title was separate from the numbered items, which made it difficult to tell what exactly, for example, the *Six Amazing Sights I Saw Today* had been. In cases like this, Mr. Portwit judged by yellowing of the paper, by the evolution of her

handwriting, or by content: Clearly, *3. Journey 2. Supertramp 1.*
Steely Dan did not go with *Six Amazing Sights*, but more likely
with *Five Most Horrific Caterwaulings I've Ever Heard*. Unfortunately, he could locate no such title and had to settle, reluctantly,
for *Five Coolest Bands*. Obviously, *2. The top of his cratered head
when he is watching his penis go inside me 1. His lips clamped
onto my breast, his eyes like a fish staring up at the ceiling* went
with *Four Funny Features of Mr. Portwit While We Are Having
Sex*, rather than with *Seven Fantasies of Mother's Torture*.

Mr. Portwit drank the last of his coffee. Grounds drained into
his mouth.

"I hate to boot you into the street, my man," Biggs said. He
brought orange juice out of the refrigerator and poured himself a
tall glass.

"You didn't boot me anywhere," Mr. Portwit said, rising from his
stool. "You asked nicely."

"You're one of a kind." Biggs sank his teeth into a fritter. As he
chewed, he added, "You should go back to your wife. She's probably worried to death."

This was the most Biggs had ever said about the situation. In
vague terms, Mr. Portwit had described "trouble on the home
front," and also that he was attempting the most protracted apology in human history, which might land him in the Guinness Book.
Biggs had laughed and poured Mr. Portwit another glass of wine.
He hadn't grasped the magnitude of the situation, but then again,
Mr. Portwit understood that one man's mountain was another
man's postcard.

"I know she's worried." Mr. Portwit rinsed his mug in the sink,
then dried it with a dish towel. "I can't do anything about that."

"You ought to call, huh?"

"A couple nights ago," Mr. Portwit said, "I'd been putting lists
together for thirteen hours, trying to keep my mind off her. I
couldn't take the suspense anymore. I drove to Portage at three in
the morning. I looked in our bedroom window, through the gap in
the curtains. I watched her sleep." He felt as if he'd just dropped
his trousers onto the floor. Biggs had no idea about his history of
peeping, but still, Mr. Portwit was embarrassed and avoided looking him in the eyes. He scanned his mind for a phrase that would
justify his salacious behavior, validate himself as a human being,

but the words weren't in his lexicon. "I don't feel worthy of her. That's about as simply as I can state it."

Biggs poured a mug of coffee. He glanced at his watch. "No guy feels worthy of his wife. Most guys have a knack for screwing up." He ran a hand over his piffling patch of remaining hair, as if to make sure it hadn't abandoned him. "We screw up over and over. The wives get mad, but they stick around. That's the way it is with Judy and me. I'm blind drunk four nights a week. She gets pissed, she forgives me. It's all part of the game."

Mr. Portwit nodded. He was recalling that evening—seeing Mary Ann through the window and feeling the palpable, trembling relief wash over him. She was alive, his lovable wifely lump among the bedclothes. In that moment, his task no longer felt urgent. The next day, he'd turned practical, performed some calculations. After phoning a Kinko's on Friday to learn the weight of one ream (500 sheets) of 8½ x 11 20 lb. white paper, the nearest estimate Dale could manufacture was that the total number of lists fell somewhere between three and four thousand. Some days he'd gotten lucky and repaired ten; other days he found the pieces for only two or three. Even at an optimistic average of eight lists per day, he calculated that it would take more than four hundred days—over a year—to finish the task. No man could remain suicidally apologetic for that long.

He'd formulated a backup plan. The fire would be just as romantic as the mailings, even though Mary Ann wouldn't be around to witness it.

Mr. Portwit kept his eyes on the linoleum, on his ten bare toes that looked like hairy dumplings. "My father cheated on my mother. Three different women that we know of."

"My point exactly."

"My mother's an intelligent woman. She knew about it. Knows about it. She never batted an eye. Never let on. I used to think she was afraid. Or weak."

Biggs leaned against the counter and grabbed his own thigh with his free hand. As if checking for ripeness, he squeezed it. "That sucks, man."

"I agree halfway," Mr. Portwit said. "What my father did sucks. But my mother . . . maybe she had the right idea."

Biggs pinched his nose and coughed lightly. "Say, Dale. You can use my shower anytime you'd like. Clean towels in the closet."

"Why did you keep my belt, Biggs?"

"Say again?"

"You hung it up behind the bar. Why?"

Biggs shrugged. "I figured you might want it back someday."

"I told you to get rid of it, but you didn't. You didn't believe that's what I wanted."

"I guess not. You were drunk."

"You were correct, Biggs," Mr. Portwit was leaving the kitchen now, heading down the hallway toward his room. "*Back then*, you were correct. But not anymore, my friend." Mary Ann's lists were not far away, and they were waiting like children to be packed and moved to a better life. "My mother knew what she was doing. She threw away the belt and never looked back!"

"Does that mean I can have it?" Biggs called.

Mr. Portwit slammed the bedroom door.

At two on Sunday afternoon he said his thank-yous and good-byes, shook Biggs' hand, and headed out. Downtown was predictably deserted. For this Mr. Portwit was grateful. He lugged the two black garbage bags over his left shoulder. *Fire is cleansing; fire frees the mind*, he thought. *After the flames, Mr. Phoenix isn't far behind.* He had jettisoned his duffel bag into the dumpster behind Main Street Café and left the Escort keys in the basket of Biggs' coffeemaker—a parting gift for his friend. It was December 19. There was no snow on the ground. The sky was clear and sunny; as much as he searched, he couldn't find a cloud. The air was as crisp and cool as a fresh bedsheet.

His clouds of breath led him east past the wig shop, the Club Soda, and the YWCA, to the railroad tracks. He walked along them for a quarter mile, deep into Kalamazoo's north side, where houses had skin disorders and shootings took place weekly, and where nobody, not a single resident, had spending money. No one would mess with him here. The people had more important things to worry about than a skinny man in a stained shirt lugging black bags like some demented Santa Claus.

At a spot that felt isolated, bounded by narrow avenues of trees, Mr. Portwit dropped his burden onto the tracks. From his pocket he retrieved a handful of matchbooks he'd taken from the Green Top. The wind blew tenderly, more period than exclamation point, so it was not difficult for Mr. Portwit to ignite a cluster of matches and drop it onto one of the bags. He lit another book and tossed it onto the second.

Far away, a siren whirred. Maybe it was the police, coming after him. A dog barked. Maybe it was his childhood dog Victor, the German shepherd, dug free by his own paws from his backyard grave in order to trot across the county and reunite with his master on this glorious day. *Fire frees the mind*, he thought. *And the sweet toxins of burning garbage bags free it even further.* He inhaled deeply, triumphantly, then doubled over in a paroxysm of coughing.

He added another book of matches to the first bag. The two flames poofed together into one robust column. He distributed the remaining matchbooks onto both fires, which swelled, crackled, hissed. Black plumes thick as tree trunks curled upward into the sky. He had planned on a blaze of absolution that would symbolically erase his mistake, but now, watching Mary Ann's past die again at his hands, there was only crushing sadness. The wind cooled the sweat atop his head; he felt a weed tickling his bare ankle. As ashes, the lists would climb into the heavens—and then what? He would still be this tiny, stranded man, rooted to the earth, obsessed with dramatic gestures no one cared to witness, gestures that he himself barely remembered after they elapsed. He confronted the fact that he wasn't torching the lists for Mary Ann. He had lied his whole life, and this was yet another whopper, another flourish, another sprig of parsley on his plate of steamed bullshit.

The fire had engulfed the bags, roaring, its heat an angry heat, looking for a person to burn.

A low whistle sounded. Not far down the tracks, peeking from behind the Kraftbrau Brew Pub, showed the nose of an approaching train. The wind fanned the flames, and a tongue of fire licked Mr. Portwit's forearm. The train sounded again, a great, nerve-jarring trombone. Surrounded by an audience of weeds and broken glass, Dale rotated in all directions but could not spot another human being from whom to solicit advice. The train grew larger, blaring *woo-woo*. And then, urgently, *woo-woo!* A distant crossing rail lowered, and the dinging *ding ding dinged*.

Like two mythological creatures, they primped for war and performed the prebattle ceremonies. The train rolled and thundered, steady and unstoppable; the twin pyres melded into one immense, twisting blaze, roaring like an airborne river of bats.

Mr. Portwit stepped closer to the fire, singeing his eyebrows, scorching his cheeks. He realized there was only one thing he could do, and that was to self-immolate, to join Mary Ann's lists on their elevator to the sky. In one poetic gesture, he might expunge the failures of his life. He would be remembered; he would go out, as the saying went, in a blaze of glory.

And if the flames didn't do the trick, the train would be right there to finish the job.

But as he stared into the convulsing, bluish-orange inferno, where the lists popped and screamed like innocent witches, he knew that by dying he would only kill Mary Ann again. He had already murdered her lists—her link to her past, to her childhood, to her bereavement for her father. Dale felt a rage growing, but it wasn't turned outward. He raged at his own predictability—typical that the great revelation in his crisis would be a selfish one. There was no glory in letting himself off the hook and leaving Mary Ann alone once again. When he'd stepped into the belt loop, at least he'd had no one who cared about him. Now it was different. How many times would Mary Ann have to die before he'd admit his shortcomings?

Mr. Portwit backed down the slope, his heels digging into the gravel, until he reached the line of weeds on level ground. There he squatted. He heard the startled cry of a woman somewhere behind him. Beyond the narrow band of trees, people had seen the smoke snaking into the sky. The train was powerless to stop, turn, or retreat. It plunged stupidly forward, the air itself trembling before it.

When it collided with the bags, a spray of orange and yellow sparks erupted. A dense black cloud swelled in all directions, swallowing the train. Half the cloud rose into the sky, and the other half—the scraps of burning paper and embers—formed a flurry of glowing anti-snow that swung and dipped in a mad, wind-borne dance. Mr. Portwit stood in the weeds with his eyes closed. He raised his arms and was baptized by the feathery black ashes of Mary Ann's life.

The freight train, tagged with graffiti (*Dee Boy Suck It Up*), lumbered on, a dignified, unflappable dinosaur. Mr. Portwit turned and walked toward the line of trees that separated the tracks from the surrounding neighborhood.

A pair of young boys scrambled down a narrow path toward him. One of the boys pointed. "Holy shit, it's on fire!" he yelled.

Mr. Portwit turned. The train was not on fire, but the weeds were. An area the size and shape of a kiddie pool glowed faintly in the daylight. The boys grabbed sticks and threw them at the blaze. They jumped and hollered, giggled and danced around it. The only thing Mr. Portwit could do was stand upright, like a good human, and cry.

Mr. Portwit emerged from the trees at the end of a cul-de-sac. From what seemed like every house, people were stepping onto their lawns, pointing at the sky, at the rain of ashes and the black cloud, gesturing and talking with what sounded like delight about the mysterious catastrophe.

Three police cruisers whisked up onto the sidewalk, blocking Mr. Portwit's path. Cops leapt from the cars with their guns pointed. They screamed to get on the ground. Mr. Portwit sat. They screamed louder, poked the air with their gun barrels, approached on bowed legs like crabs. They insisted that he needed to lay face-down, RIGHT NOW, or get his head blown off. Mr. Portwit considered standing up so they would make good on their promise, but like the torn lists, such an act would—and *should*, he knew—be misinterpreted by Mary Ann. His opportunity was over.

They wrenched Mr. Portwit's arms behind his back and locked handcuffs onto his wrists. They removed the glasses from his face and heaved him up by the biceps. A tall, large-headed detective read the Miranda rights with all the flair of a wizard incanting a spell. An anonymous officer grabbed the top of Mr. Portwit's head. When was the last time he'd felt a hand—almost tender—upon him? For better or worse, his self-enforced exile was finished. He'd been readmitted into the community of human beings. Mr. Portwit was politely shoved into the back of the police car.

He sat alone, staring at his sooty pants. His eyeballs stung.

A police officer opened the driver's door and dropped into place behind the wheel. He lifted the radio and spoke into it, using many numbers and repeating the word "suspect." The passenger door opened. A detective, wearing a pink shirt and a blue tie, with a big head of graying feathered hair, climbed inside. When the man turned, he was smiling in a way that suggested he and Mr. Portwit shared a secret joke.

"You OK back there?" he asked.

Mr. Portwit thought about it. "That's a complicated question," he answered.

The detective laughed. "Very good." The cruiser backed into the road. "There's at least one woman who is going to be *very* happy to see you, my friend," the detective said.

"I don't think you mean my mother," Mr. Portwit answered.

They laughed together. *The type of guy who makes friends wherever he goes*, thought Mr. Portwit. "Sir, may I ask your name?" he said.

"Detective Simons, KPD."

Mr. Portwit looked out the window at the sky, which had clouded over and was now as white as Mary Ann's teeth. "Nice to meet you, Detective Simons," he said. "My name is Dale."

Epilogue

May 23

The new leg was much thinner than the other one. But under a loose-fitting pair of slacks, who could tell?

"I can't tell," admitted Principal Foster. "You just look like you."

Mary Ann turned on her left heel, regarded herself in the full-length mirror mounted on the southern wall of her classroom. She didn't say it, but Principal Foster also looked the same as he always had. Better. There was a gleam in his eye that had been absent before, and it lent him a joy and wisdom that everyone at Elkhart had noticed since his first day back. A regimen of chemotherapy, the loss of body hair, a weakened immune system, and a near-death experience in the back of an ambulance—Mary Ann wondered if her own trials had been enough to put such a shine in her eyes.

"I'm not used to this thing," she said. "It hurts like hell."

"You wouldn't know it to look at your face."

Mary Ann sat down and removed the prosthetic. It was the completion of her first test ride, a two-hour stint at the end of the school day. She'd slaved for months at her walker exercises in order to trim her weight, had worn an elastic "stump shrinker" for three weeks to keep the residual limb from becoming flabby, had had a plaster cast set over the stump, then a sheet of clear thermoplastic material heated and pulled down over the plaster mold to make a preliminary socket, then three weeks of socket aligning and adjusting. After all this, she had this "definitive prosthesis" that would need further adjusting and aligning in the coming weeks. She would also require weekly training sessions to help her understand how to use the new limb.

Principal Foster carried the fake leg as they walked together out of the room. In the hallway, they passed Mrs. Passinault.

"Have a nice day, Principal Foster," Mrs. Passinault said. She looked at Mary Ann, and her lips formed a moderately pleasant *U*. "You too, Mrs. Portwit."

"You too, Mrs. Passinault," Mary Ann replied.

For the Elkhart teachers, Mary Ann's missing leg seemed to act as a daily reminder of their shame for their earlier treatment of her. They now included her in lunchtime conversations, extended invitations to candle parties and perfume parties (she rarely accepted), and even welcomed Mary Ann to the educators' conference in Charleston, which she found informative but dull. All it had taken was to lose a limb—if only she'd known years ago, she would've chopped off one of her feet!

As was their custom, Principal Foster drove Mary Ann home. His hairpiece looked quite natural.

"How long until you're back behind the wheel?" he asked.

"They say I can learn anytime I want," she said. "As soon as I'm ready." Beside her, the sidewalk scrolled like a film reel.

Principal Foster honked the horn as Mary Ann let herself in. She waved from the door, upon which she could still read, at a certain angle, the faint outline of the soap words YOU SUCK. She went inside, dropped the prosthetic on the couch, opened the drapes to let the May sunshine play on the living-room carpet. She turned on a Neville Brothers CD and drew a hot bath. While the tub filled, she stepped on the scale. Seven pounds would be added by the new leg, but her real body was down to 224 pounds.

Two twenty-four. February 24—2/24—was Mr. Portwit's birthday. She resolved to tell him about this coincidence in her next letter, which she would write this evening. He'd spent his last birthday eating what he called "a generous helping of jail cake." She didn't ask.

She climbed into the tub and closed her eyes. The undulations of the nylon-stringed guitar rolled into the bathroom like ocean waves. Mr. Portwit had been in prison for exactly five months. It was difficult to believe that so much time had passed. Their one-year wedding anniversary—the paper one—was coming up in ninety days, give or take, just in time for his first parole hearing.

At the preliminary hearing, Mr. Portwit had pled guilty to reckless endangerment for his role in Miranda Brandmal's suicide, guilty to arson for burning the trash bags, guilty to unlawful possession of a controlled substance for the Librium (he had refused to implicate Mary Ann), *not* guilty to destruction of property for the damage to the train (he argued unsuccessfully that it was incumbent upon the locomotive to stop itself).

He'd also pled guilty to intent to commit suicide—a charge he himself added to the list, citing the fact that he'd meant to throw himself upon the blaze, but only refrained because he heard children approaching. Those in attendance—Mary Ann, her mother, his mother, Bernette and Barry, Mrs. Brandmal's brother-in-law Zachary, and Biggs—gasped. This charge was dropped by the judge, but he recognized Mr. Portwit's cry for help and added psychological counseling to the eighteen-to-twenty-four-month prison term.

"Although, to be honest, *Dale*," the judge said wearily, rubbing the bridge of his nose with a handkerchief, "I was going to do that *without* this last revelation."

Mr. Portwit had stood before the court looking like an Oompa-Loompa in his bright orange jumpsuit. He found Mary Ann in the crowd, sent her a significant thumbs-up that made Mary Ann blush because everyone else had seen it, too. Evidently, he was excited to move into the minimum security prison in Lansing, with the possibility of parole after eight months. Lansing was a ninety-minute drive from Portage, but the distance didn't matter, because Mary Ann wasn't going to visit.

Before his capture, Mary Ann had had no idea when Dale would be found, but she knew it was only a matter of time. Her mended lists continued to arrive, which meant he was alive and close by. Mary Ann understood that her husband was an impatient, capricious man only obeying his most recent—however touching—harebrained scheme. The lists wouldn't last much longer. On December 9, Mary Ann called the funeral home and requested that they postpone the leg burial. The funeral director, as well as the priest, grave digger, and Mother (especially Mother) had balked, but Mary Ann turned on the tears and offered the director twenty dollars a day if he would preserve her leg for a couple of weeks, tops. He was happy to oblige; they put the leg in a refrigeration unit.

Dale was arrested ten days later.

He refused bail, the main effect of which, from Mary Ann's point of view, was that she didn't have to interact with him. Out of an anger egged on by her mother, Mary Ann had refused to speak to Dale, but she made a point to invite him, through his appointed lawyer, to her leg's funeral. Only moments after the call from Detective Simons that detailed Dale's arrest, Mary Ann had phoned the funeral home and said she was ready to get the leg out of storage.

The soonest they could be ready, the director said, was in three days.

The judge kindly let Dale attend the Wednesday service, with the provision that Dale, accompanied by an officer, would communicate with no one and would return immediately to his cell.

For Mary Ann, the embalmed appendage in the casket left her cold. She'd already come face-to-face (or, more accurately, eye-to-thigh) with it at the funeral home. She was now eager to see it put into the ground. The leg had nothing to do with her anymore. The shock of its loss had already been felt, and the sooner it was buried, the sooner she could get used to the new ways of doing things.

The amputated leg was dusted with heavy makeup to a doll-like Crayola "flesh" hue. The naked foot (a point of contention between Mary Ann and Mother, who wanted at least a frilly sock on the thing) bore rose-red toenails. The leg lay amid the plush folds of burgundy velvet.

When she and Dale finally saw each other at the wake, he was shaken by the sight of her stump.

While standing in the short line to view the open casket (only Mother, Hakim, Bernette, Barry, and Ramone had been invited), Dale glanced at the row of seats, where Mary Ann sat with Bernette and Barry. Upon seeing Mary Ann, he stood motionless for a moment, then clutched the lapels of his police chaperon's uniform for support. His face drained of color, and he wore a look of confusion and dread, as if instead of seeing his wife, he saw only the horrible absence with which he'd left her. Mary Ann felt a compulsion to run to him, to swallow him in a hug, but she was both physically and legally restricted from doing so.

Dale was also upset by the leg itself.

He knelt beside the casket. Mary Ann was near enough to hear him whispering, though she couldn't discern what he was saying. Mary Ann imagined he was recalling the way he had rubbed that calf, kissed those toes, and nuzzled that thigh. He whispered for five full minutes, his shoulders and back spasming occasionally, before being encouraged to his feet by the attending officer.

An hour later, at the grave site, as the tiny coffin descended into the ground, Dale was nowhere to be seen. He had gone back to his holding cell.

The other guests huddled around the shallow rectangular hole.

The day was overcast and dark, and flurries invaded the sky. On the invitations Mary Ann had explicitly requested that guests NOT dress for mourning. The occasion, she'd noted, was to commemorate rather than to grieve. As if to spite her, Mother wore black and cried throughout the brief service. Bernette patted Mary Ann's shoulder. Mary Ann was so livid she could only grind her teeth and stare at the priest's wattle as he spoke:

"First Corinthians tells us, 'Whether one member suffer, all the members suffer with it; or one member be honored, all the members rejoice with it.' Today we honor the member of Mary Ann Portwit: the leg that as a babe kicked inside her mother's belly, the leg that trembled as she took her first steps on this earth." He sprinkled the casket with holy water. He made the sign of the cross in the air. "What is sown is perishable, what is raised is imperishable. It is sown in dishonor, it is raised in glory. It is sown in weakness, it is raised in power. It is sown a physical body, it is raised a spiritual body."

The frigid wind mercifully drowned out the noise of Mother's weeping.

With the assistance of the metal bars she'd had installed, Mary Ann lifted herself out of the bath. Seated on the tub rim, she toweled her body. Her weight loss had shrunk her breasts somewhat, but they were still impressive. She rubbed the towel over them, thinking about the way Dale had of mashing them together, burying his face between them as if he wanted to suffocate. Then he might pour Hershey's syrup and use his manhood as a paintbrush.

She missed their messy sex. The sheets were immaculate now. During the first month of his imprisonment, she'd bought a vibrator. She put it to use, shutting her eyes and envisioning Dale. The climaxes were enjoyable, but without his bizarre exclamations ("What a truth!"), it wasn't the same. She missed their lovemaking not because it had been kinky or devious or even consistently erotic, but because it was something they did together, away from the eyes of others. She retired the "toy" to the bottom drawer of her dresser and used her fingers when necessary.

On the sofa, she lay on her back and massaged her residual limb with Tiger Balm. The stump was deeply sore, bruised far beneath the skin. She counseled herself by opening *Where Did It Go?* to the section on prostheses: "There are times when it will be frustrating, and you may become angry and begin to grieve your loss all over again."

The prosthetist had told her it would be a month—the end of

June—before she could bear the new leg for more than three hours a day. Her body needed to get used to it. The book made comparisons between a loved one's death and the loss of the limb:

When we lose a loved one it's natural for us to miss them painfully at first, but less and less as time passes. Without meaning to trivialize the experience, it's kind of like "out of sight, out of mind." When we lose a limb, out of sight out of mind may not work, because we may be reminded every day of our lives that there is nothing where our arm or leg used to be.

The front door opened, and Bernette came in, carrying a grocery bag and a stack of mail.

"Howdy," she said.

"You're chipper."

Bernette set most of the mail on the coffee table. "It's Friday," she said. "It's a *gorgeous* day. It smells like spring. Hype and I saved a baby robin. Why shouldn't I be happy? Are you?"

"That's a personal question."

"Damn right."

"I'm happy. Next question."

"There are *two* from Dale today," Bernette said. She gazed at the two envelopes she hadn't placed on the coffee table. "Should I put them with the others?"

"Please."

Bernette headed toward the kitchen, dropping the envelopes into a small wicker bowl on the dining room table(s), inside of which, Mary Ann knew, there were five other unopened letters from Mr. Portwit.

"Pork chops?" Bernette called.

"Sounds great," answered Mary Ann, sorting. Electric bill . . . MasterCard bill . . . invitation to Elkhart Elementary End-of-the-School-Year Egg Toss. She didn't want any of it. Then she was descended upon by the image of Mr. Portwit being consumed by flames. She dropped the mail. Her lips trembled; she touched her face. She recalled the two talks she'd had with Mr. Portwit at the Battle Creek Detention Center, just after his sentencing, before he was shipped to Lansing.

On Christmas Eve they had spoken on red telephones, separated by Plexiglas. Mary Ann was in a fog. The encounter felt surreal. She was seated before something that resembled a dressing-room mirror. If this was a mirror, then she was a bald, bespectacled, weary-looking man. She wondered if Dale was doing the same thing, viewing himself as a drugged-out fatass woman with one leg. She didn't ask.

It was the first time they talked since—well, since many things. He pledged to design and construct the most comely and functional bionic leg the world had ever seen, as soon as he was able. She thanked him. He apologized for the damage he had done to her lists and to her, as a person.

"Is it true," she asked, "that you were going to . . ." She had more difficulty than she'd imagined making the words.

"Yes," he said, "I was going to kill myself." He studied his free hand, first the top of it, then the palm, like a student who was having trouble finding where he'd written his cheat notes. "It wasn't the first time I tried," he said.

He told her about the hanging-by-belt attempt, providing as much detail as the twenty-minute visit would allow, beginning with the "dark cloud" after Rufus switched routes, moving backward in time to Miranda Brandmal, springing forward to the xxx bonanza and the "occasional" call girl, drifting to the present that Mary Ann knew: their meeting and courtship and his eventual love for her. Shame colored his face. He spoke quickly, without self-awareness. She'd never heard him communicate so directly, without adornment, ellipses, or riddles. In short, he sounded honest. He ended by instructing Mary Ann to get rid of Rufus.

"Drop him in the hurby curby. Don't even bother taking him out of his frame," he said. "I'm tired of ceremony. Tired of it." His eyes flitted from one spot to another, as if watching an ant scurry about on the counter. He didn't appear to be talking specifically to Mary Ann, but she listened specifically. "I kept thinking there were exact, provable causes for the way I ended up."

"You don't think that now?"

"It's not my concern to find them."

"I'm not angry," she said. "Just depressed."

"Don't be. I can't hurt you anymore."

"That's not attractive. That self-pity thing. You never had a mean bone in your body. You're just crazy, that's all. A crazy"—she began laughing—"crazy asshole." She continued laughing, which turned into blubbering. She dabbed the wet spots with tissue.

"That's my girl," Mr. Portwit said. "You feel things more than most people."

He pressed his right palm against the Plexiglas. She pressed her left palm against his, and with this gesture he became even more like a reflection.

Two days later, Oscar Portwit had passed away in his sleep, experiencing, according to the doctors, no pain. The causes for his death were *Natural.* His heart had stopped. Alive and breathing one moment, an object the next. The last contact Dale had had with his father had been the Thanksgiving dinner. Oscar hadn't been at Dale's hearing because of his health, according to Adeline, but Dale believed the old man was being the only kind of father he knew how to be: "My boy did something wrong? That's why God made punishments."

Except Oscar couldn't whale on his son anymore, so ignoring him was the next best thing.

Mary Ann was informed of the death by Adeline, via telephone. Adeline had spoken to Dale moments earlier and was upset about their conversation (although Adeline's "upset" was another person's "sedated").

"He won't come to the funeral," Adeline said.

"Are you serious?"

"I asked him ten times," she said. "I can't keep asking. He'll listen to you."

"I'll talk to him," Mary Ann said.

Mr. Portwit could not be persuaded. He told Mary Ann over the phone: "I will forever be sorry that I missed your leg's burial, but I will not regret this decision. He wouldn't, either."

"It's your mother you should be thinking about."

"Tell her I'll think about her. That's more than Dad ever did."

Mary Ann got exasperated. She made her voice sound chipper. "OK, then. I'll let her know."

"I'm sorry I ran away from your leg funeral," Dale said. "The wake did what it promised: It woke me up, and I didn't like what I saw. I had . . ."BEEEEEEEP ". . . breakdown."

"What was that?"

"They're cutting us off in thirty seconds," Dale said. "Hey, I've got some advice. The next time someone asks how you lost your leg, you tell them, 'I didn't lose it. I know exactly where it is.'"

As Bernette and Mary Ann took their seats for pork chops, the front door opened. In walked Mary Ann's mother. "I know, I know," she said, waving her free hand before her face like a swatter preempting a fly attack. "I messed up." Her left arm cradled a lidded Corningware dish. "Why do I always do this?"

"No big deal," Bernette said. She took the casserole and set it on the table. "We're just sitting down. Are these scalloped potatoes? I'm a sucker for scalloped potatoes."

"I keep thinking Friday is Saturday," Martha explained. "It won't happen again. With Hakim out of the picture, I don't have his work schedule to go by anymore." She seated herself at the table. "I swear the weeks have gotten longer, haven't they?"

"Mom, you don't have to pretend you don't know what day it is. You're allowed to drop by."

"I'm not pretending anything!" She was horrified, but mildly enough that she forgot instantly about the matter and fetched herself a place setting from the kitchen.

They ate dinner with sunlight pouring through the windows. The shift from short winter days to long summer ones was always a source of amazement. Even after the food was eaten, dishes washed, and Bernette and Martha had said their good-byes, the world outside could not be described as "dark." The Patterson boys zipped up the road on their Schwinns, a sprinkler baptized the Morgans' front lawn. Bernette and Martha walked together down the driveway, waved to each other, and climbed into their separate cars. They backed into the road. Bernette's car lights came on instantly. Martha's remained off. They both drove away.

It was time for Mary Ann's new Friday night tradition. She placed the wicker bowl-basket onto the coffee table. She pointed the remote control at the television, pushed a button, and welcomed a *Doogie Howser* marathon into her living room.

She opened the first of this week's envelopes from Mr. Portwit. There were four lists, handwritten on lined paper. In the second envelope, there were seven lists. In the third, eight. In the fourth, three. In the fifth, eleven. She stacked all the lists together. Thirty-three in all. She would read each carefully. She would select the five best, then add them to the collection in the three-ring binder. She had been performing this ritual for five months. Mr. Portwit's lists were his own; he was not attempting to rewrite or rephrase the ones he had destroyed. The most recent batch bore titles like:

Five Prison Side Dishes Best Left Unsampled

Eight Parts of Your Body I Dream of Kissing
Six Types of Fish That Appear to Have Lips, But Do Not
Five Reasons Biggs Is Really My Friend
Four Scientific Principles That Excite Me
Zero School Principals That Excite Me (Ha)
Eleven Ways Prison Life Beats Bachelorhood
Six Sentences I Wrote Just for You

Normally, his lists were folded alone inside plain white 4½ x 9½ envelopes. However, the envelope that arrived today contained three additional sheets. Mr. Portwit had written a letter. His crowded handwriting covered both sides of the pages. Mary Ann sipped from her green tea and read:

My Darling Mary Ann,

Here it is, only three months from my first parole hearing. To describe the way I miss you as a destructive cancer on my cells would be an understatement so large it could be scientifically proven erroneous. In this prison, I have on my hands, as you know, many waking hours during the course of an average day. I am allowed—even forced, you might say—to simply *think*, and I spend additional hours sharing these thoughts with Mr. Gooseman (why they can't provide a *real* psychiatrist is a constant source of irritation that I will describe in a future missive).

During these thoughts and conversations, I inevitably turn to you. Rest assured, as difficult as it is for your one-legged body to move about our house in physical reality, in my mental world you are nothing less than an acrobat, springing, leaping, and frolicking with a bucketful of peanut butter cookies in your arms. I miss our broken house, but more importantly, I miss seeing you inside our house. Have you fixed it up? In your last letter you mentioned that your mother was taking you to pick up new drapes for the living room.

I miss your smell, your skin. I miss the way your mouth turns up in a smile when I kiss your cheek. I miss the sound of rushing water, the sound of rushing water that tells me you are behind the shower curtain.

You know that I feel these things. I have told you before.

What I have not told you is this: I will not attend my parole hearing in August. I do not wish to be paroled. I have come to a decision, and my decision is that I will stay in prison for as long as they wish to keep me. I will not harm anybody to achieve a lengthier stay (in fact, I have made two good friends, to whom I will introduce you in my next letter). I will not harm myself, either. I simply will not attend the parole hearings; thus, I will not be paroled. My lawyer assures me that this is how it works.

Prison life is simpler than life outside. Brain energy is not wasted upon the tiny things. I don't wonder which clothes to wear, what time to turn off the light and go to sleep, how long to stand in front of the mirror and dig chunks from the corners of my eyes, what to say to Principal Foster, how to respond to twelve-year-old vandals without appearing psychotic. (How is Rick Fletcher, by the way? No, wait: I don't care.) In prison, I feel a therapeutic stability (though I reiterate my intent not to let the parole board in on the presence of this quality) that allows a level of reflection and peace that, quite honestly, I never thought possible.

I have mentioned this before, but I want to remind you that the inmates who surround me are not a violent sort. They are tax cheats, blackmailers, con men, forgers—intellectual criminals, I suppose. The most violent offender I have met is Richard Clark, a sixty-year-old who crushed his son with a tractor. He claims it was an accident, and I believe him. The company of these men suits me, at least in comparison to the rapists, murderers, and pedophiles of Jackson County Prison, of whom my associates love to tell stories. I am surrounded by men who had big dreams and small dreams, and in the end, they committed crimes of selfishness or carelessness; however, at least they dreamed in the first place. Honestly, the camaraderie of these "criminals" is more enriching than the company of the elementary-school teachers and parents with whom I spent the greater portion of my life.

My sole hope, my dear Mary Ann, is that you understand that Miranda Brandmal, at the time I met her, was determined to end her own life, and would have done so regardless of my presence or the pills that fell into my possession (wink, wink).

To me, these are important distinctions. I hope they are to you as well.

Realize that although I love you, I will not be leaving here until the full duration of my term. I feel undeserving of your company and, rightly or wrongly, believe that I must earn my way back into your heart and our home. My incarceration should achieve this end.

My deepest hope is that you will continue to love me and communicate with me, and that you will respect our marriage vows as

I intend to do (I admit, it is easier for me, although in certain lights, some of these men aren't bad-looking—ha ha). I have discussed the possibility of conjugal visits with my attorney, and he is going to file a formal request on my behalf in the coming weeks.

My father's passing was more troubling than I initially let on. I believe (and the on-site physician concedes the possibility) that his death is related to my recent dizzy spells, hot flashes, and shortness of breath. Still, I refuse to discuss him, or my mother, with Mr. Gooseman. I have told him, as I have told you, that since I am a firm believer in evolution, I believe humans descended from sea life. I have opened picture books from the library and pointed out to Mr. Gooseman, using numerous full-color examples, that *no* fish—and in fact virtually *no* sea creatures—have necks; that, in effect, they are designed to *always face forward.* I have repeatedly emphasized my belief that the fatal flaw of humans is our necks (a physical representation of our unhealthy need to look backward [which borders on a mania in the psychological profession, as you well know]), and our

Oops. I see that I am almost out of space. It is late, and I will not get another ration of paper until Monday. (They accuse me of wastefulness, and have even resorted to dramatically dumping my trash can to show how many crumpled sheets are only written on with a few lines.) Regardless of my troubles, rest assured you will get a hefty envelope of lists on Tuesday or Wednesday. As I've mentioned before, you should not feel obligated to keep these lists; in fact, I discourage it. I only hope that you read them and imagine me writing them as I think of you.

Sincerely,

Dale

Mary Ann folded the letter and slid it into the envelope. No parole. He would stay in prison until they were ready to let him go. She sat very still and closed her eyes. Her hand instinctively kneaded her sore stump. He wouldn't be home for another year. The jangle of nerves in her stomach, the warmth spreading across her scalp— Was it anger? Relief? She didn't know. Mostly she felt confused. In her mind she envisioned a split screen, like a bad TV show. On one side was Dale, hunched over a rickety desk, scribbling sweet nothings and Top Ten lists long after lights-out. On the other side of the screen Mary Ann saw herself: supine on the sofa, reading Dale's words, hearing his voice in her head; at the bookstore sipping tea; going to the park with Bernette and her children. She would be the amputee wife with the phantom husband.

And who knows? she thought. *He might change his mind next week.*

It took ten minutes to select the five best lists from this week's batch. The others, along with Dale's letter, she crumpled into balls and tossed behind her head, not caring where they landed. From the drawer of the end table, she withdrew the three-ring binder. The lists were already on punched paper, so it didn't take more than a moment to add them to the back of the collection.

Mary Ann kept one eye on Doogie Howser as she worked. Doogie, with arms crossed, crinkled his brow and tapped a pencil against his chin while he studied a row of X-rays. So serious. So intelligent. So boyish. So keen and hungry. So smart, and so stupid. He was not quite a man, not quite a boy; he was human, and he would make mistakes, but in the end, the world would be a better place for his efforts.

She had forgotten to close the new drapes. Truth told, the color—Sherbet Orange—had been more Mother's choice than her own. Mary Ann kept expecting them to melt.

Beyond the picture window, darkness had arrived. The street lamps created pockets of illumination, but only enough to attract swarms of bugs. Out there, there was no true light. A person's vision, her senses, couldn't be trusted. A brown jacket might turn out to be green. A snapping twig could signify a chipmunk or an ax murderer. Under cover of night, it was a misleading, frightening world.

Mary Ann grabbed her walker, pulled it toward herself, and stood into its embrace. On the screen, credits scrolled skyward over a still shot of Doogie Howser's smile.

It was no wonder, Mary Ann reasoned, that people slept at night. What was the point of being awake when there was nothing to see? She maneuvered around the coffee table, leaned forward, and swung herself toward the TV, in three easy movements. She shut it off, then tended to the window. Sherbet or not, the curtains needed to be closed. Leaving them open made her feel like she was in a goldfish bowl.

In the corner, the fake leg, propped against the wall, waited for a body.